G000092388

Make it Concrete

MAKE IT CONCRETE

Miryam Sivan

Cuidono • Brooklyn

MAKE IT CONCRETE

© 2019 Miryam Sivan

An excerpt from this novel was previously published under the title "The Keys," in *Jewish Fiction*, Toronto, Spring 2012.

Cover photo: GotovyyStock/Shutterstock
Author photo: Ellin Yassky

All rights reserved. No part of this book may be reproduced in any form or by any means, electronic or mechanical, including photocopying, recording, scanning, or by any information storage or retrieval system, without permission from the author and publisher.

ISBN: 9781944453084
eISBN: 9781944453091

Cuidono Press
Brooklyn NY

www.cuidono.com

For my grandmothers Nechama and Pila
Who lost so many and loved so well.

Contents

*

Now Europe, O Europe, my hell on earth, what shall I say of you, since you have won most of your triumphs at the expense of my limbs? O Italy, depraved and bellicose, for what shall I praise you? Famished lions have fattened themselves within your borders by tearing apart the flesh of my lambs. O France, in your luxuriant pastures my ewes have grazed poisonous herbs. O Germany, haughty, rough and mountainous, my goats were dashed to pieces as they fell from the summit of your craggy Alps. O England, my cattle drank bitter and brackish drafts from your sweet cold waters. And Spain, hypocritical, cruel and lupine, ravenous and raging wolves have been devouring my woolly flock within you.

—Samuel Usque
Consolation for the Tribulations of Israel
Ferrara 1553

Yidn, shraybt un farshraybt!

—Simon Dubnow
Riga Ghetto 1941
("Jews, write and record!")

The Caves

1

On an early morning at the end of September, the second grade children gathered in the stone courtyard of Yehuda HaNassi's burial cave. It was the most famous grave in Bet She'arim. Dark green cypress trees framed the park's manicured lawns. Limestone facades softened the harsh light of the Middle East. And along the road that twisted above the grounds, scattered stones from a synagogue, a few homes, an olive press, and a gate were all that remained of the community Rabbi Yehuda HaNassi, a prince from the line of King David, brought with him out of the cauldron of Jerusalem. 200 C.E.

Isabel Toledo stood at the edge of a large lawn. Yelling and laughing, children ran in all directions. Adults spoke in clusters. Three dogs chased one another, tumbling, barking, growling. Under a wide oak their people sat on a blanket drinking coffee from a silver thermos and watched.

"*Ema*," Uri, Isabel's seven year old son, tugged at her arm. "Do you have the book?"

Every September, a few weeks into the school year, the town held a ceremony presenting its children with their first copy of *Genesis*. Yehuda HaNassi's cave was chosen for the occasion because, as head of the Sanhedrin during the Second Kingdom of Israel, he had set himself and his scholars to writing down those parts of the Bible which until that moment in history had been transmitted verbally from teacher to student, father to son. But spoken transmission relied on safety, continuity, face to face instruction. Conditions not guaranteed under Roman rule. So they scribed the oral tradition: insurance for an uncertain future.

"*Ema*, the book!" Uri pulled at her backpack.

"Yes, of course." Isabel reached into the backpack and handed him the *Genesis* textbook. Clutching it tightly, Uri moved through the swarm of eager seven-year-olds to Idit, his teacher, and his book was added to the growing pile beside her.

Isabel's eyes swept the landscape in what Alon, her ex, mockingly referred to as her preemptive surveillance. He didn't understand that it was reflexive, that she couldn't help it, even now at a community event, in this stunning natural venue, during a relatively quiet political period. Beyond the people, beyond the dogs and trees and lawns, Isabel found shadows on the hill, indications of caves and narrow paths in the rock face. She calculated it would take thirteen minutes total from her house to here. Three minutes to put Uri and Woody in the car. Another seven to reach the park. A final three to run from the car to the second tier of caves. Just enough time to slip past the round-up at the end of her street, the roadblocks, the house-to-house searches. Just enough time, barring hesitations and unpredictable delays, since every minute was critical to escape. Unnecessary movements could diminish their chances of survival.

Isabel forced herself to stop calculating. She pulled her eyes away from the hill and its shadows and walked towards Yehuda HaNassi's burial cave. Parents and children flitted about the stone courtyard in a state of heightened expectation. Soon the ceremony would begin. Isabel spied a felled Doric column at the back and went and sat on it. The cold stone soothed her. Other adults began to gather round.

Isabel stared at the tall arches and low rectangular doors to the entrance of HaNassi's cave. Soon after they became lovers Zakhi had brought her here. To the park. To the caves. He loved these limestone doors carved to resemble wooden slats, metal bolts, and hinges.

"The common construction material at the start of the Common Era," Zakhi said. "Watch this." He moved a heavy stone door back and forth. "Two thousand years later and the hinges are still operable. Impossible to replicate such craftsmanship today." He grinned proudly as if he were the stonemason responsible for such beauty.

It took time for the assembly of children, parents, grandparents, and teachers to move into the courtyard and calm down. It took time for the ceremony to begin. Isabel sat on the cold stone pillar and realized she had no idea what to expect. Uri had come home the week before with a square of white linen and instructions from Idit: parents were to sew a cover for the *Genesis* textbook. Isabel had not been asked to do anything like this for her two older children. She flipped through the textbook's pages. There seemed to be very few changes in the dozen plus years since Lia and Yael were in second grade. The colors seemed brighter, yes, and the reproductions sharper. But God was still God. Not a character exactly, not a myth, nor merely an historical personage. A simple given. Creator and Master of the Universe. The stories of Creation, of Babel, the Flood, of Abraham the first monotheist and his family, all presented matter-of-factly. Faith left off the page. A not unwise policy in their region of fundamentalism and violence.

When Lia, now twenty-three, and Yael, now nineteen, were in second grade, they lived on kibbutz. Jewish holidays were celebrated as agriculture festivals. The girls came home with their *Genesis* textbooks without fanfare or solemnity, just one of many textbooks to be worked through that year. But now they lived in town, and Uri went to the neighborhood school, and the novelty of this rite of passage—the invitation for seven-year-old children to join the conversation going on among Jews for thousands of years—was compounded for Isabel by not having an Israeli childhood of her own.

She had gone to P.S. 9 in New York. Every morning at nine o'clock sharp the school bell rang. The children rose from their wooden desks and faced the American flag in the corner of the classroom. Following cues piped in through the PA system, they placed their right hands over their hearts, pledged allegiance to the flag and to the United States of America and to the Republic for which it stands, one nation, under God, indivisible, with liberty and justice for all. Then, too, God wasn't a subject but a given. And Isabel learned to tell her right hand from her left.

Of course Isabel did as Idit instructed. She sewed the square of white linen into a book jacket. In the middle she embroidered two tablets resembling the ones Moses brought down from the mountain. She chain stitched the numbers one to ten on them in gold thread. In the bottom left corner, she added a small silver candelabrum. And above it, in blue and silver thread, she stitched Uri's name. All in all the book cover came out better than expected and Uri loved it.

Isabel leaned her head back and took in the thick autumn-blue sky. An early coolness flushed the air. Large clouds drifted overhead. She thought of Zakhi kissing her good-bye the day before. They had stood outside the Winkler house in the neighboring village. Leaning against his truck she saw a large bank of clouds. The first in many months.

"The rains are coming," she said.

Zakhi turned towards the house under construction. "An early rain'll be disastrous. We're far from closing up the house. Stone mason's holding everything up."

"Without the stone sills the blind frames can't be fitted," Isabel mimicked Zakhi. "Which holds up the plasterer who can't seal the gaps between the frames and the walls, and then other trades, like dear Zakhi the electrician, can't come in and finish his work."

Zakhi laughed out loud.

"Construction's a three dimensional jigsaw puzzle," she delivered lines she'd heard him say over the last two years. "Each piece overlaid and built on the other. One contractor's delinquency," her voice dropped dramatically, "paralyzes all."

"You're good, Isabel Toledo."

"Good enough to get a job?"

"Career change?"

"Maybe."

"Jaim Benjamin's book?"

"Killing me."

"Softly." Zakhi leaned into her and kissed her mouth. "Back to the mines." He turned back to the Winkler house under construction.

And Isabel drove back to her house and her desk. To World War Two. To Jaim Benjamin's life. To northern Greece. To Nazis. To her fifteenth ghostwrite in twenty years.

"You're pale, Isabel. I'm worried about you." Molly squeezed in next to Isabel on the cold Doric column.

"Huh?"

"You. Pale as a ghost. What's going on?"

"I'm fine, really."

Molly stared at her. She was Isabel's best friend and a shrink and knew her as well as anyone. Maybe better. They met years ago through their children. Yael and Molly's middle son, Yiftach, were in the same junior high and high school class. Now Uri was with Molly's youngest son, Eden. Their second school cycle together as moms. Molly was originally from Dublin. These two English-speaking immigrants had found each other, to their mutual and great relief.

"Don't believe you." Molly continued to stare at her.

Isabel didn't answer. She was in no mood to be chided. Eventually the second grade teachers gathered their pupils and sat them down in neat groups. Eventually the seven year olds and their families calmed themselves enough for the mayor of the town to address them. And it was his presence—standing before them in his crisp white shirt and maroon tie—that did the trick. Silence in the face of his ultimate authority. The mayor!

Uri kept turning around. Each time Isabel gave him huge smiles. Such a beautiful child. Silky auburn hair, grey almond shaped eyes, and a small upturned nose. Like Alon. With a face like that he could have survived the war. But his skin, pale in winter, tanned easily in summer, like Suri's, Isabel's Ukrainian-born mother. And like Lia, her eldest. These two fair children of hers didn't resemble Isabel or her father's Toledo clan at all. Only Yael, her middle child, looked like them. Olive skin. Heavy lidded dark eyes. Thick black lashes. A long face defined by high cheek bones and a narrow chin. Iconographic. Like a woman in an El Greco painting. A Jewish woman from Toledo itself. The Jerusalem of Spain.

It took some time for Isabel to understand that Uri kept looking back because he was searching for Alon. Isabel was suddenly self-conscious that she was the only one of their family there. Other

5

children's parents, grandparents, and siblings had come to celebrate with them. But Lia was in India and was due back in a week, days before her semester began. Yael was in the army, her request to leave base denied. Alon's parents were dead. As was Dave, Isabel's father. Suri, the only grandparent, lived in New York and wasn't due to visit Israel until the following summer. And Alon? Mr. Segev was late as usual.

With every turn of Uri's head Isabel's heart stung. Every nod reeked of disappointment. Each held breath an acknowledgment that sometimes things didn't work out. How to explain to Uri that families were created in good faith. That children were made to be loved, often within the framework of the family. But when the frame broke, and the family dispersed, the child remained there, somehow, still contained within the picture.

The mayor stood next to the cave's open doors. He cleared his throat and smiled at the children. He caught the eyes of those closest to him. His smile, a straight lined toothy grin, was a cross between Mr. Rogers's and Mr. Ed's. American references Isabel would have to explain to her Israeli children and to Molly. All tittering stopped.

"I want to welcome here this morning, all the second grade children of our town, their parents and other family members, their teachers, and school principals. Every year when I come to this ceremony of presenting each child with his or her very first Bible, I am overcome with the power of our connection as a people to this book, to this language, to this land."

Molly let out a small groan. Isabel put her hand on Molly's knee. "No political commentary now," she whispered.

"Everything here is politics. Everything."

"Molly behave."

She nodded. She would cooperate.

"We are gathered here today before the burial cave of one of the greatest Jewish minds that ever lived." The mayor beamed, happy to have such esteemed company in his small town. "Rabbi Yehuda HaNassi. Judah the Prince. He wrote down the oral tradition, the *Mishna*, in Hebrew that is the model for the Hebrew we speak today. It is my privilege to be a part of this ongoing chain of transmission.

6

And today, when you children receive your own *Genesis*, you will become part of this chain.

"Good luck in your studies. You are among the millions and billions of stars God promised to Abraham when he said, 'Look now toward Heaven and count the stars, if you are able to, and He said to him, So shall thy seed be.' You are children of the future about to embark on the journey of learning the book of our people. I wish you all a fruitful and enriching adventure."

Tears welled up unexpectedly in Isabel's eyes when the children filed past their teachers and reached up for their books nestled in white linen. The ancient and the present merged and Isabel remembered that this was one of the reasons she moved here. Isabel looked over at Molly. Despite herself her eyes were damp too. The children smiled widely, proud of their own achievement of reaching second grade, of their entrance into this larger world of the mythical and mighty Sanhedrin and of history. A hand fell on Isabel's shoulder. Startled she turned and saw Alon. He too wiped tears from his cheeks.

"Since when do you fall for religious-nationalist speeches?" Isabel asked.

"We're Diaspora. We're excused." Molly gave Alon a quick kiss on the cheek.

"But a son-of-a-kibbutz like you?" Isabel grinned.

"I guess you infected me." Alon grinned back.

"*Aba.*" Uri ran to them and Alon picked the child up. He kissed his mouth and forehead, held him close. Old new versions of the same face. Uri shoved the book at Alon.

"Just beautiful. *Ema* sewed the cover?"

Uri nodded yes.

"Apparently not all schools are like the ones on kibbutz," Isabel said.

Alon shrugged his shoulders. "Greek to me."

"Did the pony arrive?" Uri asked Alon.

"Yes, a real beauty."

"I want to see him," Uri demanded. "You promised I could help train him."

"Okay then. Let's just clear it with the boss," Alon said.

7

"Uri can go to kibbutz," Isabel said. Hours of work waited at her desk. Better to have the child occupied. "But have him back by six, okay." She glanced at her watch.

"No problem. Let's do it." Alon slid the boy to the ground.

Isabel bent down on one knee to kiss Uri. "Congratulations, my big boy. I'm very proud of you. Now you can teach me to read the Bible in Hebrew. Your sisters didn't have the patience."

"I will, *Ema*, I promise." He hugged her tightly around the neck. Gave her a long serious kiss on the cheek.

"Thank you, love." They walked towards the parking lot. The dogs rested in the shade. Their people sat on a blanket and ate sandwiches. Isabel thought of Jaim Benjamin trekking through the hills bordering Yugoslavia. 1943. The burning in his chest for his mother who sent him into the mountains sure that the people there would give him refuge. She put bread, olives, water, a few photographs, and her wedding ring into a large shawl and ordered him to walk and not look back. A few days later Florina's few hundred Jews were sent to death camps in Poland.

Alon and Uri got into Alon's truck. Isabel waved good-bye and waited by her car. Molly and Eden drove by.

"Going home?" Molly asked, slowing the car down.

"Sure."

"You need a rest, darling."

Isabel looked up at the sky. A cloud with a hole in its middle like an open eye drifted along the blue dome. Storks flew toward Africa in a rolling V. Isabel took a notepad from her bag. *Do storks winter in Madagascar?*

2

Isabel didn't want to go home. She didn't want to be inside Jaim Benjamin's life. She was tired of the war. The terror. The losses. The haunting. Weeks ago she admitted to Emanuel that a skulking trepidation had taken over her work days. Even some of her nights. She regretted her words as soon as she spoke.

"Time to stop, Izzie," Emanuel said. He was a mathematician. And the official boyfriend. "I calculate you've been in this Holocaust business too long."

"Yeah, but someone's got to do it. Someone's got to push silence around." Isabel fumed. Emanuel's words reminded her of Alon who discouraged ghosting from the get go. And Alon's words reminded her of Dave who throughout high school and college told her to leave the past alone. Look to the future Isabel, Dave would say to her whenever she tried to talk to him about European history, the past is a greedy storm.

Isabel knew that Emanuel was not Dave and that he truly had her best interests at heart. From the first time she met him at an exhibition opening in town four years earlier, she had sensed that here was a man strong enough to be kind. He had delicate handsome features and soft grey curls down to his neck. An academic with a bit of the bohemian about him. And she had said yes at the end of the evening when he asked if he could see her again. But lately he had begun pointing out things that were not part of the script of their relationship: that they should travel more for pleasure; that they should drink less wine; that they should move in together; that she should stop ghosting or at least take a break from it. It was alarming how often he returned to these last two points. Because even after four years of intimacy, Isabel didn't want them to live together. And she didn't want to stop ghosting, though she suspected Emanuel was not entirely wrong on this one. Twenty years of slipping into survivors' lives, a warm body between cold sheets, was taking its toll on her. And that mortified her. How dare she complain of hardship? The dead and the survivors were owed too much.

Isabel looked around Bet She'arim and felt it was too beautiful a day to leave the park for the darkness of her desk. She had a sudden yen for Zakhi and a short reprieve before returning to German-occupied Greece. Zakhi had just come back from Thailand and Isabel couldn't get enough of him. She had missed him and suddenly, out of nowhere, the fourteen-year age gap between them taunted her. Suddenly their relationship was all risk with no safety net. She never used to think about Zakhi and other, younger women. She just enjoyed their time together. But now she needed him more. He had become a ballast to her life on the seam of then and now. The dead and near dead. The living and the walking wounded. The loops of memory. He was also the playmate that helped her buck the staid safety of Emanuel.

Isabel stepped away from the parking lot and back across the large green lawn. She stopped by the playing dogs and called Zakhi.

"You free now?"

"Fortune shines upon us, Isabel Toledo," Zakhi answered. "I'm leaving the building supply store in town and can be in the park in five."

She waited on a wood bench by the Cave of the Coffins, next court over from Yehudah HaNassi's, and debated whether to tell Zakhi about the gas station attendant the day before who ordered her to move to the right. In German. And when Isabel didn't budge, he screamed at her, amplifying her terror and paralysis. Then suddenly his shouting was Hebrew and she drove the car to the adjacent aisle of pumps. She could share this with Zakhi because he would never tell her to stop ghosting. Zakhi understood her commitment. He was haunted too.

Zakhi's truck pulled into the parking lot. From the bench, Isabel watched him step out. He glanced at his cell phone, slid it into the back pocket of his low riding jeans, and turned towards the lawn. Long strides in heavy boots. He also looked up at the hill. Like her. He watched the dogs chase each other among the oak trees. His gait was purposeful. His hips pumped forward. The man exuded sex.

He found her easily enough. The park had emptied since the ceremony. They didn't talk. Not even hello. When he held out his large calloused hand she took it and he pulled her to her feet and hugged her tightly.

"I missed you," he said.

It had only been twenty-four hours. Isabel smiled and took a deep breath of the smell of his neck. Holding hands they walked to the Cave of Coffins and bent low to pass through the short narrow door. The bright September morning did not give way easily to the cool dimness inside and it took their eyes a few moments to adjust. Silently they continued down the cave's long-spined corridor and passed shadowed niches filled with stone sarcophagi. At the corridor's end they entered a large tall space and stood close, shoulders touching. Isabel finally spoke.

"I love those chisel scores." She raised her chin towards the pock-marked walls and looked up at the high ceiling.

"All carved out by hand." Zakhi walked around the large alcove, taking in details and dimensions. "Somebody important was buried here."

Isabel leaned against the damp wall. She could literally spend days watching this man move.

"Function follows form," he said. "The builders simply and ingeniously enlarged the natural limestone bays."

"When you were in Thailand, I came here a lot. It's cool . . . relief from the heat . . . from my work." She stopped herself but wanted to tell him so badly. Zakhi wouldn't judge her like Emanuel and Suri. Even Lia gave her odd looks when they Skyped. All the way from India.

But she couldn't, wouldn't, talk now. What if Thailand had made Zakhi change his mind about the war, about her ghosting, about her? People went through changes when they travelled. They had insights. New perspectives. She wouldn't say a word. She couldn't afford to hear Emanuel's-Alon's-Dave's words come out of Zakhi's mouth.

"You came with Woody I assume." He stopped near her and then walked round the cave again. "We're really deep inside the hill, right?" Zakhi stopped and stared at her. "You know how much I like being deep inside," and flashed her a mischievous sexy grin. Isabel laughed greedily, adoring his foreplay. He went and stood next to an ancient seven-branched bas relief candelabrum carved on the back wall, sizing it up.

"Looks like a modern interpretation of primitive art, no?"

"Yes," Isabel said, paying closer attention to the plain blocky candelabrum. It stood out as different among the highly ornamented sarcophagi. Yet here it was. A man-size marker indicating that the bones buried in this hillside belonged to the children of Israel.

"Impressive." Zakhi made his way back to her, coursing casually in and out of a loud pool of Spanish tourists that suddenly filled the space. "Wonder what their overrun costs were?"

Isabel laughed again and took Zakhi's hand. They walked back down the corridor and through each one of the many ante chambers. At seventy-five meters square, the Cave of the Coffins was by far the largest in the necropolis.

"This coffin belongs to Kyra Mega, wife of Rabbi Joshua, son of Levi Shalom." Isabel used her cellphone flashlight to read the inscription. "And that one, Yudan, son of Rabbi Hillel. Look here, the goddess Nike," she flashed the light on a winged female creature carved on a large coffin in the corner.

"Victory is at hand." Zakhi drew her into a large dark niche with haphazardly stacked coffins.

"The archaeologists haven't made order in here yet," Isabel said.

"Perfect."

Zakhi led her towards the back. A small rectangle cut high into the wall let in a thin cone of natural light.

"All these bas reliefs—bulls, lions, crocodiles, cows, eagles, even Aphrodite there, proof, look." Isabel pointed here and there. "Jews have always been transnational."

Zakhi pulled her to him. Kissed and licked her lips. She had missed this, missed him. Two months without his touch, without his eyes, without his laughter, and his smile. He moved them deeper into the hollow, screening them behind the last row of coffins and lifted her legs around his waist. When he slid his hands under her dress, he let out a long low whistle.

"Ready for action." His lips pressed against hers and ran his hands over her naked buttocks. "Just how I like it," he whispered into her mouth.

Like a cat going up a tree Isabel's legs wrapped around Zakhi. He undid his jeans, took hold of some of her weight, and when he entered her, her moan reverberated against the many surfaces of stone. She moved her hands from Zakhi's neck and pushed back against the cool stone of the coffin. Along the cover's decorative edge her fingers read *aleph*—א—*chet*—ח. Zakhi pitched into her and she stopped reaching for script. His physical power, his gentility and wildness, lured her to stillness. His tradesman hands that jack hammered concrete block walls, laid cable, spliced wires, and worked with live current unseamed her. Zakhi moved back and forth watching her buckle and whimper. When they were done, they held on to each other quietly. Isabel's fingers read the stone again. Aleph, chet, yod, nuun, ayin, mem. אחינעם. The resting place of Achinoam.

Zakhi kissed Isabel long and hard on her open lips. With one hand he held her spent body. With the other he stroked her calves, thighs, calling her skin to life.

"I really missed you," he said. "Under the palm trees, in hammocks, over cocktails, my dear, I thought of Isabel hunched over her keyboard day after day."

She smiled. Pulled him closer.

"But maybe it's time to stop."

Her heart dropped to her stomach. Here it was. Finally. The breakup that was written into the script from the first time they met.

"Seriously. A few months in Thailand, a rest from work, would do you a world of good."

She was relieved but also annoyed. Why did everyone want her to stop writing? "When Uri's done with the army, I'll be free. For now I'm here."

Zakhi slackened his hold and slowly her legs slipped to the ground. He slapped her backside lightly. Her dress fell back into place. He sat down on the coffin.

"Isn't it sacrilegious to have sex in a graveyard? Here's a righteous perfumer. And there, rabbis, their families, their virgin daughters and nieces."

Isabel scanned Zakhi's face. A refugee from a religious family, were the teachings of his fathers' peeking through? Was he mocking them or paying homage? Zakhi lived like a heathen but cited Scripture like other men cite sports.

"First, Zakhi Kandel, dearest." Isabel's finger traced the sharp outline of his handsome sun browned face, "no one's buried here right now. No righteous perfumers. No virgin daughters. Them bones been removed hundreds of years ago. Second, I like sex in graveyards. Peaceful in a compressed kind of way. And third, in case any souls are hovering around, then we're providing a bit of entertainment. Think of it as a mitzvah."

She inclined toward Zakhi—her friend and lover—found his mouth, pulled him up from sitting towards her. She pressed herself full length against him. "Again," she murmured and stroked his smooth shaven head. She wanted to lose herself. "Again," she hummed knowing she should be working. The book's deadline's fast upon her. But she sought sanctuary in the park. In Zakhi's strong

13

hands. In the wide chest she had missed. In the gravelly voice that told her about construction projects, books, and the latest government insanity.

While he was away, she had suffered his absence silently. Afraid to admit to herself how much and not able to share it with Molly who didn't want to hear about Zakhi. Molly wanted Isabel to grow up, was how she so tactfully put it, and move in with Emanuel. On those rare occasions when Isabel did mention Zakhi, Molly reminded her that fourteen years separated them. Nearly one life cycle apart. Isabel was forty-seven with three children. Zakhi was thirty-three and had it all ahead of him: falling in love, building a life with a chosen mate, making all the usual mistakes one makes in marriage, and gaining all the usual miracles associated with children and—unless or until it fell apart—domestic peace. As if Isabel didn't know all this. As if she weren't terrified of this attachment.

Isabel lifted Zakhi's loose cotton shirt and ran her fingertips lightly over his mocha-soft skin. She adored his skin. The first time they lay naked together, two years ago, she couldn't stop stroking him. She asked if he were Yemenite or Sephardi, like the Toledos. But he said no. His family were Dark Russians from the Pale of Settlement.

"Again," Isabel hummed a third time. A little louder, just a little more, just a little longer. In the cave's dimness, in the screened recess behind the coffins, she placed his hands on her breasts. Their recreation a balm to her turbulence. Zakhi lifted Isabel up against the coffin. She wrapped her legs around him, again, closed her eyes, and whispered, "Help me drive away the ghosts."

3

Isabel drove quickly from Bet She'arim to her house on the other side of town. Foot hard on the gas even on the narrow turns. Now that the school ceremony was over, now that she had been with Zakhi, she had no excuse not to get back to work. Joseph Schine's deadline heckled her: *Pages, Isabel, I need pages, pages.*

Fields of sunflowers spiked up on one side of the winding road.

Dancing cypresses on the other. This landscape of soft hills, modest groves of oak and olive trees, a passing goat herd and shepherd, looked like Provence. Same colors, same textures. Yet when suddenly the earth and skies reverberated with lightening grey metal, the mechanical thunder of F-16s and low flying helicopters ferrying wounded soldiers to Haifa, then one knew, despite the silver greens of trees, the blue brilliant sky sheltering Jewish and Bedouin villages, the goats, shepherds, the teenagers on horses, the short hills running toward the Carmel mountain range and on to the sea, that this was not Provence but the State of Israel going to battle once again.

Isabel pulled into her driveway and dashed into the house. She gave Woody a quick pat on the belly and beelined straight to the desk without looking right or left. If she paused for one second, she might never make it. *Pages, Isabel, I need pages, pages.* Schine's refrain towed her to the computer. Owner, chief editor, art coordinator, public relations manager, and sole distributor of Schine Publishing, a publication house dedicated to Holocaust testimonials, Schine squeezed her like a constrictor. His thick Polish accent, like Suri's, like her aunts Zizi and Lola, jammed the New York-Galilee line, book after book, year after year. He insisted she comply with his draconian production schedule. Six to eight months from survivor interview to completed manuscript. No flexibility or frills. And she complied. Laid herself down on Schine's conveyor belt.

"Why?" Emanuel asked.

"Why?" Lia asked.

"I think it's perfectly awful," Suri the survivor weighed in time and again. Suri had been against this work from the very beginning. "Live life, Isabel. Use your imagination to create new worlds, ones with beauty and love and adventure."

Luckily Dave was already dead when she began ghosting or she was sure to have been subject to the usual speech: "Why European history? The past is a greedy storm Isabel." He would frown as he spoke, intent on displaying disappointment. "Why not computers? Be part of the cutting edge, part of the future." He would bob his head as if to push towards the future.

"Let the dead rest. Let the pain settle." Suri's mouth tightened and turned away when Isabel talked about her books. Through her silence she said again and again that her own life story would not be shared nor written down.

But Isabel had no rest. Once she wrote Rosa Levi's life she was hooked. She and Alon and the girls lived on kibbutz then and Rosa talked to her. About the war. About the Jews. About her life. Finally someone willing to talk and, like a restorative torrent, her words became the powerful antidote to Suri's stifling muteness. Finally answers to questions. Finally details, descriptions, tears. After that there was no stopping her.

Isabel opened the computer. She was behind schedule, which was totally unusual for her. All of the previous books she had written for Schine were produced and delivered on time. But not this one. Not this time. Which is why she hadn't answered Schine's badgering calls all week. Years ago she gave up telling him to stop calling her all the time, that his anxiety and pressure didn't help the process. He had to trust she'd meet the deadline. And she had for fourteen books over the past twenty years. But the word relax was not in Schine's vocabulary. He treated every manuscript like it was the last boat out of Europe.

Isabel had sat with Jaim in April in New York. Now it was the beginning of October. Seventy-five percent should have been done by now but only the first third was. She told Schine two weeks ago that she was winding up the second third. She lied. No choice. She scrolled down through the pages. Scanned the sentences. Jaim Benjamin on a scrubby hill walked a herd of twenty goats back down to the village. The sun was setting. The goats moved slowly. Bellies full. Ready to lie down for the night. The pen was enclosed with wood slats. It was covered in tin. Large dogs slept with them. Wolves and raptors hunted at night.

Jaim washed his face, arms, and chest from a large bucket near the well. Inside the small house, the Ivanovs, the elderly couple whose family has known his for generations, waited for him. The Jews of Florina came from Spain following the Expulsion in 1492. They lived peacefully and well among their Christian neighbors. They sold fabrics and *charuji* shoes. Jaim Benjamin and Isabel laughed how from Spain to Florina to Lodz to New York, Jews were forever in the garment business.

Olives, hard cheese, flat bread waited on the table. A noise startled the animals in the hutch. The dogs growled. Jaim rose from his chair to see what or who might be disturbing them. The old man gestured for him to stay and went out by himself. Nazi beasts, men and dogs, patrolled the hamlets at night. It was too risky for Jaim to talk to them. He looked like a mountain peasant after six months of hard labor and simple living but didn't sound like one.

When Jaim recalled this moment, Isabel told him that she too lived near goats and passed them on her nightly walk with Woody. To her they looked like old Jewish men.

"The old Jewish men you have in mind are from Eastern European shtetls. Old Jewish men from Greece look different. We are Sephardi, you know. Darker, broader, in face and body. We look like you look, Isabel, like your father and grandfather probably looked. It's a shame you know so little about our history." Jaim Benjamin dared her to venture into this other dimension of her past. To venture into her father's story. But she wouldn't. She couldn't. And she basically didn't want to. Dave Toledo was and would remain on the margins on her life.

And remembering this chat, Isabel pushed away from the desk and went into the kitchen to start cooking. Yael would be home in two days. The fridge needed to be stocked. Isabel knew they fed the soldiers on base, but watching Yael eat, you'd think they didn't. She put up a pot of basmati rice. She roasted red peppers and eggplants. She sifted through orange lentils for a soup. She soaked cannellini and kidney beans in water. On Friday she would put them in a slow cooker with onions, garlic, potatoes, carrots, and bulgur. A vegetarian *hamin*, or *cholent* as Suri called it, for Saturday's lunch. She felt better and decided to call Lia in India. It had been a week since they spoke and she missed her terribly. When they tried to reach her the night before—Uri wanted to talk to her before the *Genesis* ceremony—the call didn't go through. Not unusual. Plenty of places in the world didn't have good reception. And now again Lia's phone rang and rang and rang.

Isabel made herself a cold coffee and went to sit on the porch swing. Tomorrow morning she would make up for today's delinquency by waking up extra early and planting herself by the desk. She was behind, true, but she would catch up. She needed a good run of typing to make the deadline. It wasn't clear to her why after so many books it was this one, Jaim's life in Greece during the war, with no actual scenes of ghettos, *aktions*, transports, or camps, that was hardest for her. Maybe she was just tired. Too many lives. Too much atrocity. Maybe it was the shared Spanish heritage or the link Jaim Benjamin made between the Inquisition and the Holocaust. Emanuel said Jaim Benjamin's book was going slowly because of Dave.

"And you don't want to go there."

"You're a mathematician, not a shrink," Isabel countered when Emanuel offered this interpretation.

"Still, it all adds up," he said gently but with conviction.

Emanuel might be right. But Isabel didn't want to admit it. Dave was long gone. So was the pain of his bitter absence from her childhood and from Suri's life. When it came to Dave Isabel agreed with Suri. Gone was gone. Let the dead rest.

Isabel drank some coffee and opened the tablet to read the news. When she read and then reread the headline all wind was sucked out of her. *Bomb found on tracks in Himachal Pradesh.* She read out loud to understand better. *Mountain Railways of India. En route to Chandigarh. One bomb went off before train crossed. Second bomb detonated by Bomb Disposal Squad.* Her guts ran cold and she continued reading: *It is not yet known how many injured from sudden halt in service.*

She started heaving. Her heart hurt. Lia was there. She said she wanted to see Le Corbusier's urban design. That explained the unanswered phone. Maybe there were hostages. It was just a matter of time before Jews were separated from the others. Then the Israelis from the Jews. Terrorists would negotiate for their lives. Or kill them off one by one after rape and mutilation to send the world a message. Isabel clutched her stomach. She staggered to the lawn.

"No," she cried to the tall trees in the yard. "No, not Lia." She rushed from one end of the property to another. An alarmed Woody stayed close to her heels. How could this be happening?

"No, no, no!" she wailed out loud. "I told her to stay home and rest. She works so hard. What is she looking for in India?" Isabel screamed at the yawning blue sky. It was so beautiful she hated it. She wouldn't live if something happened to one of her children. Dread rippled through her and she collapsed near the pomegranate tree.

The phone rang. Isabel pulled it out from her pocket. And listened.

"Isabel?" Suri asked. "Isabel is that you?"

"What?"

"Honey, are you crying?"

"What?"

"What what? What's going on?"

"Lia!"

"Lia?"

"Lia's on the train with the bomb . . . Suri . . . I can't . . ."

"Isabel, Isabel, listen to me." Suri was stern. "Stop all this right now. Lia's in an ashram. Not on a train."

Isabel fought to breathe evenly. Really?

"Honey, Lia's in an ashram in Kerala." Suri repeated herself slowly. Softly.

"How do you know?"

"Because I spoke to her a few days ago. She called to wish me a happy birthday. She knew she wouldn't be able to call me from the ashram on my birthday. Such a thoughtful person."

"Lia's in an ashram?"

"Yes, in Kerala."

"In an ashram in Kerala? You sure?" Isabel started to laugh and cry at the same time. "I can't believe . . ."

"Isabel, sweetheart, you don't sound well. And not just now. Lately. I don't want to talk about your work, you know my thoughts about that, but you need a vacation. When Lia comes back from India, you and Emanuel should go away. Just the two of you. To rest. To sightsee. To spoil one another. Like your father and I used to."

Isabel wiped her eyes and nose on her arm. Yes, she thought, just like that bi-annual charade of closeness. That was exactly the kind of relationship she wished for herself.

"Lia's in an ashram in Kerala?" she cried with joy. "You're sure?"

"Yes. Yes. Are you better now?"

"I don't know what came over me." Isabel stood and pulled her shoulders back. "You're right. Lia told me she was going to Kerala, but I forgot. I can't keep track of her plans. I can't believe I worried so much."

"Shh. I love you. Is Uri there?"

"He's with Alon . . . wait, here he is, coming through the front door."

And as Uri chatted on the phone with his grandmother in New York, Isabel washed her face and straightened out her clothing. She made a quick salad for supper. After hearing all about the pony, she put Uri in the bath, then bed, then joined him under the covers to read his favorite new chapter book. He had made the blanket into a tent and held the book in one hand and a flashlight in the other. She opened the book to where they had left off the night before.

"We're in a cave, *Ema*. Like Bet She'arim." Uri turned the flashlight to his face when he spoke. Then turned it on her abruptly as if it were a microphone and this an interview. Her turn to talk.

"A cave?"

"Yes." He turned the light on his face. "And we're hiding from the enemy."

"Uri, let's read the book." Terror rekindled in her. She was in a cave with a child or two or even three. Protecting them. Praying they'd be quiet. Patrols outside. Dogs sniffing them out. She felt suffocated.

"*Ema?*" he shined the flashlight on her face again and stared at her.

"I don't feel well." Isabel pulled the blanket off and breathed deeply into the dark room. "I need a minute." She left the bed and went into the bathroom to drink.

When she returned Uri lay on his side, facing the wall, spooning with Woody, the blanket pulled up to his neck. She had ruined it for him. She lay down behind him and stretched her arm over him and the dog. "Do you want me to tell you a story from when I was little?"

He shook his head yes.

"There's a place in the middle of New York called Rockefeller Center. And in the winter, my father, your grandfather Dave, liked to go ice skating there. I liked it too, though Grandma Suri didn't. She said she couldn't get the hang of the skates and waited for us in a restaurant nearby, or sometimes she didn't come at all. Special time for me and my father. Do you remember we went there last summer?"

Uri nodded slightly.

"Well, I had an ice skating outfit. A jacket and short skirt made from black velvet and custom white boots. I think Dave thought I'd be some fancy figure skater or something. But I fell all the time and made holes in my stockings." She laughed softly. Pulled in tighter to Uri and Woody. "Do you remember there's an enormous gold statue there, against one of the walls? Prometheus bringing fire to . . ."

She didn't know how long her phone rang, but suddenly she heard it, tumbled out of bed and staggered to her bedroom to answer.

"I'm outside," Emanuel said. Judging by his tone he had been there awhile.

"Sorry, I fell asleep." Isabel shuffled to the door. "I'm really sorry, it's been a rough day . . ." She opened it for him.

Emanuel also looked tired but smiled. "If I had a key I wouldn't need to wake you up, Issie. I'd just join you in bed."

"Please don't start now."

"Fine."

*

The year they built their house in town Isabel and Alon's marriage fell apart but Isabel was too busy falling in love with concrete to notice. On pour days she waited anxiously for the mixers to arrive and Alon acted like a jilted lover. He didn't know why she spent so much time on the construction site and complained she neglected the family. He didn't understand why she refused to change her last name from Toledo to Segev. All the other women he knew took their husbands' names. He claimed this was another sign she never really cared for him. Isabel waved his complaints away. Alon had stopped understanding her. She had explained to him many times why a woman would choose not to give up her birth family's name and become subsumed in her husband's tribe. Then he complained bitterly about the ghosting. But when she discovered the magic of construction, he lost all hope of ever being a dominant player in her life again.

And funnily enough it was this unexpected passion that cemented her relationship with Zakhi. He understood her love of concrete and always invited her to witness pour days on his construction sites. A week after the *Genesis* ceremony, Isabel dropped Uri off at school and drove to the Winkler site. It was a pour day. She turned into the village. The Winkler plot, on a hillock at the end of a lane of new homes, had a dramatic view of shifting grades of field and mountain. Isabel drove into the pastoral beauty when suddenly dogs exploded on either side of her car. They barked frantically. They bared their teeth. They dared her to touch them. "*When you get to the gate you'll have to run . . .*" Every time Isabel entered the village she knew it was coming and every time the dogs took her by surprise. And terrified her. "*And the furies kept on screaming, Schneller! Schneller!*" Isabel pressed down on the gas and horn simultaneously. Nonplussed, the dogs flanked her tires and bumpers. When the car squealed to a halt on the gravel of the Winkler property, they stopped too, high from the chase. Not even waiting for her to cut the engine, they made sharp U-turns and were back in their driveways, panting, sated, waiting for the next car.

Isabel closed her eyes. She placed her forehead against the steering wheel. It wasn't just the dogs' fierceness that troubled her. But her own. Every time she ran the gauntlet she craved hitting back. A small leg caught under a heavy tire. A rump clipped by the front fender. She controlled herself but also hated herself for wanting to hurt them.

She sat in her car a moment longer to compose herself. Zakhi's truck was there. So was Moshe's, the plasterer. Since Isabel had been visiting Zakhi on sites for two years she knew some of the contractors he worked with regularly. She got out of her car and walked to the western and southern facades of the house. The scaffolding was in place and the naked concrete block walls were being dressed in their grey petticoat. From color samples on the wall, Isabel could see that after the grey a soft yellow exterior plaster would be applied. The dress. Slowly she walked back towards a large opening that would eventually be the front door but stopped when he heard Zakhi shouting.

"I don't care who's dying this week. Nothing's completed. Nothing. What's installed needs going over. I haven't approved one piece of stone you've laid." Silence. Obviously Sucrat the stone mason was defending himself.

Zakhi walked out of the house holding his phone. His scowl became a smile when he saw Isabel. He came towards her and together they looked towards the road, waiting for the concrete mixers. Isabel was nervous. And excited. Zakhi got a call and walked away to take it. He was a gentleman and never yelled at his contractors near her. When he came back he handed her a cell phone. "Call the concrete company for me, dear. Let's make sure they show up today. If not, I'm going to totally lose it."

Isabel took the phone and dialed the number. The phone rang on the other end. She never remembered seeing Zakhi so unnerved. Maybe it was because he was not only the electrician but project manager, supervising construction from excavation to carpentry. Maybe it was too much for him. He was so easy going when he was only responsible for the electrical work. Or maybe another woman was playing with his heart.

The ringing continued. Isabel closed the line and pressed redial with more force than was necessary. Zakhi's antagonism was contagious. In the momentary quiet between each ring, indignation snapped through her. She closed the line again. Pressed redial. How could a concrete company's office not answer at eight in the morning? Day light hours were critical. Morning hours even more so. It was not summer but the days were still warm. Dehydration compromised concrete's strength. Zakhi would be watering the newly poured surfaces at regular intervals over the next few days, slowing the curing process.

Isabel closed the phone line. Each time she pressed redial, her nerves surged. She wanted nothing more than to throw the phone to the ground. To stomp on it. And then she saw them. Large and serene like elephants, two concrete mixers rolled noisily down the narrow village lane. The ground rumbled under their weight. Their fat elliptical drums turned round and round, keeping the aggregate mixed and moist. They were so large and so imposing that even the dogs knew better than to give chase. They stood in their driveways to stake out their territory, but were rooted in place. Zakhi came to stand by her. Isabel purred with excitement. The masonry crew stepped forward to meet the mixers.

After twenty minutes of prep, concrete began to flow from the drums. A metal pipe held high by a brontosaurus-like crane swallowed it and channeled it to a thick rubber hose. Isabel rocked with anticipation. The head of the crew seized the hose and used all the weight and force of his body to control the heavy surge of grey lava that rushed out of the bucking black hose.

"A beast," Isabel said, awed yet again by the power and rush of the concrete.

The workers used long metal rakes to spread the concrete evenly throughout the wooden forms on the ground. These were the outdoor walkways circumventing the house. The second concrete mixer pulled up. The crew filled vertical columns and horizontal slabs for a small cottage at the edge of the yard. The concrete would harden in a few hours. Enough to step on within twenty-four.

"*Tohu vivohu*," Isabel said rapturously to a distracted Zakhi. What was he thinking about so intently? "The primordial matter of Genesis. Swirling chaos. Fast flowing matter dividing into form."

Zakhi smiled at her, not moved at this moment by the poetry or her passion. His phone rang. He moved out of earshot.

When Lia and Yael studied the Book of Exodus in third grade, Isabel read along with them in an English translation. They learned that Bezalel was commanded to build the portable tabernacle for the Ten Commandments. All the strict building specifications were laid out—from exterior walls to interior partitions, from floors to roof, from lighting fixtures to sacrificial ornaments and vessels— straight from the Lord's mouth. No room for change orders, ornery or delinquent contractors. Bezalel was in charge of it all. Bezalel the artisan. Bezalel the artist. Bezalel the project manager. Bezalel son of Uri.

The crew finished with the concrete slabs and wooden forms. Meantime Moshe and his team mixed lime, cement, and sand for the plaster and worked on the western facade. The concrete mixers with their emptied drums turned away. The dogs watched them rumble towards the gate, still daunted by their mass.

"Is something wrong with me?" Zakhi walked back to her. "Is it so wrong to expect people to show up for work, and once here to work?" They watched Sucrat's young assistants get into their truck and drive away. "He has the nerve to say that the kid with the blue shirt is his son and has wonderful hands. That I should give him a chance." Zakhi looked as if he were about to cry.

"I'm sorry." Isabel kissed him lightly on the cheek. "Can we meet tomorrow? Maybe I can cheer you up?" She smiled playfully.

Zakhi nodded and dialed Sucrat again. She heard the phone not being picked up and walked to her car. She did not have energy for the dogs and drove slowly in the opposite direction, taking the long route all around the village.

The Libels

1

Isabel had said yes right away when Itka Schwartz invited her to the commemorative dinner in Prague. A chance to run away from Schine and his *pages, Isabel, I need pages, pages.* A respite from Emanuel. Lia, just back from India, would stay home with Uri. And in a few days her children would join her in Prague for a brief family vacation. She wanted Yael to come too. Not that big a deal anymore to request permission to leave the base and country for a short spell. But Yael said that when she took time off, she'd be heading to Eilat with friends. The brilliant blue Red Sea, the purple orange mountains, the snorkeling, the hookahs, civilization a step behind, that was what she called a vacation.

So for now Isabel was on her own among Prague's heavy greys. No one to care for but herself in this city charged with beauty and echoes. She decided to focus on the beauty this visit. Back burner the echoes, the heavy tread of history. From the plane she welcomed the wide Vltava River. The carved stone bridges. The terracotta roofs. The Castle perched on a hill. How lovely! The long leash of home slackened.

And she would see Jiri.

*

After a quick shower at the hotel, Isabel made her way down Celetná Street. She had been here enough times to swim in the pleasure of familiarity. She paused in front of one of Kafka's former residences, right next door to Jiri's studio. Kafka lived here from the time of his bar-mitzvah until his early twenties. 1896–1907. Did the fierce black spires of the Church of Our Lady before Týn also induce tremors of the hunted in him? How Franz loved and suffered his native city.

"Not this trip," she rebuked herself out loud. This was a vacation. Focus on the beauty. "History away." Isabel ran into the lobby of Jiri's building and bounded up the stairs to the top floor. She arrived out of breath and happy.

"Sorry I kept you waiting," Jiri opened the studio door after a moment's delay, looking groggy and preoccupied. "I'm working on an article. Nineteenth-century nature paintings at the National." Jiri had taken her to that museum last time she was in town. Top of Wenceslas Square. "Boring shit." Waved her into the room. "Coffee?" He placed a pot of water on a small electric burner.

They sat on a hard wood bench by the window. Smiling and checking each other out. Despite his wrinkled clothing and tired face, Jiri looked his usual sensual self. His light blue eyes and sandy hair, the deep character lines that edged his cheeks, pleased Isabel. This was good. Passion with another man. A distraction. An emotional albeit temporary wedge between herself and Emanuel. Between herself and Zakhi. And she liked Jiri. Simple fact. She liked him a lot.

Jiri sat quietly and didn't stop smiling at her. Isabel looked back at him, then out to the world. Our Lady's ribbed vaults, her tall arched stained glass, and menacing black spires filled the sky. Silence dragged on. Last time they met was four months ago. Awkward moments of reconnection.

"Show me how your uncircumcised member works," Isabel spoke suddenly, delicately, and turned into the room. Turned into the man. She took small sips of tepid coffee as Jiri opened his pants. His hand moved slowly, methodically. When his penis filled with blood, she

27

went over and remembered him. She kissed his wide lined face. His skin smelled of morning shave and a light musk cologne. She kissed his neck. His hair was buzzed close to the skull, Israeli style— not that he knew that—and as they kissed, and as he removed her clothing, she moved her hands over his velvet scalp. Silly clichés came over her during sex. Sometimes in the general loss of control they spilled out.

"My Czech charger," Isabel moaned and closed her eyes. She bent forward toward the floor as Jiri took her nipple into his mouth. She felt him move deeply into her. "Oh, Prague pony."

Jiri burst out laughing. Isabel hung her head in shame but Jiri couldn't stop laughing.

"You're going to lose your erection," Isabel retorted sharply and focused on a large knot in the dark wood floor. Normally Jiri's laughter would have been received as a playful challenge. A higher benchmark to meet. But now it brought Isabel down. Her usual bravado and sense of humor abandoned her. She felt spooked instead.

Jiri saw her unease, slipped out, took her by the hand, and led her to a small mattress in a shadowed corner of the room. He arranged himself on it and gently pulled her down beside him. He kissed her neck, her breasts. Gentle, gentle. Isabel turned her head towards the window. Black spires sliced the sky. Jiri's lips moved along her body.

"This is for you my precious pussy, my Jewish," he paused at her pubes, "jam pot."

She laughed out loud, pulled him up, looked into his eyes, and breathed with him. Outside skies clouded over grey. Jiri entered her again.

"Just like your mother's house in New York." Jiri drew himself in and out slowly, rhythmically, teasing out her pleasure. "Same parquet wood floors, same porcelain sink." He moved harder and faster, memories of their first coupling enflaming them. Jiri watched her face change with excitement. When she came he followed so softly she was not sure he had.

"*Neni zač,*" Isabel whispered and held him against her.

"Shh." He tucked his head under her arm. Their braided limbs soft and contented in the dim light of a Prague autumn.

*

In the initial stages of a book Isabel's tears and rage often translated into a fierce appetite for life. After a long day breathing in 'that Holocaust *drek*' as Molly called it (Isabel loved Yiddish in an Irish brogue), she sought out music, dance, and mainly sex. The night she met Jiri Stipek, six months ago in April, she was primed to be with a man.

It was a small noisy pub on Houston Street. Her third day of sitting with Jaim Benjamin. Hours of listening to stories. Of asking questions. Of taking it in. A global-warming hot spell fried the city. At the bar, she sat next to this sculptor from Prague. In his late thirties, married with two small children, he was in New York with the works of several Central European artists whose work was being shown at a gallery in Chelsea.

Isabel told him about her trips to Prague and Karlovy Vary. She flirted and declared that the Vinohrady apartments reminded her of the Upper West Side. Same parquet wood floors. High ceilings. Wall moldings and ceiling medallions. Same large white porcelain sinks and tubs. She invited him to Suri's to corroborate the affinity. *Prosim.*

Isabel hadn't brought a strange man to her mother's apartment since high school. And she could because Suri and her boyfriend, Hal, were visiting friends in Montauk. On the way uptown Isabel led Jiri to the metal slip between subway cars. She leaned him against the cool stainless steel carriage and watched tracks flash through the barrier of swinging chains. They rocked back and forth.

"I haven't slept with a woman other than my wife in many years. But I'll make an exception for you, Isabel Toledo." Jiri stroked her hair and pulled her close. "You're very beautiful. Like a woman from Spain." He stroked her ass. Kissed her mouth. "And a gentleman cannot exactly say no to a lady's direct request. *Prosim.*"

Isabel undressed Jiri in her childhood bedroom and was immediately besieged by his hairless, muscular, beautifully proportioned, silk-skinned torso, his uncircumcised loveliness. Raised in New York and living in Israel since early adulthood, Isabel was not accustomed to such male members. Hello world. She pushed her tongue into his mouth and murmured her few Czech words over and over again. *Dobrý den. Prosim. Děkuji.* Good day. Please. Thank you.

29

⋆

"When are you coming to visit me in Israel?" Isabel asked. She and Jiri remained tucked into one another on the small mattress in the corner of his studio. Her back pushed against the wall of cold exposed bricks. In the building next door she imagined Kafka once leaned against these very same bricks on the wall's other side.

"And your husband?"

"I'm not married."

"Your boyfriend?"

"Emanuel? What about him?"

"Aren't you in love?"

"Does it matter?"

"I thought you were a couple."

"We are and aren't." She looked up at the loose strips of paint on the ceiling. "I'm attached to Emanuel. I love him, but I don't want to live with him. I have a busy enough domestic life with my children. Besides, I bore easily. Park a man in my house and within six months I'll never want to have sex with him again. I'm restless. Or just plain awful."

"You don't ever need to be bored, Isabel Toledo. Come visit me in Prague whenever you want."

Isabel rolled on top of him and glanced at the small clock on the table. In an hour she was meeting Itka Schwartz at the Intercontinental Hotel. Time enough for another round. While she moaned no, no, not as in don't, or stop, but as in don't stop, Jiri pounded yes and yes and yes. Grey light and gothic gloom filled the room. She closed her eyes to not see the corralling of Jews into Josefov. Twelfth century. No. She opened her eyes and stared at the brick wall. The Pope ordered a wall built around them. Thirteenth century. No. Trains and wooden slats exploded in her mind alongside the spot inside of her Jiri insisted on reaching. By force of will, out of terror and desperation, Isabel's mind became a black screen. Focus on the body she told herself. Only the body. Banish history's wretchedness. Pleasure instead. Only the body. Whimpering and making a big fool of herself, she finally came, sweaty and exhausted from the effort of wrestling on two fronts. Jiri laced his thick arm around her waist and held her limp body suspended. She was like a piece of stone he looked over to sculpt. She twisted up at the waist. They kissed. They kissed some more. Sets of kisses dug into soft wet mouths. With his lips Jiri said he adored her. That she revved him up. That she was always welcome to his body. She moved her lips over his. Pressing. Sucking. Tasting. Responded that she adored him too. He enlivened her.

By a crazed white porcelain sink Jiri sponged her clean and dried her with a small towel. She dressed quickly and hurried out to the streets to find Itka before her meeting with the mayor's representative. No matter that Isabel only knew a few words in Czech, Itka wanted her by her side. "You are my voice, Isabel. Part of my life story. You are my backbone now." Itka explained herself referring to her memoir that Isabel had written a few years back. Since then they had become close friends. The previous winter Itka invited Isabel for a pampering weekend at the Karlovy Vary spa, and four months ago Isabel came to Prague for the Czech-language publication party of Itka's book. Post-Communist rule, Itka and her husband Ivan, originally from Bratislava, had an apartment in the city and went back and forth between Bat Yam and Prague. A tentative truce with the past.

Isabel stopped for a moment by the entrance of the Church of Our Lady before Týn. Tycho Brahe's crypt was inside. She felt a sudden urge to peek at the bronze statue of him with a globe in one hand, and a sword in the other. A man willing to fight for his re-visioning of the cosmos. 1601. But Itka waited and Isabel had no more time for indulgences.

2

"Our synagogues have become museums, relics, shells emptied of life. Just like the Nazis intended," the commemorative dinner's first guest of honor thundered from the dais. "But we're not extinct as the Nazis predicted." He stared out at the people in the large banquet hall, most of whom were in their seventies and eighties. Wrinkled faces. Thinning hair. Slow reflexes. Long memories. They came from rebuilt lives in the United States, England, Israel. Some from neighboring

Germany and other European countries. A number of people Isabel's age were also present. Children accompanying parents. "But in this city it appears as if we are." He paused.

People stirred. Murmured. Was he being lauded or criticized? Was his anger a healthy house cleaning or an opening of Pandora's Box?

"Remember, my fellow Bohemians. Remember that they partially succeeded with their plan. They wiped us out of here." Slowly he returned to his seat. Isabel stared at the table centerpiece of red and white carnations. Poured herself some more wine. Usually the mood was reflective, elegiac at these kinds of commemorative events. Horrors alluded to. Heroism lauded. Direct mention of specific atrocities avoided. But this man took no pains to hide emotions or particulars. With his words, he allowed for anger, not reconciliation, to saturate the air of the banquet hall.

Another man in an expensive suit approached the dais. "For nearly 800 years the Jews in Praha, were forced to wear special hats, a yellow patch, or Star of David when they left the ghetto for a few hours." He spoke softly, in excellent almost non-accented American English. "In 1710, Fredrick William I allowed those Jews willing to pay 8,000 thaler to move about the city without the yellow tag. That is about 36,000 dollars in today's currency. Few could afford such a generous offer. And then in 1781, the Emperor Joseph I issued the Toleration Edict. Civil rights." A little louder. "Finally accepted, we thought, members of the Empire, citizens of Bohemia, able to live outside the cramped ghetto." His voice quivered. "But no. One hundred and fifty years later, no time at all in world history, a snap of the fingers, we're ordered to wear the yellow star again, to return to the ghetto." He banged the table with a clenched hand. His words tumbled and then burst forth. "But in this ghetto, in Terezin, they don't let us live our restricted lives. No, in Terezin they intend for us to die, and we do, by disease, starvation, thirst, from heartbreak, and despair. Those strong enough to survive these plagues are sent to Auschwitz to play against its odds." He clutched the podium. His face reddened.

"I didn't come here today to accuse." His voice shook. It was softer. "I didn't come here to . . . I want to say I'm sorry about my anger, my pain, but I'm not. I was sent to Terezin in 1942 and haven't been back to Europe since my liberation from Auschwitz on January 27, 1945. It's very hard after so many years." He paused. "Very hard . . . but I'm here with old friends and former classmates of mine, of my brothers and sisters. When I think of the hundreds, the thousands who are not here . . ."

He cried uncontrollably. His wife and another man came up to the podium and led him to his seat. Isabel glanced over at Itka. Her perennial smile was gone. Her eyes shone with tears. Itka had turned eleven soon after the war began. At fifteen her family was taken to Terezin. At seventeen Germany was defeated. None of her immediate relatives survived. Itka had seen two performances of Krása's *Brundibar* in Terezin. Watching them helped her hold on to a sliver of hope. Maybe she'd be with her parents again. She survived Terezin with her Uncle Bruno. Bruno spent time with Ottla Kafka in the ghetto cum camp until she volunteered to accompany a children's transport to Auschwitz. Years later Itka realized Ottla was Franz Kafka's youngest sister. Itka's husband took hold of his wife's hand and held it firmly.

Grief kicked up in Isabel as she watched them. After forty years, the communist lid had lifted and grievances were finally being aired. Isabel knew what was coming. Property seizures. Round-ups. Transport lists. Hostile, unreceptive neighbors. Ghettos. Labor camps. Concentration camps. The trace which remained of centuries old communities. The long history of Bohemian anti-Semitism. The murder of Jews from Bohemia, Moravia, Slovakia, Silesia, and Sudetenland. Frowns and fists would punctuate sentences.

Isabel downed her glass of wine and poured another.

Isabel left the memorial dinner before the official good-nights, begging off a night cap, telling Itka she didn't feel well, blaming it on the wine.

As she floated back to the hotel she recalled her first visit to Auschwitz-Birkenau the summer between high school and college. She had just turned eighteen and spent a month volunteering on a desert kibbutz. Then she toured Europe with another American volunteer. In Rome she decided to go to Poland. Spontaneously. No obvious reason why except that nearly all of Suri's family had been transported there in cattle cars from the walled city of Kamenets-Podolski. And there they died. Her travelling companion went to Holland.

In Poland Isabel was waylaid by the concentration camps. She staggered before the piles of booty. She breathed in the smell of Zyklon B trapped in heaps of greying-brown hair. She sat down amidst the rubble of gas chambers and ovens. Toed fields of ash and bone. A number of consequential life decisions came to her then in those killing fields.

First: she would return to live in Israel after completing college. Which she did. Within a year of graduation she married Alon. Within two she nursed Lia.

Second: she would dedicate her life to the memory of the murdered millions. Which she began to do eight years after moving to Israel. Impulsively she ghosted the life story of Rosa Levi, her co-worker in the kibbutz kitchen, and never looked back. She had found her niche.

Third: she would make sure that she, and any children she had, would become adept at self-defense. Martial arts and firearms. Which they were. Lia, Yael, and Isabel possessed black belts in karate. Uri began his training the year before.

Sometimes as they stood in the kitchen, Isabel threw one of her tall strong daughters off balance with a surprise *ashibaray*. The arch of her foot smacked the girl's shin and her leg lifted off the ground just enough to knock her on her ass when Isabel added a small push.

"Oh yeah?" Lia or Yael on their feet immediately came after her poised to return the blow. Isabel ran from them, laughing hard, round and round the work island they went. If Uri came into the room and saw one of his sisters chasing their mother, he knew they were sparring. He'd come around from the other side and jump on Isabel. Tackling her to the floor, they'd tickle her until she peed her pants.

And there were times, as she waited in the car for Uri to come out from karate class, that she thought about Bella, Suri's mother, who knew nothing of self-defense. Or of guns. Or offensive or defensive strategies. Bella knew nothing about mass murder and ideologically driven expulsion. She lived in Kamenets-Podolski and kept a kosher home. She loved her children and respected her hard working husband. Bella, not unlike hundreds of thousands of women her age all across Europe, remembered the First World War, though she had only been a child. When the second one began she expected a tragic repeat of those earlier devastating hostilities. Food shortages. Men conscripted. Arrogant soldiers. Only this time it was worse. Within days of this second German occupation, appalling decrees were published against the Jews. Their movements restricted. Their work lives demolished. They weren't allowed to own objects of value. Including jewelry. Including pets.

Eventually they were moved into a ghetto. Then the strong were taken to labor camps. The rest by truck to the woods. There they dug their own graves. Stripped naked. Neighbor next to neighbor. Mothers hid children between exposed limbs. *They made our mothers strip in front of us. Here mothers are no longer mothers to their children.* Charlotte Delbo observing the worst. German soldiers shot these Jews and neatly filled the pits. Even murder could be aesthetic and orderly.

Watching Uri run towards the car in his white *karate gi*, a yellow belt tied tightly around his small waist, Isabel felt secure, even belligerent. She started the car. Bella hadn't stood a chance. The first large-scale action of the Final Solution slammed into Kamenets-Podolski on August 27 and 28, 1941. 23,600 Jews from the ghetto massacred in two days.

Even with all the wine from the commemoration dinner in her blood, Isabel slept badly. Not as uneasily as Gregor Samsa, but still when her phone rang at ten in the morning, she felt only half-human. Her limbs almost too heavy to move. Her back uncooperative. Somehow she managed to lurch over to the other side of the bed to stop the loud chirping. A call from home.

"*Ema*, where's the bicycle helmet?" Uri asked.

"I'll call you back." She didn't want him to hear her low hoarse, practically unintelligible, voice. She wanted to wash her face, rinse her mouth, clear her throat.

"No time, *Ema*, we're leaving now. Where is it?" His impatience was not just about the helmet. He didn't want her to hang up. Isabel tried to summon the contents of the hall closet in her mind but couldn't. She tried to move her voice into the normal range and just about managed to do so when Lia called out that she found it.

"I miss you, *Ema*," Uri said quickly.

Of course he did. She had travelled a lot this year. The helmet was just an excuse to call.

"I love you," Isabel crooned. "My favorite boy. See you tomorrow morning."

"I love you too."

Isabel closed the phone. Despite her stiff back she managed to turn over in the large bed. Shreds of violence from a dream came to her. Fragments of fear. She tossed and tangled the sheets and pulled herself to standing, grumpy, combative, hauling a serious headache.

3

Isabel hit the streets. She needed a café with good coffee and internet access. A rarity in Europe. Maybe something arrived from Schine. Or from Jaim Benjamin. She made a deal with herself: check mail now and not again for the rest of the trip.

Isabel walked towards Old Town Square. Kafka's face popped up on billboards, tee-shirts, posters, calendars, cards, and coffee mugs. Kafka who felt displaced in his native city, who suffered a diaspora within a diaspora within a diaspora—a Jew among Christians, a German language writer in a Czech speaking country, an artist among the bourgeoisie—had been elevated in recent decades to the pantheon of local geniuses and saints. She passed the building where he was born. It was now a museum. Behind the plate glass window of what was once his family's first floor apartment a large poster of his thin face stared out.

She stopped momentarily to stare back at his intelligent dark Jew eyes. She felt nothing. This was just a flat poster, an homage more to capitalism than to Kafka's vision of a world rife with brutality, futility, and irrationality. She continued to a café down the street, remembering good coffee there. It was closed until noon. She walked past Jiri's studio and didn't buzz. He had work to do. Then past the

Gymnasium where Kafka went to school. Not far from there was a café with passable coffee that also offered fresh, not boxed, milk upon request.

As Isabel drank the hot strong coffee, she took out her notepad and tried to switch geographies. To think of the structure of Jaim Benjamin's book. To work. To keep up even in this foreign locale. Even on vacation. Even with a wicked headache from last night's wine and rage. *Pages, Isabel I need pages, pages.* Even here. But Kafka eclipsed Schine. His silhouette watched her from the back of a tee-shirt at a table next to hers. She tried to stare past him, to get a foothold in the hills running back from the Aegean. But Kafka dragged her back to the landlocked damp planes of Czechoslovakia. And to nearby Poland. She glared at Franz stamped white on the black tee-shirt and considered Josef K. who Kafka created in 1914, inspired by the Mendel Beiliss trial for 'ritual murder' in Kiev. 1911. Isabel asked the waitress for more milk to dilute the muddy bitter coffee. Begun in England in 1144, ritual murder, also known as the blood libel, quickly became a European favorite. Sometimes small scale slaughters accompanied the charge. Sometimes larger, state-sponsored events. Chmielnicki. 1648–1649. Kishinev. Easter 1903. Shiraz. 1910. Kielce. 1946.

Josef K. wasn't accused of killing and using a Christian child's blood for Passover bread. Though he was summoned to court and told to secure a lawyer and come up with a defense for something equally ridiculous: an unidentified crime. Terror overwhelmed him at moments. If found guilty he might be given the death penalty. But most of the time Josef K. put the officials who tracked him out of his mind. He couldn't accept that justice was a matter of expediency and politics. He went to work at the bank. Took his meals at the small restaurants he favored. Had coffee at one of Prague's many cafés. And reasoned that episodic contact with the anonymous system that had somehow latched on to him indicated he might in the end be overlooked or spared. But of course growing up in a Europe all too eager not to let its Jews have happy endings, Kafka didn't let his Josef K. (both of them, writer and character, named after the Emperor Franz Josef) off the hook so easily. At the end of *The Trial* two men dressed in black lead Josef K. away from his room. Old supporting actors, he explains the scene to himself, still unwilling to accept the intrusion of the absurd into his well-ordered Prussian life. These men don't know how to respond when Josef K. asks them which theater they belong to. "Theater?" they ask and take him to an isolated quarry. There they stab him in the heart. "Like a dog," Josef K. says with his last breath. Like a dog.

Isabel finished her coffee and opened a bottle of sparkling water. The bubbles were so lively they practically hurt going down. She drank slowly. In booming British English the man with Kafka on his back ordered another Pilsner. It was not yet noon.

She opened her notepad. Smoothed down a page. Began a list. Lists composed her. On the practical side, Jaim Benjamin's story was being transcribed in clear correct American English. And it was half done. One hundred and twenty pages to be precise. Jaim Benjamin's few comments on the chapters he reviewed made for little additional work. Schine's draconian schedule would be met. Jaim Benjamin added a note that he felt lighter with the telling. A rock removed from his heart. All pluses this side of the ledger.

On the other—her pen paused above the page—were years of stories thrown up like fortress walls. She began drawing minus signs as if they were words in a sentence. One and then another, another, another to the right edge of the page, then back to the start of the next line. One, then another, another, another --------------------
----
----------------------------- back to the left side of the page to start again.

Isabel poured more bubbly water into the glass. No matter that sentences and paragraphs emerged, that schedule milestones were being met more or less, long periods of silence plagued her. The emotional core of Jaim Benjamin's story eluded her and it was her job to get to the heart and soul of the story. The people who commissioned her to write their life stories were not interested in dry historical accounts. Library shelves, archives, the internet were jam-packed with books and reports stocked with comprehensive facts, lists, speeches, and correspondence. Make the pain real, Jaim Benjamin had said when they first sat together in New York. Do what Aristotle said only literature could: enable readers to understand experience *in extremis*. As if she didn't know this. What Kafka did with his many metamorphoses of K.

And she could do this. Had been doing this for two decades. From the last vision of a father standing on a street corner in a long brown coat, Isabel exposed a child's avalanche of anguish and loss. She had described a pediatric hospital being cleared out by German soldiers. Children too slow to rise from their beds and walk the hallways were tossed out the window. She had come in close to a mother's feelings as she stood on the pavement below watching children fly like broken kites from second and third story windows. It was only possible to come in close. But close was better than nowhere at all.

For twenty years now Isabel had plunged into emotional pits and used specific names and cartographies to write her way out. But now she felt lost in the there, the here, in both places, in neither place. She was way off the path. Had gone astray. Because of Jaim Benjamin's story. Because he tossed her from one *lebensraum* to another. 450 years apart. From Isabella to Bella. From Dave to Suri.

Isabel opened the back of her notepad to a page filled with words. Inadvertently and unbidden, words written on the plane. Suri forbade Isabel to write Bella's story. Suri forbade Isabel to know Suri's story. So it went without saying that Suri forbade Isabel to write Suri's story. Suri hated the industry of memory. She called Schine a publisher of holokitsch. Isabel stared at the page that felt like a product of automatic writing. She was afraid to read it. Suri and Bella: *Verboten.* Taboo. Shame. Guilt. Fear. Frustration. Compulsion.

Suri named me Isabel, after Bella, her mother, who died naked and trembling in a freshly dug pit in a Ukrainian forest clearing. But whenever I consider my name, it's not just my grandmother who comes to mind, but the meaning of her name, the Latin root: beautiful. For Suri's sister, Aunt Lola has assured me that Bella, their mother, was not. The one photograph they managed to hold on to through those terrible hard years, shows a woman in her late twenties with thick black hair gathered in the back. She has a broad face and light colored eyes. Fatigue lines have already found a home around her thin mouth. This is a woman who though not beautiful, would have come to be called handsome as she grew older, had she the opportunity to.

A mélange of emotion propelled Isabel out of the café chair. She put a few coins on the table. The walls of the world tilted toward her. The man with Kafka on his back growled for more Pilsner. Isabel rushed towards the street. Fresh air. Suddenly, pointedly, her body ached for Zakhi because he accepted her need to dive into toxic waters. Sauntering down uneven cobblestone streets, Isabel shook her head hard to free it of what ifs. What if Suri would secretly be relieved if Isabel told her story? What if Zakhi and Isabel committed to each other knowing she would grow old before him?

Isabel crossed Old Town Square again. A large brown statue of the golem welcomed visitors to Josefov, the old Jewish quarter. She stopped to ponder this commercial face lift. From grotesque Frankenstein-creature, he had morphed into a cuddly Pillsbury Dough Boy-Hulk hybrid. Gone were centuries of a locked ghetto. Of lynchings. Of loathsome accusations. Gruesome punishments. Standing calmly by a sign pointing to the Staronová Synagogue, the golem statue held a tray with tourist brochures. No longer needed to fight the scourge of the blood libel, the Jewish golem had been reborn into a non-denominational concierge. How hospitable.

The quiet Saturday morning streets of Vinohrady filled with people walking dogs. As Isabel told Jiri the first night they met, this neighborhood reminded her of the Upper West Side. And remembering that conversation, she pictured Suri reading a book on a bench along Riverside Drive. She and Hal liked to take in the river breeze under the trees.

Since working on Jaim Benjamin's book, no, actually it began with Itka's life story, Suri's bowdlerization had become an agony for Isabel. Others welcomed talking about their past. Lots of children received answers to their questions about the war. They knew their parents' histories. Learned about extended families. For some, this information landed on them even before they began asking questions. But all Isabel ever got was a stunning reserve. The script dictated that Suri was the survivor whose veneer Isabel the daughter needed to protect. That meant not penetrating it. Not asking questions. But now it was harder. Suri's veneer suffocated Isabel. Last time she was in New York she fought for air and they fought. First time ever. Because Isabel asked questions.

"How did Bella know to send you east to Russia? So few people understood what was about to happen . . . how did she?"

"Isabel, sweetheart, life is beautiful, live it, and leave the dead alone." Suri took a delicate sip of wine. Her eyes looked up from the rim of her wine glass and met Isabel's. They told her flat out to mind her own business.

The same message she had been receiving for the past thirty years. When she was sixteen Dave told her that Suri survived the war in Siberia, having full responsibility for her three younger siblings. She was a child herself and foraged for food and fuel. Then their brother Shiya died. That was the first time Isabel had heard about Shiya. Her Aunts Zizi and Lola hinted at miseries. At missing their parents. Their lost siblings, aunts, uncles, cousins, friends. But they were careful not to talk when Suri was around. And Isabel never pressed for more information yet when she thought of Suri somehow surviving Siberia, the images and color on the screen faded to an undifferentiated black, as if stored in an encrypted file whose password she didn't possess. She, her aunts, her father, all felt the delicate balance of Suri's frailty and acted from an overwhelming need to shelter her. But when she would be in New York in a few months' time to sit with Jaim Benjamin on the final draft of his book, Isabel knew that it would also be time to bully the status quo of decades.

"The dead don't leave me alone." Isabel had stared at Suri during their last visit.

"Rubbish." Suri got up from the table, took her wine glass, and went into the other room. Vivaldi's "Four Seasons" filled the house.

*

Isabel sat on a bench in a small park in Vinohrady. Many people and dogs were out on this beautiful day. She missed Woody and looked for Jack Russells. A man and a Rhodesian Ridgeback walked by. An old woman with two pugs passed. They stopped. One dog lifted his leg, his pee barely missed Isabel's shoes. The old woman giggled like a girl at her naughty pup. Isabel was not amused. The woman hurried away with her mini ruffians. Isabel took out the notepad again.

Looked at the contraband Bella-murder-in-the-woods paragraph. So few lines. So much guilt. She jumped three clean pages.

I am becoming a ghost. The hard lines by which I know myself, as if gone over with an eraser, slowly disappear.

The words scared her and she looked up just as a handsome pair of men entered the park with a pair of equally handsome Jack Russells. Ah, here they were. One dog was white and brown like Woody. The other white, brown, and black. Isabel sat up, put away notepad and pencil, and awaited their approach. Quality dog moments restored equanimity. And she was desperate for some.

Years back Molly told her that she ghosted because of Suri's veto. As if she didn't know this. But Molly was only partially right. She ghosted because of Suri but also because of Rosa. Rosa Levi. For six hours every day Isabel and Rosa sat next to each other at a stainless steel work table in the kibbutz kitchen peeling, dicing, and mixing vegetables for a thousand people's breakfasts, lunches, and dinners. Isabel's timid questions drew out the war and camp tales curled inside Rosa for decades. Rosa's responses emerged first in small ripples then in large knock down waves that overwhelmed them. Some days Rosa left the kitchen early crushed by the load of sense memories.

After a few months Isabel asked Rosa if she could write her story down. In English. And Aunt Zizi found Schine. When the book came out a year later it was translated into Hebrew by another kibbutz member. Then Rosa began to speak at local schools. Not long after that Schine contacted Isabel and asked if she'd be interested in writing another book. She said yes and had been saying yes for twenty years. And not because of Suri, but because each one of these people had an important story to tell.

The Jack Russells and their people walked next to Isabel's bench. Her hand fell and the dogs rushed to sniff it. She scratched their heads. The men chattered to her in Czech. She smiled. Her hand on the dogs.

"English?"

They shook their heads no. Laughed. Gave the dogs small signals on the leash. Visiting time was over.

4

As soon as Isabel entered the Shwartz's elegant apartment, Itka complimented her on her new dress and shoes. Like most women from Prague, Itka believed in self-grooming. Her blond hair was always styled. Graceful dresses flattered her sensuous hips and bosom. Many years Isabel's senior, she had taken upon herself the project of sprucing up Isabel's country ways with manicures, pedicures, expensive hair colors and cuts, high-end clothing. As a woman ages and loses the beauty of youth, she must compensate with good clothing and care, Itka instructed her ghostwriter and friend. Isabel went on field trips with Itka to boutiques and cosmeticians. And learned.

"So I'll look good at my desk," Isabel had teased her. "And for the goats in my neighborhood." But nevertheless she learned and especially when she travelled for work and sat with clients, Isabel stepped up her game.

After last night's dinner they had all had enough of the war and were careful to talk about everything but. When the topic of beaches came up, Isabel described the beauty of the sea and Phoenician ruins of Achziv. As usual, wine was a favorite subject. Some time was spent talking about Israel's excellent run over the past few years. Isabel kept up with the pleasant conversation. Manners were important but she also found herself fending off images of Jaim Benjamin's mountain village. Of Kafka's dark lanes. The golem's stealth. Bella's murder in the woods. Her unease did not fade and she beat a hasty departure as soon as it was polite to. On her way back to the hotel she was once again laid low by the tourist booths. Usually she laughed them off but now their ruthless merchandising of Kafka and the golem clawed at her. When she got to her room, she drew the curtains and crawled under the covers.

And didn't feel much better when she returned to the streets hours later. The *fin de siècle* renovation of Josefov failed to keep taut the boundary between medieval Easter massacres and today. With more dissonance than harmony Isabel bounced between the former ghetto walls like a note on a staff. Kafka had told his good friend Janouch that despite the makeover *we walk about as in a dream, and we ourselves are only a ghost of former times.* The ghetto's woes declared themselves like bones and ash in lax earth. Isabel's gut contracted with the estrangement of Franz Kafka, Josef K., K., Gregor Samsa. She too felt misshapen. Not literally as a dog or giant beetle, but as a Jew living in the shadow of the blood libel and now, courtesy of Jaim Benjamin, the Inquisition. *Under orders from Pope Paul IV, Jews couldn't use titles such as Signor or Don. 1555.* Jaim wrote this at the bottom of one page. And on the next: *Germany's Nuremberg Laws did same with Herr, with Frau. 1935.* The overlay of histories grabbed at Isabel's heels. She stumbled. Walked even faster. Just to keep moving.

"But it's not then. Ghetto. Gestapo. Transports," Isabel spoke out loud into the empty alley. "I am here now. Cell phones. High speed travel. Internet."

She stole around a corner, looked nervously to all sides, appraising what she was not sure. She pressed her hands hard against the building and its rough brick surface returned her to the moment.

"Reality check: children arriving tomorrow morning. We'll tour. Eat a lot. Have fun." Isabel reassured herself with words spoken out loud. To hear them. Feel their concrete shape. They helped keep her afloat for a moment but then time's warp pulled her. Josefov shifted. The undertow of imagining, no, it was much more than imagining, the actual feel of torments, violence and loss dragged her to the sandy bottom. She struggled to remain upright. To not slide down the prickly brick wall. She searched for chewing gum inside her bag. The sharp spray of mint in her mouth steadied her. Somewhat. She chewed hard. Swallowed saliva. Then set out again.

Isabel stuck close to the buildings. Rage and loathing washed over her for those who sold Kafka and golem trinkets. Pariahs who grew rich on Josefov's legends. Dead Jews exploited for a quick buck. She opened her mouth to scream. She wanted to lose control. Smash stands. Trample clay golem figurines. Abraham in Ur destroying his father's idol shop. She wanted to mount a soapbox and tell the real story. How once, right before daybreak, Rabbi Loewe's golem discovered men planting the body of a dead Christian child near the carpenter's home. The Rabbi was summoned. The Constable sent for. That one time justice was served. A blip on the screen.

Isabel made her way towards the river. A sign over a doorway displayed a hulking black figure. The Golem Restaurant. A small dark café with pastries in the window. She ran from it and found herself outside squat Altneuschule. Its outsized brick gable shaped like a saw's sharp teeth gave the diminutive synagogue a menacing air.

For once there was no long line of tourists and Isabel rushed inside. She scanned the walls for a door. What she wouldn't give to see the golem's remains, to coax them back to life. Local legend had it that the stairs to the attic were demolished after a German soldier died trying to pry open its door. Jacob's ladder retracted. A place of no return. But she didn't believe it. That neat tie-up fit too well with the overall revisionism on display. The attic was here. The door and stairs to the attic were here. Probably blocked off by sheetrock. The golem's remains were here. All one had to do was find the way.

Isabel circled the synagogue. She knocked lightly on thick walls searching for the lighter sound of a new wall. With each turn around the dark room she picked up speed and her headache returned. Except for the brief hundred years that separated their construction, this space had nothing in common with the airy sanctuary of Toledo's El Transito Synagogue, yet for a moment Isabel felt suspended between both. So close and yet so far apart from each other.

The guard at the entrance watched her. She began to sweat. He might call the authorities. They would send her somewhere. She tried to blend in with the wall. And when that didn't work, she looked up confidently. Play the part. Act naturally. History seized her. Which was why she needed to see Rabbi Loewe's pile of dirt. For just one second. It would release her. It was the antidote to the piles at Auschwitz. To the screams inside brisk winds.

Isabel's phone rang. She answered but said nothing.

"Can you talk?" Jiri asked.

She could but didn't.

"Meet me in half an hour at the foot of the Charles Bridge, Old Town side. I have something to show you." Jiri hung up before she said hello.

Frightened by the guard, Isabel left the synagogue and made her way indirectly to the Bridge, just in case she was being followed. One lane led to another. She grazed the walls making sure not to trip on the slippery cobblestones. She avoided eye contact. These narrow stone streets were like Toledo's, they were Toledo's. Bohemia and Castile-La Mancha enclosed her.

The persistent dusk kept the street lights off and shadows long. A large misshapen figure appeared on a wall. Probably another café using the golem as logo. She approached and only saw cracked plaster and a small window secured with metal whorls. Then suddenly again, out of the corner of her eye, movement. She turned her head quickly. Too late. Nothing to see. And absolutely no café sign or mark on the wall.

Surreptitiously Isabel lurched towards the Vltava. The golem was not a pile of dirt in a closed off synagogue attic. It was alive and mobile in the Old City's streets. And it yearned to be seen by the right person. And here she was. The one to see it. She made her way to the water. Suddenly. There it was again. A large squarish form running under the bridge's fat legs. Jewish history, so blatantly cyclical, bad things always came round. Why not something good?

"Why not a return of the golem?" Isabel said out loud and ran after it. The darkening outline of roofs, spires, tortured metalwork, and gargoyles loomed above. She looked for a foothold in the riverbank wall. But suddenly couldn't move. Someone had taken firm hold of her arm.

"Aahh," Isabel moaned. They had come for her. Who would let her children know?

Jiri pulled her back. She collapsed against him. Saved. He kissed her lightly on the cheek and led her away. Isabel glanced back momentarily to remember where and how while Jiri took her down a narrow lane by the river quay. Because he held her hand so firmly, she wanted to tell him that she was losing the battle against the whispers of pogroms, lurking golems, Crusader massacres, and Kafka watching the Hilsner blood-libel riots from his bedroom window. 1899. But she lacked courage. She didn't want Jiri to know her ghost self and maybe what she saw was not real and would fade like an image in a dream in the remaining night hours. Could be that by morning she'd realize she had seen a shadow or a passing cloud. It was just her mind hostage to twisted inbred remembrances.

Better not to say anything to Jiri who was leading her up a set of narrow steps. An old apartment had been converted into an art gallery. Immediately she recognized two of his pieces. *The River Styx.* A highly polished black stone composed into a vertical slab with a narrow groove. A phallic and vaginal road block to death. The other piece, *Investigations*, was sculpted out of light brown stone. A child crouched low as if looking at ants on the ground. Jiri brought her over to a third piece made of pale wood. A soft curved back. Subtle planes on a turned down face that could be a woman's. She read the name: *Toledo.* Jiri waited beside her.

"So beautiful." Isabel hugged him. "I'm honored. Thank you."

"Thank you." He held her close. "Enough formalities. Now beer."

They walked to a nearby pub in the middle of Old Town. Tourists swarmed outside like bees around a hive, but the pub was filled mainly with locals. Apparently this place wasn't listed in the guidebooks. Busts of large elk, moose, and stag hung on the walls. Waitresses with profound cleavage brought tall mugs of Pilsner to the heavy wood tables. They drank until midnight. When Jiri dropped her off at the hotel, she kissed him passionately under a streetlamp. She didn't care that Prague was essentially a small town and he a married native son.

Exhausted, Isabel fell asleep immediately and slept well. The half liters of Pilsner smoothed the bumps and canyons in her mind. She woke not from disturbing dreams, but from what felt like none at all. By the time she met Lia and Uri at the airport later that morning she had all but forgotten the golem sightings of the day before. The very blue sky and high yellow sun cordoned off the past and its grief.

They parked their bags at the hotel and headed out to Old Town and Charles Bridge. Thirty statues of saints on pedestals presided proud and lonely along the bridge's balustrade. Uri wanted to know about each one. Isabel explained as best she could what saints were but she didn't even come close to satisfying his appetite for details. She knew some life stories. Like that of St. Francis of Assisi. But others, like St. Luthgard and St. Crucifix, were unfamiliar. He was, to put it mildly, very disappointed in her. They made their way through the smash of tourists, painters, and souvenir sellers to the middle of the bridge. A very large Jesus on the cross made Uri come to a complete stop.

"Who is this?" he asked dramatically, staring at the emaciated man flanked by Mary and the apostle John. "He's got nails in his hands and feet! And there's Hebrew." Excitedly Uri read the words blazing gold above the man's head, "קדוש," and on either side of the cross, "קדוש. קדוש." Holy. Holy. Holy.

"According to the prophet Isaiah the angels celebrate God singing Holy Holy Holy," Isabel explained.

Lia read out the Hebrew that encircled the torso of the tortured man and that completed the gilded necklace of words: "יהוה צבאות." YHVH is the Lord of Hosts.

"I don't understand." Uri kept his eyes on Jesus. "Who is he and why does he know Hebrew?"

"Angels speak Hebrew," Lia said.

Uri stared up at Lia and back again at the tall statue of a dying man. A look of astonishment on his face. "He's an angel?"

"Not exactly," Isabel said, not sure how to begin to explain Jesus of Nazareth to him. "Itka told me that in 1700, when these statues were put up, the Jewish community was forced to supply the gold for these words." She spoke in Hebrew, not wanting to be overheard by passersby. Not wanting to be misunderstood. Not wanting to offend. Or endanger the children. "Elias Backoffen, a Jew from the ghetto, was accused of desecrating a crucifix in a church."

"So collective punishment's not a new invention." Lia shook her head back like a horse throwing off reins. "Guess we learned our methods well from our tormentors."

"Those are the letters with the goats." Uri pointed excitedly to the YHVH. "That's one of God's secret names. Idit told us that on Yom Kippur one goat was killed in the desert. And one with God's secret name was killed in the Temple."

"Idit taught you that?" Isabel asked surprised. Lia and Yael learned nothing about Temple rites when they were in grammar school.

"Yes. Was he sacrificed too?" Uri looked up at the man on the cross.

Lia and Isabel looked at one another. The child was smart. He had what Suri called a *yiddisher kop*.

"Sacrificed in a way, but not on Yom Kippur. That man is Jesus of Nazareth," Isabel spoke carefully. Slowly. Still in Hebrew. "Yes," she responded to Uri's eyes opening wide, "lived right near us. Jesus lived when the Romans ruled Israel, a little before Yehuda HaNassi's time. He was a big teacher, a revolutionary even. The rabbis hated him. The Romans killed him. Some say he was the son of god."

"And a billion people agree with this," Lia chimed in. "It's called Christianity."

"How can anyone be the son of God?" Uri asked. "God doesn't have a body."

"They say the spirit of god entered his mother Miryam, the woman standing next to him. She became pregnant with Jesus."

"So he's a half god, like Hercules?"

"No, not really. He's considered a full god. They say he's the messiah," Isabel added.

Uri looked back up at the sad dying man. Then he looked away at the sky stretching out beyond the dark outlines of the bridge's statuaries. His face was stern.

"What d'you mean, the messiah?" His shoulders rose to his ears and his palms lifted to the sky, making him look like a miniature Tevye from a Sholem Aleichem story.

Lia and Isabel burst out laughing.

"What's so funny?"

"Nothing," Isabel controlled herself. "It's an excellent question."

Lia bent down to hug him. Uri's posture was funny, but the subtext of his words was not. The voice of Jewish dissent. An almost instinctive, fastidious, decidedly not-humorous resistance to the revision of the ancient religion. A Jew's simple no. A stubborn insistence. *What d'you mean, the messiah?* And millennia of bloodshed in response.

5

On their third day of wandering the streets on both sides of the Vltava River, Isabel decided they had had enough. It was time for nature, for a glorious forest. Time to go to Karlštejn one hour away from the center by coach. Uri's mood changed as soon as they drove past the Communist-era concrete apartment blocks at the edge of the city. Suddenly there was green. Fields, pastures, then mountains. He chattered on, made funny faces from the seat in front. After days of frowning, a half smile emerged on Isabel's face too when they rolled more deeply into the countryside. The golem, a phantom limb left behind in some dark alley, ceased to throb. With the bus safely ensconced in the greens of the not-urban, Uri began to hum. He had been an amazing sport for days now, especially since tramping in and out of buildings did not yield much emotional payback for a seven-year-old. But he had followed Isabel obediently into Hradčany Castle and Ottla Kafka's diminutive cottage on Alchemist's Way. He had wandered with her through flamboyant Baroque and Rococo churches, the likes of which he and his Israeli sister had never seen before. He sat quietly through chamber music performances in these churches, Bach on organ, Vivaldi on strings. And in between there was endless walking on cobbled streets, broken up by a serene boat ride up the Vltava to see Gehry's playful Dancing House on the medieval riverbank. Only now, seeing his face fill with light and lightness, did Isabel realize how the city had weighed on him. Like her girls, Uri was raised on and near farms, surrounded by animals and verdant fields. He knew them. Needed them.

What kept him going were the shops with candy in glass cases sold by weight. He made selections by pressing a specific number of fingers near a particular chocolate or licorice. Then he watched closely as the saleslady deposited the pieces into a little white bag. But Jesus also played his part. After that first day on Charles Bridge, Uri didn't ask any more questions about the man from Nazareth, but it was clear that ubiquitous displays all over the city of the tortured man on the cross fascinated him.

The bus stopped not far from the fourteenth-century castle. They strolled up a path through an old thicket of trees. Sweet pine saturated the air. Uri walked ahead with a local woman and her Wire-Haired Dachshund. Uri usually made instant friends with people and their dogs. A family trait.

"Look. The buildings are built one on top of the other. Like steps," Isabel said to Lia as they approached the castle. "And that tower. Massive. What beautiful off-white plaster. Not possible to reach that quality of plaster anymore."

"I like those elegant black roofs and turrets." Lia kept an eye on Uri who walked ahead with the woman and her dog.

On an English speaking tour of Karlštejn the guide informed them that the castle was built to house King Charles IV's collection of holy relics and the coronation jewels of the Roman Empire. Up staircases and through rooms, they trailed behind him and his hard-to-follow accent into small dark chambers. They looked out narrow windows set into thick walls. They ducked through short door openings. He continually banged doors open and shut as they entered and exited each room.

"Vandalism and theft over the years force the castle management to keep the small tour groups isolated," he explained.

"A bizarre method of crowd control," Lia whispered to her mother.

"Typical medieval construction," Isabel whispered back when they entered the tenth identical room. She stopped listening to the guide's laconic explanations.

He perked up unexpectedly on the stairs to the Great Tower. "You are now in the Chapel of the Holy Cross." He managed a smile. "Please notice the semi-precious stones decorating the vaults. They are set in the shape of crosses. This is the most expensive and luxurious part of the castle, consecrated in 1357. And these panel paintings, 129 in total, make up the largest collection of its kind in the world. Here are portraits of saints, prophets, and angels. Some will be familiar to you. Theodoric was court painter to the Holy Roman Emperor, Charles IV. The first Czech painter to be recognized for his art." The small English speaking group wandered beneath Master Theodoric's work.

The guide threw open the door on the far wall. Time to move on. The group passed through. The guide banged the door shut.

In the last room of the tour, Uri stood before a wooden sculpture of Jesus on the cross. Bright red blood dripped down the dying body. Deep folds of pain combed his face. Eyelids opened fractionally. The body was slack with resignation. Isabel watched Uri take it all in. He folded his small hand into hers.

"*Ema*, what if they're right?"

She was stunned. By the power of persuasion. This impressionable, curious, and open-minded seven-year-old had been inundated with churches, statues, paintings, frescoes, even tapestries of Jesus on the Cross for three days now. The medium and the message converged as they had throughout history to make the masses believe in the son sacrificed by the father for the world to know salvation.

"What if they're right?" Uri asked again. This was not a rhetorical question. Children did not ask rhetorical questions.

"What if?" she answered. "No one knows for certain. It's a matter of what you believe, Uri, more than what is right or not right. Those who believe this, advertise it to persuade everyone it's true. Like seeing Coca-Cola posters everywhere and suddenly you're thirsty and want a Coke."

"It's not exactly the same thing," Lia threw in. "The desire to have spirituality in your life is not *just* a matter of suggestion. It comes from within. Religion developed out of a genuine need for meaning."

"To want to understand why we're here and what to do about it, okay." Isabel turned to Lia and left Uri in the dust of the habitual disagreement with her first born. "But to say it's one god over another, and that there's a messiah, or saints, or many gods, or only one, is a matter of information dissemination. And power."

"Nobody knows really, sweetheart." Isabel turned back to Uri and his question. "Christians believe Jesus is god and messiah. Jews believe god is without form and they're still waiting for the messiah. Some people don't believe in god at all."

"Yeah, like you." Uri snorted.

"Yeah, like me. Look the door's open. We've got to keep up." She nudged him forward.

On the way back down the mountain they walked through the

small village of Karlštejn. A diminutive lane lined with souvenir shops and pubs pouring draft from early morning. Uri ran ahead to look at the display of kites.

"Why did you tell Uri you don't believe in god?" Lia asked.

"Because he wanted to know. Why should I lie? I didn't with you or Yael."

"We never asked those kinds of questions."

"Kibbutz was anti-religious and mocking. Anyway, Uri's different. Don't you remember when he asked why god made us? How old was he?"

"Three and a half."

"He thinks about these things. Maybe he'll become a rabbi or a philosopher."

"Or guru," Lia grinned.

Uri came running toward them clutching a bright red kite.

"Can I have it, *Ema*? Please, *prosim*?"

He ran around them with the kite. Red like the matador's cloth. Like Christ's blood.

6

The last day in the beautiful city of Prague was the Jewish day. Isabel always saved Jewish sites for the end of any trip to a European city. Why ruin a good vacation? Dave, who seemed to hold a personal grudge against history, still liked to point out: "From a Jewish point of view, Europe is one big graveyard." Not knowing how her children would react, Isabel decided to postpone their encounter with this particular history until the end of the visit. They had seen the sites. They had had their fun. Now they could see what had happened to the Jews.

Waking early they went straight to perennially crowded Josefov.

"I'll explain who the golem is later." Anticipating Uri's stream of questions, Isabel held his hand and pulled him past the large doughy statue of the golem at the entrance to the quarter.

"Golem?"

"Later."

At first her children were not impressed. They were accustomed to seeing much older buildings. And the stone streets were like those back home in Jerusalem and Acco. But the six synagogues on Maiselova Street—the only structures left standing after the vast renovation—got their attention.

"Look." Uri pointed to a clock with Hebrew letters.

"Old Town Hall," Isabel said. "The clock hands run backwards, right to left like Hebrew."

"Built in 1586," Lia read from a pamphlet she picked up in the hotel lobby, "and renovated with this Baroque pink facade 200 years later."

Down the alley, they passed tourist stalls selling small oil paintings of Josefov's narrow stone streets, dolls of Hasidic men and children clutching gold coins, and clay golem figurines in a myriad of sizes.

Lia stopped and lifted up a Hasidic doll. "I don't believe this."

"Like the men in Jerusalem," Uri said.

"I just don't believe this." Lia glared at the vendor.

"What are they doing here?" Uri asked.

Concern plowed through Isabel. They had barely touched the surface of the ghetto and already her children were freaking out. They stared at Isabel. She didn't answer.

"*Ema*?" Uri asked.

"Mom?" Lia asked.

"Yes, these dolls are dressed like Hasidic men from Jerusalem and Bnei Brak and Brooklyn and Antwerpen and other parts of the world. This look originally comes from Poland. Not that far from here actually."

"And the coins?" Lia asked heatedly, as if Isabel were responsible for Exhibit One of anti-Semitism.

"The coins are vulgar, I'm with you on that. If you ask the guy selling them, he won't even understand why it's offensive. For many of these people Jews and money go together."

"But this place is *Judenrein*. Jews don't live here anymore."

"Lia, honey, we have the whole day to get through. Please." She tilted her head in Uri's direction.

"It's just disgusting. If they could, they'd kill us again."

"Who killed who?" Uri's ears on fire.

"The Holocaust, Uri." Lia put the doll back and glowered at the merchant again. "Then we were vermin. Now we're dolls."

"Lia, please."

"Here too?" Uri asked.

"Yes, here too, Uri." Maybe it wasn't a good idea to have them join her on this brief holiday. She didn't know if she could face history and be strong for them at the same time.

As if reading her mind, Lia bent low to talk to her little brother. "Uri honey, where we're walking lots of Jews used to live. For hundreds of years. Then the Germans came and killed everyone. But there's still a lot of interest in Jews. See these dolls, and the golem Mom will tell you about."

"Necro-nostalgia," Isabel whispered.

"What Mom?"

"Necro-nostalgia," Isabel said louder. Rows of male dolls in long black coats wearing fur shtreimels, long black beards and knickers, with hooked noses and clutching large gold coins to their chests, stared blankly into space.

The children watched her. She shook her head to stay present, focused, but tears filled her eyes anyway. "Let's go." Isabel straightened her back. "The Altneuschule's over there."

Uri took her hand.

"Called Staronová in Czech. Europe's oldest active synagogue. Built in 1270," Lia read the brochure as they stood in the long entrance line. "When it was built Jews were not allowed to be architects. So a Christian designed it."

"Looks like Shrek's house." Uri was excited.

"You're right." Isabel saw the low building, its heavy-hanging eaves and saw-toothed gable, through the child's eyes. Indeed, a dwelling fit for an ogre.

Once inside they wandered around the dim medieval sanctuary. Isabel slipped away into the women's gallery seeking repose. But the space was too narrow and dark for that. Women who might want to pray along with the men of their community were sandwiched between thick walls and basically could feel on their bodies this reluctant concession to their presence. There was little air and slits in the thick wall provided minimum visibility into the main sanctuary. Lia and Uri joined her.

"These days services are held irregularly, and few women come." Isabel felt a need to rationalize the inhospitable and demeaning space to her daughter.

"That's obvious. This place is as spiritual as a dungeon." Lia frowned.

The three of them squinted through the slits. People milled under Gothic stone bays and around heavy octagonal pillars. Twelve narrow windows in the exterior walls, one for each Israelite tribe, let in negligible amounts of light. Retrofitted large and ornate electric chandeliers hardly helped. The place was dark, gloomy, and depressing.

After a couple of minutes, Lia got up. "We're done." She took Uri's hand and they left.

Isabel remained and steadied herself. She worried. If the Hasidic doll with the coin brought them low, how would they react to the Pinkas Synagogue? And the cemetery? She watched Uri drag Lia to see a glass case against the far wall. Maybe they should skip the rest of the Jewish quarter? Go to the city's anemic zoo instead?

"Mom." With her hand Lia summoned Isabel to come quick.

Isabel came out from behind the restraining wall of the women's section and walked over to them standing by a memorial case she had never noticed before.

"Ema, it's like the ten commandments." Uri pointed at the shape of the two cases. "Like what you sewed for my book."

"And look." Lia pointed at the names in the glass case. "Franz Kafka."

"Huh?" Isabel felt lightheaded.

"Says here," Lia read from the brochure, "that Kafka had his bar-mitzvah in this synagogue and on the new moon of the month of Sivan, the anniversary of his death, the light near his name is turned on."

Isabel grabbed the edge of the case to steady herself. Why should Kafka's *yahrtzeit* take her by surprise? Why should it affect her so? He was born in this city, grew up here, and lived here for nearly his entire life. But how did she not know this when she knew so much about him and his Prague? Isabel looked for the ark on the eastern wall.

Empty now of Torah scrolls it was the shooting gallery he described in the well-known letter to his father. From this vantage point, sitting in this synagogue's pews, Kafka drew certain conclusions about appearances, hypocrisy, and the lack of true affection.

"Pretty cool. You really like his work, right Mom?"

Isabel nodded. Swept into a draft of revenants, she stared at his name and leaned more of her weight on the glass case. No big deal she scolded herself. Just another fact. Another bit of history. Let it sweep through you, no, over you, she instructed herself. Keep it together.

"You okay?" Lia tugged at Isabel's sleeve. "Ready to go? Uri's already outside."

Isabel forced herself to move, to shake off the pain of the rejecting father and the snubbed homeland. To join her children. To return to here and now. By the time they reached the Pinkas Synagogue on nearby Siroka Street she was back. Though more nervous than ever. What if they fell apart here? What if pain coagulated and choked them? She paused outside.

Lia looked at her. "We're tougher than you think, Mom. It's you I'm worried about."

The walls of the Pinkas Synagogue were covered ceiling to floor with the handwritten names of the 77,297 Jews from Bohemia and Moravia who died in the ghettos and camps. Uri had just mastered his Latin letters and read the wall, starting from the top. Cities. Towns. First names. Last names. Dates of birth. Deportation dates— the last known piece of information about the dead. Isabel stopped Uri after a few names. He read too slowly. Much remained to be seen that day.

They climbed the stairs to the synagogue's second floor. Isabel on one side of Uri, Lia on the other, and made their way slowly past display cases containing some of the 4,000 drawings, paintings, and poems created by Jewish children in Terezin. Isabel legs shook. She walked to a window for some air. Left Uri in Lia's care.

The city's pitched roofs were so pretty. Terracotta soothed the eyes. Of course Uri knew about the Holocaust. The year before he came home on Holocaust Remembrance Day and asked her if she knew that children had been taken in trains built for cows to camps where they were gassed and burned. Isabel had forgotten that Israel's state school curriculum exposed Jewish children to this information so early. When Lia came home in first grade with this same information and many questions, Isabel was shocked. Why so young? Why so early? The teacher pointed out that the children who were transported, gassed, and burned were not exactly spared this information.

And just like Lia and Yael, Uri insisted on knowing whether anyone in their family had been taken away in cattle cars and gassed to death. And as with the girls, Isabel began the conversation that would probably go on for the rest of their lives about Grandma Suri's mother, Bella Weiss, and her sister Raizel, Aunt Zizi's twin, and baby brother Sholem, and the walled town of Kamenets-Podolski. And when Uri insisted on knowing if anyone in their family had actually died in the camps, Isabel said yes and named more names for nothing less would satisfy him.

"Great-grandmother Bella's sisters went into the gas chambers?" His eyes lit up. "And their children? Aunts, uncles, cousins? Wow. So many."

And as with Lia and Yael, Isabel reminded Uri that having family killed in the concentration camps and in the Ukrainian woods wasn't like winning the lottery. There was nothing good about it. And like his sisters he said of course, he knew. But still this was *his* family. History had come a little closer to him that day. Grandma Suri's mother! Grandma Suri's brother and sister!

Slowly Lia and Uri made their way past the children's drawings and poems in the glass cases. Isabel remained by the window and watched. Uri had no questions. Isabel didn't know whether this was good or bad. Soon enough they were done and together they descended the stairs.

They toured the remaining four synagogues in the quarter. Despite Isabel's antipathy, they wandered through the craft stalls in Old Town Square and bought small gifts for Alon, Yael, Emanuel, and Suri. Then they went to the Old Cemetery.

For 350 years Prague's Jews buried their dead in the Old Cemetery. 12,000 tombstones stacked one against the other. One hundred thousand graves burrowing twelve stories deep in less than a quarter acre. The MaHaRaL—Rabbi Judah Loewe ben Bezalel—artisan, kabbalist, creator and destroyer of the infamous golem, its most famous VIP.

"Like *Star Trek*." Uri pointed enthusiastically to hands carved on a gravestone held up like two fans directed toward one another. The first and second fingers coupled, split from the coupled third and fourth. "Spock and the Vulcans do that."

"When the priests bless Israel," Isabel explained, "they hold their hands like that. Gene Rodenberry borrowed stuff from Judaism."

"Cool." Uri was captivated.

On this sunny day the cemetery was especially crowded. The narrow paths around the graves almost too busy to walk on. Everyone it seemed had followed the travel guides' advice and arrived early. The *Starý židovský hřbitov*, or Old Jewish Cemetery, was the largest tourist attraction in Prague. Isabel had been twice before. Each time, once even during a light snow, the place overflowed with visitors fascinated by the site of a people as restricted in death as they had been in life. A necropolis ghetto.

In 1787 even the municipal authorities realized that there was a limit to urban density and closed the Old Cemetery and opened a new one in Zizkov. Then in 1890 a Jewish section adjacent to the large Christian cemetery in Strašnice opened. Kafka and his parents were buried there. Dying from tuberculosis in 1924 spared Franz the ghettos and concentration camps where his three sisters were murdered less than twenty years later.

On her first trip to Prague Isabel visited Kafka's grave in Strašnice with its ivy trimmed perimeter walls, spacious plots, and untended gravestones. She was surrounded by Ashkenazi names from her American childhood: Schwartz, Roth, Miller, Horowitz, Applebaum, Eisner. Those whose ancestors were lucky enough to get out before the war, lived and prospered on the banks of the Hudson, in the L.A. basin, in other parts of Europe, and Israel. But here in Prague, only two generations managed to be buried in Strašnice's New Cemetery. All activity stopped in the early 1940s. The next generation went up in smoke in the ovens of Terezin, Chełmno, and Auschwitz-Birkenau. An alternative solution to urban density.

They walked toward the Maharal's grave. Though crammed close to the others, its headstone was taller, wider, and grander than its neighbors. A large acorn at the top acted as a beacon. Columns with pomegranate capitols framed the headstone shaped into two tablets, like the memorial case in the Altneuschule, like the stone Moses brought down with him from the mountain top. Religious Jews, some praying, some crying, encircled the grave.

"Who's the Maharal? What's a golem?" Uri demanded to know. "And the slips of paper . . ." He pointed to them jammed into the grave's crannies. "Does he get messages to God faster?"

The three of them stood closely together beside the heavily trafficked tombstone. As quickly and as simply as possible, and again in Hebrew, though here many of the Jewish visitors would understand her explanation, Isabel gave Uri another thumbnail sketch of history. This time of European anti-Semitism. On this his last day in the city, she recounted that Jews were hated, feared, and locked into the ghetto at night, and often killed.

"Rabbi Loewe created a superhero to protect them. A golem made from mud, water and holy words. It had no soul but could understand language. I read somewhere that his name was Yosele."

Lia and Uri laughed.

"But in the end Rabbi Loewe had to undo the golem. Superheroes can grow too large and become too powerful. From forces of good they can become agents of destruction."

"Like the Hulk!" Uri called out.

"Exactly," Isabel answered. "Legend says that the dust and soil of the golem's remains are in the Altneuschule's attic."

"The Shrek building?"

"Yes."

"Let's go back and see it."

"Can't."

"Why? I want to." He turned slightly, ready to run back to the synagogue.

"There's no way into the attic."

"I'll find a way. Please, *Ema*, let's go now and try. Please."

"Uri," Isabel said firmly. "It's off limits. No one's allowed. Okay? No one." She paused. She wanted to tell him she already tried, but that might encourage him.

He was quiet. And upset. Isabel started to walk away from the grave. They followed.

"Only very holy people can make a golem. The rest of us have to know our place." Isabel put her hand on his shoulder. He shook it off but after a moment stared up at her. He wanted to understand.

"Why is it so crowded in here?" He stopped and gazed at the hundreds and thousands of gravestones leaning one against the other.

"Because they wouldn't give Jews more land." Lia took over.

"But why? Couldn't they just buy it? Were they poor?"

"It wasn't a question of money. Correct me if I'm wrong, Mom."

Why did Lia and Yael always call her Mom, whereas Uri insists on the Hebrew, *Ema*? Why had she never wondered about this before? Why did she call her parents Suri and Dave? Why had she never wondered about that?

"They wanted to be mean," Lia said to Uri. "They wanted to make life hard for the Jews. They wanted to be hurtful."

"Who?"

"The people who ruled the place."

"The people who believe Jesus is god and messiah?" he probed quietly.

"Yes."

Uri looked up at the tall trees that grew by the outer walls of the cemetery. He was quiet. They continued to bump into people on the tombstone paths. Suddenly Uri took Isabel's hand.

"*Ema*, I don't feel good."

Isabel looked down at Uri's pale face. She took him in her arms and found a small concrete ledge by the wall. She sat down on it with him in her lap. "What's wrong, sweetheart?"

"Don't know." He looked down at the ground. His eyes filled with tears.

"What?" She asked though she knew. She caressed his face. Lia stroked his soft hair. He looked as if he were about to throw up. Isabel took out a water bottle from the backpack. Slid him down beside her.

"Please drink, Uri. You need to drink."

Reluctantly, he let her spill some water into his mouth. "I just don't feel good here." He leaned over into Lia who cradled him.

Isabel surveyed the tombstones that made her son sick to his stomach. One rabbi's feeble effort to change the course of their wretched history with a superhero brought in at the height of a season of blood libels, was tragic and pathetic. Just think of the odds. Where was good King Wenceslas when the Jews needed him?

Lia rocked Uri in her arms and hummed softly. Isabel swallowed hard and closed her eyes so they wouldn't see her cry.

"According to the *Protocols of the Elders of Zion*," Lia read aloud from the brochure, "in this cemetery the rabbis met to plot Jewish world-wide domination."

"Lia, please."

Uri was quiet next to them and scratched his head. Isabel watched. His hand went down and then up again to his head. She pulled him to her and began to examine his head for lice. Her face tensed and her fingers worked quickly and harshly.

"Ema," Lia said and pulled Uri from Isabel's hands. "He's okay. I checked his head last night. Get a grip."

Isabel stared at Lia and dropped the hysteria that had risen so quickly in her. Lice on the head or body brought death. A zero tolerance vigilance.

"Okay. Sorry." Isabel put a loving hand on Uri's thigh.

"Are we going to Terezin later?" Lia asked.

"No time." Isabel looked to the gravestones in front of them. "It's a full day trip."

It was Terezin, not this cemetery, that side-swiped Isabel on her first visit to Prague. It was identified as a ghetto, so she hadn't prepared herself emotionally. To see ovens. Yet there they were. Even worse were their straps. She couldn't get over the straps. A retro-fit in the middle of the war to prevent the wood ovens from bursting since they hadn't been designed to withstand the extreme heat of continuous operation. So many bodies to burn. So little time.

"But you were there, no?" Lia asked more gently this time.

Isabel's face registered many emotions.

"Yes," she answered slowly. "The *Arbeit Macht Frei* entrance sign there is not made of metal. It's written with black paint on the town's stone gate." She paused. "Painted on. As if any place could be made into a death camp."

Isabel looked at Uri's unhappy face. "Enough. Enough." She forced herself to smile. "Uri, I thought of another word to add to the Czech/check game we played yesterday on the bus." She lured the boy and his sister out of sadness. "Here goes: check out the Czech hat-check girl giving us the check in Czech. That's five times. Bet you can't beat that."

Uri looked up at his mother. He was weak but couldn't resist the challenge. His eyes flashed. He raised his head from Lia's lap. "Check out the Czech hat-check girl checking our check in Czech." He jumped to standing. Quick as lightening, his mind off the horror. "That's six."

Lia laughed. "I have another, get ready you two. Reality check: check out the Czech hat-check woman checking our check in Czech. Count 'em. That's seven."

"I'll get another." Uri put his elbow in one palm, his chin in the other, striking a contemplative pose.

Isabel stared at the graves crammed together like too many crooked teeth in a mouth. Not far from where they sat was the oldest grave in the cemetery. 1439. Avigdor Kara: rabbi, poet, physician. One of the few 3,000 ghetto dwellers to survive the infamous 1389 Easter pogrom, two years before the decimation in Andalucia. Local priests declared Jews had desecrated the Host. One of the more popular accusations. Competitor to the blood libel. Pogrom: an unholy communion of righteousness and terror. Nothing makes you free.

"I did it!" Uri danced in front of the tombstones. "Reality check: check out the Czech hat-check woman checking our check-in check in Czech in the Czech Republic. That's not eight, that's nine. Count 'em! Check-mate! Ten!" and he burst into a fit of laughter.

The Sites

1

On the plane ride east Isabel watched her children sleep. The boy, still a child at seven. The girl, a woman, old enough to be a mother herself at twenty-three. Both under Isabel's wing and protection yet her body felt weak. Her fortitude these last few days was breached yesterday in the cemetery with Uri's breakdown. She tried to camouflage it by talking a lot: to Lia about her upcoming academic year and to Uri about the new pony on kibbutz.

This morning on the metro on their way to Television Tower she was exposed. A pair of black uniformed inspectors made their way straight to them. Ice packed her limbs. Her hands shook feeling for the tickets in her back pocket.

"I've got them, Mom." Lia calmly handed the over the metro tickets.

The inspector who took the tickets looked down at them and up at the three of them. Isabel couldn't understand. They were anonymous tickets. Not passports with photos. His hand moved inside his jacket. She stopped breathing. He said something in Czech. His hand remained inside his jacket. He said something again. Maybe she knew the words. Maybe not. All she could hear was the din of passing trains. Her eyes remained riveted on his hands. The one by his holster. The other hidden inside his jacket.

"I'm sorry we speak English." Lia smiled.

"Your tickets good for half hour more."

"Yes. We know." She smiled some more.

The other inspector stepped closer.

"We'll take a taxi later," Isabel said.

The two officers spoke together softly. Isabel's world reduced to two tall men in black uniforms. No doubt they carried handcuffs. No doubt they carried weapons. No doubt they carried bad intentions. The children were fair haired, light eyed and skinned. But her? She was clearly not Central European. And they watched her closely as they spoke. She'd go peacefully if they ordered her to. As long as the children were unharmed. Yes, she shifted in her seat, she'd go . . .

"*Dobrý den*." The inspector handed the tickets back to Lia and moved towards the end of the car.

Isabel's head dropped. She breathed deeply. Lia took her hand.

Later she packed for their Cinderella flight back home and kept checking and double and triple checking that their tickets and passports were together and handy in her bag. She needed to be ready just in case. *Dokumenten!*

They landed in Israel at 4:30 a.m. Isabel slept until noon. Then she ran errands: food shopping, annual car inspection, retrieving Woody from Molly's, stopping at the post box. At two she made lunch and woke the children. At two-thirty Alon called to speak to them. At three Emanuel called to speak to her.

She walked out to the yard. Woody stayed close behind. He loved Molly and her household of boys but it was important to him that Isabel realized that he missed her. Very much. That she better not get any ideas of taking everyone away again anytime soon.

"Emanuel," Isabel spoke softly so Lia wouldn't hear. "Among the tombstones, in Prague, it was like being tracked in the hills of Greece."

She watched blue sky move around white clouds. She was nervous telling him, because his response was inevitable. But she would not stop ghosting and she needed to tell someone and Zakhi wasn't answering. Because it was Sunday she wouldn't call Molly. It usually took her a full day to regain composure when Yiftach returned to his combat unit. Molly was totally unequipped for the emotional disconnect that made saying good-bye to soldier children easier for other parents. Not that it was ever really easy for anyone.

"I'm getting lost in the haunted alleyways of my mind. I fear persecution all the time," she whispered to Emanuel and sat on the swing, sinking into the position that if she couldn't share this kind of emotional dissonance with him then what was she doing with him?

Woody jumped into her lap. He made a quick circle, dropped into a comfortable pose with his head resting on her knee, and looked out. "Round-ups, *aktions*, a random bullet in the head. This morning." She paused. This was rough. "I went to get my car inspected in Ramat Yishai. Not Prague. Here. At home. The clerk asked me to hand over my papers and I started to shake." Embarrassed and worried, nevertheless the words gave her courage. "She told me to wait a moment and went into the back. I felt faint and had to talk myself into calming down. What could be wrong? I mean really. A blinker? A brake pad?"

"I'm really worried, Issie," Emanuel said calmly.

"You understand, I had to tell myself, out loud, that I won't be sent anywhere if my car fails inspection." She wailed quietly. Lia and Uri couldn't know she was losing it. "By the time the clerk returned to the window I could barely hold off a full blown anxiety attack. I could hardly stand or breathe."

"Your system's had enough."

Isabel was quiet.

"I'm not letting you off so easily anymore. Isabel, we're going to talk about this tonight."

"Okay," she said reflexively just to get the conversation over with. "See you later."

She closed the phone. Moved Woody over and laid down on the swing. On the one hand, she was happy Emanuel was coming over later. On the other, she wouldn't listen to him. Sure, he was the "real" partner, the one the children knew and were fond of. The one Isabel went out into the world with. He was wonderful and she loved him. Really she did, but she also knew that he didn't totally get her. He didn't understand the muck she was mired in. He wanted her to let the dead lie. To let herself off the hook. To let him into her world

66

more. And because Isabel knew his intentions were good, and that he genuinely cared for her and her children, and because he was basically just a decent man, she didn't automatically dismiss his point of view. She couldn't afford to do this anymore. The work was taking its toll on her.

She wanted to talk to Zakhi. He felt her. He drew out the words, caught them, matched them with his own. He was not leery of the wounds. But she wouldn't call again. Though she wanted to. Really wanted to. But there was a limit to what she could demand or expect. He was probably working right now. Or with another woman. A younger woman. A lament swelled in her. She had to let Zakhi go. She had to give Emanuel more space. Start acting your age, Molly repeated perfunctorily. What did that really mean? Isabel had no idea. She pulled Woody close.

After lunch Isabel cleaned up, settled Uri in front of the TV, told Lia she had some more errands to run, and got into the car with Woody. She drove to the Winkler construction site. She couldn't help herself. She hadn't heard from Zakhi and needed to see him if only for a brief embrace. On the way she stopped in the neighboring village to buy lentils and almonds. When she passed the wood goat pens she remembered Jaim Benjamin in the Greek hills. She watched her Bedouin neighbors clean their yards, feed their animals, mind their toddlers. Would they hide her children if they were being hunted? Would she theirs?

Woody and Isabel continued to the next village. They turned down the Winklers' lane. The dogs rose slow-motion in their driveways. They smelled, before they could actually see, the mighty pint-size Woodrow. And then the gauntlet erupted. Wild vicious runs at the car. Riotous barking. Teeth snapped at the tires. A couple of small dogs catapulted themselves into the air to catch a glimpse of Woody who stood tall and bold, his front paws positioned belligerently on the dash. He howled back at his adversaries and glanced over at Isabel. He wanted her to drive harder into the heat of battle. But she had no fight in her. She laid off the horn, off the pedal, and gave way to the rods, rifle butts, the kapos' fists at the camp's gate. She slowed to feel the blows. Maximum exposure. Woody barked loudly at her. How dare she give in?

"Okay," Isabel yelled. "Okay." A frantic attempt to dispel the ghosts. "These surrounds are beautiful like a European landscape. Yes. And yet it's not Europe. Yes. And even Europe is no longer *that* Europe!" She gave gas recklessly and leaned on the horn. Woody howled with delight.

Pulling onto the Winklers' gravel driveway, she braked roughly. She opened the door and Woody flew out ready to take on his adversaries. But the pugnacious dogs had already retreated to their driveways. Only one truck was at the site and it was not Zakhi's. Isabel walked into the unfinished house. Sucrat was installing the stone windowsills.

"Hi," Isabel said to him and stood in the middle of the Great Room. "Do you know where Zakhi is?"

Sucrat looked up briefly and shook his head no. Last week Zakhi had threatened to throw Sucrat off the job. Obviously they worked it out—for now. Like his namesake, Socrates, Sucrat knew nothing. Not where Zakhi was, nor the finish date for the stone sills and saddles.

Woody ran all over the first floor looking for Zakhi. His small athletic body took the steps two at a time. He ran in and out of every room on the second floor and practically flew back down to Isabel to file his report. Three barks in quick succession. No Zakhi.

Sucrat walked by cleaning his hands on an old towel. Two p.m. was a bit early to end the work day. But who was she to question his comings and goings.

"Good-bye," Isabel said as he walked out. Maybe he didn't hear. Maybe he didn't like women on the site. Maybe he knew she would tell Zakhi about his early departure.

Isabel walked upstairs to the second floor. The entire western wall of the master bedroom's en suite bathroom was still open to the view. Zakhi told her that in a few weeks a curved glass block wall would be installed there. Hopefully before the rains. The room then would be flushed with diffuse light. A suggestion of the green hills drawn inside.

In this rural landscape she saw countryside similar to that which had provided refuge for fifteen-year-old Jaim Benjamin in Nazi-occupied Greece. Soft hills, goats, kitchen gardens. She sat in the opening that waited for a stone sill and glass block wall. The sky was bright blue.

How did skies look behind barbed wire? How did the green of leaves smell? Suddenly Zakhi walked into the bathroom whistling.

"What a lovely surprise." He sat down beside her in the wall pocket. A quick kiss on the lips. "How was Prague? Hey Woody." He rubbed the dog's head. "You okay?"

"I . . . it was . . . yeah, everything's good." She looked out at the fields. He'd read her in a second if he saw her face. As much as she wanted this, she also didn't. "Socrates was here."

"Who?"

"Sucrat. Your stone mason. He was here when I showed up and left not long ago."

"I know. I gave him so much hell. If he doesn't show up every day and finish, I'll throw his ass off the job. And withhold money." Zakhi took her hand and sucked on the tips of her fingers. He pulled her close and gave her a long kiss on the mouth.

Isabel lingered on his mouth then pulled back slightly. "Yeah, but he left early. It's two p.m. Do you know where your contractor is?" she whispered sexily.

"Exactly." He laughed and held her closer.

"Jaim Benjamin's book's unraveling me, Zakhi." Isabel said it. There it was. She leaned into him and let go into his embrace.

"I know you're looking for a new career. Come work with me and keep the contractors in line."

Isabel felt his warm chest under her cheek and laughed. Yes, this was where she needed to be. Right here. Just here. Nothing more was necessary. World go away. They held one another and stared out at the land. A small herd of cows grazed in the far distance. The fields nearby lay fallow, a few weeks respite before winter's sowing.

"Since you're here, want to help?"

She smiled. "Sure."

From his jeans pocket Zakhi took out a piece of blue chalk. "I need to mark out the walls. Tomorrow I'll jackhammer."

"Conduit channels?"

"Yup."

"You know I love it when you do that," Isabel said.

They laughed conspiratorially and turned away from the fields and their appetites. Zakhi led the way downstairs to the kitchen. He bent down to measure the wall and marked the spot for an outlet not too close to where the sink would be. Raised an eyebrow. "How's this?"

"Good."

"Did you see your friend in Prague?"

She hesitated. "Itka, sure. I went there to be with her at the commemoration dinner. It wasn't easy."

"Not her. Your man friend."

"What about him?"

"Did you see him?"

"Huh?"

"Just wondering."

Her heart clenched. Zakhi had never mentioned Jiri before. Why now? Maybe he wasn't so indifferent to what they had going and to her other dalliances? The age difference, an obvious obstacle, no? Could he be also falling for her? Unlikely. Zaki was just being playful.

"Jealousy doesn't become you, sweetheart." Isabel laughed on purpose. Made light of the emotional connection. Protect. Pad the vulnerability.

"Not jealous. Just curious."

"Good thing Emanuel's not so curious."

"He can't be. He's your cover."

"My what?"

"Come on," Zakhi said. "Help me here."

She followed after him into the utility room off the kitchen. What were they actually saying to one another? Emanuel a cover for what? Zakhi just curious about what, why? Zakhi handed her the plans and measured from the corner to the window. She watched him work. His back muscles lengthened with the stretch of his arms pulling open the measuring tape. His shirt, smudged with dirt, had a small rip in the shoulder. His work boots were scuffed and dusty. The snap of the tape back into its case aroused her. She wanted him.

When Alon and Isabel built their house in town, the maleness of the construction site and the virility on display—manual and power tools, hand-built walls, roofs, tractors, the bobcat, the boots, the rough clothing, the concrete and plaster powder—were like erotic fairy dust for Isabel. She went every day to map the progress, which also became an exhilarating escape from her desk.

Zakhi moved along the wall. Measuring and marking. Tomorrow he would jack hammer the conduit channels. His hair, his shoulders and back, the crinkles in the skin of his hands and neck, would be covered with bits of concrete and dust. Isabel wanted to return then. To touch him amidst the rubble, feel the smooth and rough bits simultaneously. But Schine's hunger for pages still strapped her to the desk. She looked at her watch.

"Zakhi, I've got to go. Prague put a dent in the production schedule. And Lia has a new boyfriend coming to dinner."

"Love's good for all." Zakhi hugged her tightly and bent down to give Woody a rub.

"I'm off then." Isabel retreated from the room. The pull of the front door at her back. "But I really want to stay." She really wanted to stay.

"You go on already." Zakhi reached into his pocket for his ringing phone. "Nail those mother fuckers in the Greek hills." He looked at his phone, waved bye, and walked into the other room to take the call.

2

Isabel had little more than an hour before Emanuel's arrival. Against his advice she would not take the day off but sat down to write. *Pages, Isabel, I need pages, pages.* She opened Jaim Benjamin's file. The lines she wrote the day before leaving for Prague sounded okay. Not great but passable. A lump rose in the back of her throat. Day after day, week after week, she sat and put words down. She outlined the trajectory of events and filled in the details. She knew what she was doing. She'd done it fourteen times before. But something remained terribly off and time away did not help.

Jaim Benjamin brought her to Spain and she didn't want to go there. Jaim Benjamin brought her to Dave Toledo, her father, dead now twenty-three years and she didn't want to go there. Definitely not there. Her childhood one dark cloud of Dave's moods punctuated by light family vacations in exotic and not-so-exotic beach locales, even after he left them and relocated to California. Even after he blamed

Suri for their only child's relocation to Israel. How unfair was that. But Dave had to blame someone and couldn't very well hold history accountable.

Like a somnambulant, Isabel read again what she wrote. *The neighbors brought a broken radio to Jaim. Maybe he knew how to fix it?* She couldn't work today. Closing the file she opened a new one. From memory she typed. *Suri named me Isabel, after Bella, her mother, who died naked and trembling in a freshly dug pit in a Ukrainian forest clearing.*

Isabel scrolled down to a new page. Because of the lump in her throat, because of Suri's painful silence and Dave's loud ire, she would write Bella's story. Set out a plot line to muddle. And not some incidental hiccup. But intentionally. Deliberately. She had quite a bit of information to work with. For years she gleaned facts about Bella and the rest of Suri's family from Zizi and Lola and from other cousins in Israel. She would connect the dots and pieces and watch a story emerge.

Isabel concentrated on the clicking of the keys. On the sound of slow typing. She kept looking at Woody and the lethargic cats. Did they know what she was doing?

"It's not really Bella's story," she blurted out after a new paragraph appeared on the screen. The dog turned his eyes toward her. The cats didn't even bother. "It's not based on transcripts. Not even on many facts." Woody's eyes shifted back and forth self-consciously, showing her the whites. "My fingers are writing. Not me." Woody closed his eyes and turned his head. Permission granted. Isabel plunged into a sea of words.

Rumor had it that Jews were being offered refuge in Madagascar. Himmler's plan for the relocation of Europe's Jews to Africa. Summer 1940. I managed to make it to the Black Sea and from there across Georgia to the Caspian. I travelled south through Iran to the Arabian Sea. From sea to shining sea as they say in America. From there a boat took us to the Indian Ocean where we reached Madagascar along with a few hundred Jews who seized this brief window of opportunity when expulsion was once again the solution to Europe's Jewish Problem.

Himmler himself said: "However cruel and tragic each individual case may be, this method is still the mildest and the best, if one rejects the Bolshevik method of physical extermination of a people out of inner conviction as un-German and impossible."

I took baby Sholem, my youngest, and Raizel, one of my three year old twins, and began walking east and south. Suri, already a little mother at ten, had already left Kamenets-Podolski with the rest of the children—Shiya, eight, Lola, six, and Zizi, three, the more difficult twin—and fled north and east. She had to. Without delay. Zizi threw tantrums whenever she saw a German army officer in tall black shiny boots. I received one letter since this terrible parting. My neighbor received a letter from her son. A group of youngsters from our city, Suri and the smaller children included, were together and on their way to Siberia.

I live, if it can be called living, among the monkeys and in the heat of Madagascar. A child suckles on each breast. I beg one of the men to bring me water. My husband was killed on the first day of the German occupation of our city. An example to us that a Jew didn't have to do anything specific to be killed. His mere existence reason enough. 'At which theater are you playing?' Josef K. asked the men in black before they drove a knife into his heart.

That day I stood by the table in my small kitchen peeling potatoes. Suri and Shiya helped. The smaller children slept in the living room on blankets on the floor so we could hear them easily. My brother-in-law, Dovid, came staggering in, blinded by tears, tearing hairs out of his beard.

"Dehargene, dehargene Yoskele," Dovid mumbled in Yiddish. They killed him, they killed Yoskele, and collapsed on the floor. Within seconds, the kitchen filled with people, reviving Dovid, reviving me who fell beside him. Suri carefully put the knives away. She wrapped the potatoes in a cloth so they wouldn't brown. She took Shiya to the other room where she made him read his Hebrew letters out loud. The twins woke first. Raizel and Zizi. With their large green eyes they toddled over to Suri and asked why so many people were in the house. Suri told them that Tati had an accident and everyone was sad. Zizi, not one for holding in her suspicions nor her pain, began screaming at the top of her lungs that she wanted Tati and no one else. I heard my baby cry and ran into the living room. I took her in my arms, gave her a breast *full of milk and told her not to worry, that Tati would be with us again one day in Gan Eden.*

Isabel closed the file and the computer. She was writing the history that was. She was writing the history that wasn't. She saw herself reflected in the turned off black computer screen. A Spanish-Ukrainian-American Jew in Israel. A child of a war refugee seeking refuge in words. A ghost in her own story.

The backdrop of silence that choked her parents' lives threatened her own. But she would have none of it. She would talk and tell and listen and see. She would ghost and ghost until the contours of story and self filled with form, light, and color. Suri could criticize and run but she could not hide. After Isabel's third book, written for a woman who had fled Lithuania and found asylum in Shanghai, Suri ambushed her daughter. She had come to Israel for a long visit after Dave's death. Before she met Hal.

"You're picking at wounds, Isabel. It's unbecoming."

Isabel defended herself gently. In those days she was very gentle with her Suri. But firm. And clear. "For the people who want to tell their stories, my words drain emotional cesspools. For them, Suri, these words have the magical power to restore life."

"Fancy notions. Let it alone, Isabel. Let it alone." And though Dave was already dead by then, and years earlier had abandoned them for his new life, and even though Isabel was an adult with two children of her own, Suri whisked him out of the garret. "Your father said you were too concerned with past sorrows. These books feed your morbid preoccupation. Sweetheart, why not write happy books with your wonderful talent?"

"Other families' stories fill the empty pockets of my own," Isabel spit out boldly, knowing even then what Molly kept saying now. And just as quickly Isabel backed down. She had hurt Suri. Saw it all over her face. This wasn't allowed. Normal adolescent rebelliousness was not on her family's menu. Nor the defiance of young adulthood. Isabel couldn't tell her mother to go to hell like most of her friends did. Suri had already been there. And barely survived.

Isabel was not allowed to be hurtful but had to protect Suri above all else. Above her own pain too. For Suri's badly sealed pain, as Nelly

Sachs described it, was always on the edge of bursting forth again. So be gentle, Sachs wrote, when you teach us to live again. And Isabel was gentle. She was a child who suffered silently, who made little trouble for her mother.

But her own badly sealed pain was bursting. Now she needed to know what happened in Siberia. What could be so awful that a lifelong moratorium had been declared? What kind of secrets was Suri protecting? Who was this woman who was her mother?

Isabel stopped turning in her chair. She listened to the comforting sounds of her house. The dishwasher ran. The fan hummed. A cat purred at the edge of the desk. Woody snored lightly on the door saddle. Suddenly a loud boom shook everything. She looked up and out the window though there was nothing informative in the sky and tree tops. She kept her head tilted upwards. Senses attuned. Waited for another boom. When it came she would know it was a jet breaking the sound barrier. And if it didn't come, then a bomb. She waited calmly. Only the sounds of domesticity persisted. The dishwasher. The fan. The animals. The phone.

"Did you hear that?" she asked Emanuel.

"What?"

"Sounded like a bomb. The whole house shook."

"I'm still in Haifa. Nothing here."

"Probably not a bomb then. I'll check the news. Dinner's at seven. Lia's new friend Asaf's coming."

"The Indian one?" Emanuel asked.

"Do you mean the one she met in India, or if he's Indian?" she teased.

"Maybe. Maybe both. Why not? Plenty of Indians to meet in India."

They laughed. Emanuel's sense of humor, his soul quietness, and his natural generosity made her feel good about herself. The way he seemed to unconditionally accept her. He would look at her and say simply, consistently: yes. And the latest suggestion to give up ghosting was not because he was against it, as Suri and Alon were, as Dave most certainly would have been. Emanuel just thought she was suffering. He wanted her to be happy and this gave her a great feeling of security. About herself, about him, about life in general.

There was a sudden quiet on the line. Emanuel wanted to say more. Which happened a lot lately. His words ready to launch but a lack of practice blocked them. Lucky for her.

"See you later then," Isabel said. "I've got to make order in the house and start cooking."

"Okay, love," he said, "Later."

Emanuel let things be. He let her be. When he irritated her she thought it was weakness and passivity. When she irritated herself, she thought it was a solid generosity. Lately she was irritated with both of them. Whenever she imagined Emanuel in her home, morning, noon, and night, she thought of Zakhi in the woods, among the stones of ancient sites, in the houses he built. She thought of men she met at bars in New York and other cities, of other adventures, of wide horizons. She had had her fill of enclosures with Alon. He had always tried to recast her into something she wasn't. The kibbutz girlfriend. The kibbutz wife. The kibbutz member. And he actively discouraged ghosting. Not because he thought it was morbid. But because he thought she wasn't a good enough writer to contain the pain. But Alon was mistaken. About that. About her. About a lot of things. A born pessimist. Or maybe just timidity in the face of the big world. Alon's sights were considerably lower. Cow sheds. Fields. Small homes. His kibbutz versus Isabel's Manhattan upbringing. For her the boundaries of the possible swept the sky.

But Emanuel was not Alon. Why not go all the way with him?

3

When Isabel came downstairs Lia was sitting on the couch with Uri. She called out a quick hello and headed to the kitchen to organize food on the counter. Uri read from *Millions of Cats*. They loved this book about a lonely old couple who wanted a cat. The old man ventured to the land of cats and saw, "Cats here, cats there, cats and kittens everywhere, hundreds of cats, thousands of cats, millions and billions and trillions of cats." Uri laughed when he finished reading this line. His favorite. Overwhelmed by choice, the old man agreed they could all come and he led them home in a Pied Piper procession. His wife was stunned. How could they care for so many? When the old couple decided to keep only the prettiest, the cats began to war viciously. Biting, scratching, clawing, shrieking, crying. After a long while, quiet returned. The old couple ventured outside. The cats had all vanished except for one frightened rather ugly kitten. They took him in, poor little kitty, and cared for him. In no time he was healthy, beautiful, adored. Their beloved cat.

Maybe the ugly duckling redeemed appealed to Uri. Though he was anything but. Maybe the sounds and rhythms lured him: *hundreds of cats, thousands of cats, millions and billions and trillions of cats.* Or maybe the half dozen or so cats that lived with them endeared this tale to his heart. They had two house cats: Himalayan Benny and red Luciana. The others lived in the yard. Uri liked to dance around them singing *hundreds of cats, thousands of cats, millions and billions and trillions of cats.* He scooped up one at a time and serenaded her, but they wouldn't follow him in a line like the cats in the book. Lia consoled him, saying they weren't eager to go anywhere because they already had such a good home.

"Lia, Uri, can you guys please help me with dinner?"

When they came in to the kitchen, Isabel planted Uri on a high stool by the island. His job was to wash and check each lettuce leaf thoroughly for bugs. Especially close to the core. Lia made the marinade for the grilled fish. Isabel made potato salad, green salad dressing, pasta. For Uri. No doubt he would turn his nose up at all other food. He remained devoted to noodles of all shapes and red sauce.

"How did you meet your friend Asaf?" Isabel rinsed bowls and spoons.

"On a steep mountain road to Dharamkot. On my way to meditation at Tushita. I whistled and suddenly someone whistled along in perfect harmony."

"What were you whistling?"

"*Sa Li'at.*"

"Ah, now that's a surprise. That he knew a Hebrew song."

"No, many Israelis there. But I was surprised at the loveliness and accuracy of his harmonies." She paused.

Isabel knew that Lia thought she was trying to dampen her enthusiasm for this new man. But she wasn't. Really she wasn't. She didn't mean anything by her questions and comments. She was just curious. Sometimes curiosity was just that and she suddenly remembered Zakhi's curiosity about Jiri. But truth was she was more than simply curious. She was also concerned. Lia hadn't been so excited about a man in years. And the last time it had ended badly.

"Okay, go on." Isabel looked at her directly to make sure she understood. She was interested in the story itself. *Sans* critique.

Not needing much encouragement, Lia smiled and took a deep breath. "When I turned around to see who was whistling like that I saw the most beautiful man I have ever laid eyes on. Don't roll your eyes like that. I mean, the most beautiful for me. Not one of those Hollywood hunks you get all gooey over."

"I do not . . ."

Uri ran around the kitchen. "Oo la la, Lia's in love. Lia's in love." He made kissing noises with his lips. Then swooped down and lifted poor Woody off the floor and planted loud kisses on his head. The dog squirmed in his arms but Uri held tight. He was in love.

"I think this is the man I was born for." Lia walked over to Isabel. Brought her face in close. "How's that for enthusiasm Ms. Easy-does-it? Ms. Conservative in matters of the heart?"

Isabel didn't want to squabble with Lia. Of course she was happy for her. She had basically been alone since that last boyfriend. But Isabel was also stunned by Lia's certainty. How protective Isabel felt, but she did the only thing she could. She smiled.

"He whistled along with me for fifteen minutes. It felt like forever. A good forever."

It took an hour to get the entire meal, the house, and Uri ready. Isabel came out of the shower and heard the doorbell. When she made her way downstairs she felt clean and recharged after a night flight and a day begun groggily at noon. Everyone was in the living room sipping one of the fruity iced cocktails Lia loved to blend up. Emanuel was on the couch playing backgammon with Uri. Lia picked dead leaves from the ficus tree. Asaf leafed through a family photo album. Woody leaned into him and received a respectable head rub.

Asaf stood to greet Isabel when she entered the room. Fortunately she was accustomed to life's strange byways and didn't gasp. Though she was startled. Asaf certainly was beautiful. Lia was right, but her daughter did not detail his beauty. Asaf was tall, very tall. He was thin, very thin. He had large black eyes, a small straight nose, a long narrow face, full lips, and thick dark brown dreadlocks down to his waist. Down to his waist. He wore turquoise cotton pants and a knee-length white tunic. A tattoo running serpentine along his left arm was visible under the cloth. Earrings pierced both ears and a small ring nestled in an eyebrow. Lia's love? He leaned down to kiss Isabel elegantly on both cheeks.

"Great to meet you," she managed to say and settled in beside him on the couch. Lia handed her a tall glass of mango and pineapple juice laced with arak. "Lia told me about your time together in India. Seems like it was quite the experience."

She hated how that sounded. The doltish adult interrogating the suitor. But she couldn't help it. She looked at him. His size. His clothing. His hair. What kind of compatibility was there between these two? Lia so smart and sophisticated. And Asaf . . . she didn't want her daughters to make the mistake she made when she married their father, Alon the farmer. Romantic for a few years, but when the charm of the *different than me* wore off and there wasn't much to talk about . . . but who knew who Asaf was and what thoughts transversed his brain under those long thick dreadlocks. Who knew what he had done and planned to do in his life other than meet young women whistling on a country road in Dharmsala.

"I started the fish already, Mom." Lia passed behind the couch and touched her lightly on the shoulder. "We can come to the table."

"Thanks honey." Isabel didn't know whether to be happy that after three years Lia had finally allowed her heart to be roused again, or whether to be aghast that it was for this man. When she passed Emanuel with the salad bowl in hand, she bent down to kiss him hello fully, softly, on the lips. They smiled. He touched her discretely on the backside as she walked away. A promise of things to come.

Some days Isabel felt guilty, but only slightly, about having sex with other men. She never lied to Emanuel because he never asked. If he did she would say that Zakhi was more than a friend. In fact he was even more than a lover. But Emanuel never asked, and truth be told she never asked him about other women either. Who knew where he was when he wasn't at work or with her? And the idea of Emanuel with another woman calmed her conscience but it also startled her. She had become accustomed to thinking that the reins of their relationship were in her hands. Could she be mistaken? How would she react to Emanuel not wanting to be with her? Not possible, she shrugged off the thought and went to sit down at the head of the table.

Emanuel took hold of the dinner conversation, playing the role of inquisitive parent. Through Asaf's answers they learned that his family was from Tel Aviv. He had three brothers. One older, a neurologist, married with two children. Two younger. One studied medicine in Jerusalem. And the youngest an army paramedic. All the while Isabel tried to calculate his age. An older brother married, thirty-two? A younger studying medicine, twenty-five?

"And what did you do in the army?" Emanuel asked.

Aah. The ultimate question. Isabel stopped doing the math. How she hated this question. When she moved to Israel at twenty-two, she received an automatic exemption from the army because she and Alon married right away. And within a few months she was pregnant to boot. So she didn't understand army ways and rejected army service as a cross-section profile of a person's character since so many young people got stuck doing jobs they hated. But hers was a minority opinion in a country where the majority of young men and women served.

"*Oketz.*" Asaf looked up from his plate.

"Like Lia!" Isabel responded.

This was what they had in common. The dogs. Love of animals. When Lia was in the K-9 unit, Isabel and the children would visit her and the dogs on their base up north. When Lia's dog, Dido, a Belgian Malinois, died in a roadside bomb in the West Bank, Isabel attended her funeral at the canine military cemetery. It would have been someone's son had the dog not gone ahead. And, yes, children of all ages, people of all religions, all sides of these provocative borders, were wounded and died every day in this bloody intractable conflict. Isabel suffered the pain of this status quo and raged against what felt too often like a deliberate stalemate. The contrived state of war. But maybe because of this contrivance, this god damn theater, it was easier to cry over the lost dogs. Shepherds, Ridgebacks, Canaanis,

Malinois, Rottweilers, mixed-breeds alike. Poignantly, innocently, unquestioningly sacrificing their lives for the people they loved.

"We also have the Technion in common." Lia looked at Emanuel who taught mathematics there.

"Another coincidence!" Isabel felt herself warming to this strangely coifed and dressed young man.

"Degree in?" Emanuel asked.

"Chemical Engineering," Asaf answered.

"He has a Ph.D. in Chemical Engineering," Lia boasted.

Their eyes opened wide. This Rasta Hindu-like figure a Doctor of Chemical Engineering?

"So you're all doctors in your family," Isabel managed to say.

"Guess so." Asaf moved more salad onto his plate. He hadn't touched the fish. Probably vegan. "My mother and my older brother, medical. My younger brother too, soon. And Ori who's in the army is on track as a paramedic. My father's a retired physicist."

"He finished all his degrees in five years. Bachelor's to Ph.D. Asaf's brilliant." Lia smiled at her beau.

"And you're working . . . ?" How did a doctor of chemical engineering spend so much time in India?

"I'm not working in my field. Found I didn't really like it."

"Oh."

"In India . . . ?" Emanuel asked.

"I planned on staying in Kerala through the winter but came back to Israel because of Lia. Now that I'm here I guess I'll scout around for something. Maybe teach at one of the colleges." He leaned toward Uri. "Challenge you to a game of backgammon. Lia tells me you're formidable."

"You're on." Uri paused. "What's formidable?" He stumbled over the long word.

"Awesome," Asaf said and the two boys pushed back their chairs and left the table. Uri ran to get the board.

Lia cleared the plates. Emanuel and Isabel remained seated.

"What to make of it all," she asked Emanuel. They smiled.

"Who's to say one has to use a degree to further a career?" Emanuel asked back.

"Who's to say one has to have a career?" she added, went into the kitchen, and put her arms around Lia. "I really like him."

"I know your reservations, Mom. I know the way you think." Lia stacked plates in the dishwasher. "He's freelancing through life, etc. etc. But don't worry. Look at the family he comes from."

"We'll see." She rinsed out bowls. "Just enjoy it for now. The future will present itself. But he's very interesting. And attractive. But what do you do with all that hair in bed?"

Lia punched Isabel in the arm playfully. Isabel recalled Jaim Benjamin's unexpected comment during their last interview. A decade earlier his wife of forty years had left the house without much notice or ado and no room for negotiation. She wanted something else. Something to make her happier. Jaim Benjamin said: "Women come into marriages thinking they can change their men. And men come into marriages expecting their wives never to change." A closing comment on a life endured more by sticking to the shadows than by venturing into the light of unkind day.

"This afternoon I looked up and wondered how the blue sky looks from inside a camp's barbed wire fence." Isabel sat next to Emanuel on the couch after finishing up in the kitchen. Lia and Asaf had read to Uri and tucked him in. Now they were on their way to camp out with friends by the Sea of Galilee. Isabel held Emanuel's hand. He pressed her fingers and didn't speak.

"Sometimes I'm so busy I forget to eat. That happen to you?" she slumped against him. "And when I'm practically faint from hunger, I tell myself to stop complaining. I should be grateful I'm not living on starvation rations of watery soup and moldy bread." She closed her eyes. "Jaim Benjamin's book is just hard. Feels like iron chains are attached to the sentences." She opened her eyes to look at Emanuel. Yes, he was listening carefully. "I have a rough outline of events. The journey to the mountains. It was dangerous. Germans knew Jews would try to use this route to escape. His two years moving from family to family. He occasionally helped another Jew who slipped across the border from Yugoslavia. And after the war. Returning to Florina. But filling in these broad lines . . . I don't know what's come over me."

"You do know," Emanuel said and brought her hand to his mouth.

"It's really really and I mean really time to take a break. Think of it as a sabbatical."

Isabel leaned into him more heavily. "Jaim Benjamin came to New York under the Greek quota."

Emanuel kissed her on the brow. Then on the cheek. Then on the lips. She slipped into his warm mouth and let herself go in his strong arms.

"Let it rest awhile, Issie."

"Maybe," she whispered.

"Definitely." He tugged her to her feet, up the stairs, and to bed.

The Dogs

1

A few weeks later they lost Woody. It was an early Saturday morning and as they loaded the car before the three-hour drive to Yael's army base in the desert, no one could recall when he was last seen. Uri claimed the dog slept with him and pointed to an indentation on the pillow. Lia said he greeted her at the front door at three a.m. Emanuel last remembered him at dinner. And Isabel just couldn't recall though she usually tucked in the house and did an animal check, a door and window check, a child check, before sinking into bed with a book and cup of tea.

But she wasn't sure she did one the night before. She was drunk from the bottle of Pinot Grigio she had finished off, the bottle Emanuel always bought for her at duty-free when he visited his daughters in Sweden. Uri had brushed his teeth and changed into pajamas. He went under the covers and Isabel followed, too exhausted from the long work day and wine to worry about Lia on the roads meeting friends at a local kibbutz pub. Did Isabel sneak a house inventory in there somewhere, before she fell into bed and the covers followed?

In the morning, after a long espresso and two aspirin, Isabel loaded the car with magazines, pears, barbecue potato chips, chewing gum, cookies, and English avocado soap (another duty-free coup). When she threw the collapsible water bowl into the back seat she noticed that Woody was not hovering around the car. He who always sensed a road trip usually threw his little body up and down in ecstatic somersaults when Isabel tossed the water bowl into the mix. That dog was born for the road.

How could Isabel have forgotten to check for him? Where could he have gotten himself off to? Yael often teased Isabel that she loved Woody more than her children and Isabel would say that wasn't true, she loved all her children the same. Woody was just one of them. And Lia teased that after Isabel got the Holocaust out of her system, she should write an Israeli *Travels with Voodie*. A travelogue with a dark side, filled with anecdotes of people who feared and hated dogs, and were perfectly comfortable being cruel to them. This cruelty was Lia's pet peeve. For a high school research project she investigated the prejudices against the so-called unclean canine rampant in Judaism and Islam in the Middle East. The spike in the number of dogs tossed out of households before Ramadan had veterinary services all across the region calling for education and reform. The malice towards 'unkosher' dogs in many Orthodox Jewish communities in Israel elicited similar cries and pleas.

Once on a Jerusalem street Lia used karate to protect a dog. The girls were in high school, Uri was still in a pram. As far as Isabel knew it was the only time in Lia's life that she actually used these hard-won skills of hers. They had walked by a man jabbing a small dog with a long pole. Scattered garbage messed the sidewalk.

"What do you think you're doing?" Lia stepped towards the man.

Isabel kept her eyes on the pole. This simple question set in motion a confrontation that began with words and ended in blows. At first the man turned his face away. By his black pants and jacket, white shirt and black hat, he was self-identified as ultra-Orthodox. A Haredi Jew. One of god's fearful. Maybe he was uncomfortable talking to a woman from outside his world. Maybe he was unhappy being challenged.

Lia asked again. "What do you think you're doing?"

He turned to face the young woman, a girl really, who had the nerve to meddle in his business.

"Yu talkin' to me?" he asked like DeNiro in a Yiddish-washed Hebrew. If Isabel weren't nervous she would have burst out laughing and maybe he sensed her amusement because his upper lip curled and the hand not holding the pole clenched into a fist. As if in a movie he raised his arm and brought the pole down in slow motion over Lia's head. Isabel watched and saw the pole freeze in mid-air. Lia had caught the top end and held fast.

"Rashi taught that because dogs kept silent during the Exodus they would be rewarded. Treated kindly, not cruelly."

She was not mocking the man but instructing him. He grimaced dangerously. A cornered animal. Isabel prepared to step in. The man grabbed the stick with both hands and tried to pull it from Lia's grip but she was too fast for him. With a twist she wrenched the pole out of his hands, flipped it and wedged it under his chin. She pushed him against a tall garbage container, the pole held tight against his windpipe.

"Do you like that?" Lia brought her face close to his. She pushed down harder on the pole.

The man's eyes rolled back in their sockets. Even though his hands held fast to the pole, he became meek. Isabel went and put her hand on Lia's shoulder. It was enough. Lia backed away and threw the pole into the street. She bundled the little dog up in her arms.

As they walked away the man yelled, "Satan's children. Monkeys. Garbage."

"I can go back and kick that guy's ass." Yael stopped to scowl at him. At fourteen she was already taller than Isabel, taller even than Lia. A black belt in karate. A formidable fighter. They burst out laughing and after a moment's hesitation kept walking.

On a bench on the Ben Yehuda pedestrian mall, they waited for the right people to adopt the little dog. This didn't take long. A young couple, recently engaged, stopped to play with him and fell in love. Lia had ready a list of instructions, including an immediate visit to the veterinarian, then they sent them on their way. The holy family.

Woodrow, an integral part of the Toledo-Segev family, always accompanied them on excursions. He was a rich source of anecdote. A magnet for adventure. Where could he be?

"I'll check the neighbors' yards. Uri, check all the closets in the house. Maybe he's locked in somewhere." Isabel ran next door.

"I'll go to the *wadi*." Lia headed to the woods in the back of the house.

"I'll stay here." Emanuel leaned against the car. "In case he shows up."

But he didn't. After fifteen minutes of searching, they congregated back by the car.

"He's probably with a female." Emanuel tried to cheer them up. "You know how males are, especially the real dogs. He'll be here when we get back, wondering what took us so long. Demanding supper."

"But he never disappears like this." Isabel stared into space. She was tipping at the edge of panic. Woody. Her little one. Her constant companion.

"We can't go without him. Yael really wants to see him." Lia was firm.

"Maybe one of the men from Thailand ate him," Uri whispered.

"Uri," Lia said sternly. "Mom, how can you let him say things like that?"

"Uri, don't say things like that. Thai people don't eat dogs. A terrible stereotype." The words spilled out mechanically. The weight of Woody's absence grew. Worry tore through her. He must be found.

"But I saw it on the children's news last week. Some Thai men caught dogs in wooden traps in the Golan and cooked them for supper."

"Ugh, I can't believe it." Lia paced the length of the driveway.

"Culturally relative, Lia." Emanuel shrugged his shoulders. "Cows off limits in India and here nothing's better than a fat juicy steak."

"But why show this stuff to children? Next they'll be saying that some other ethnic group grabs little children and boils them in kettles with potatoes and carrots."

"Hansel and Gretel!" Uri shouted proudly.

"Okay, and the blood libel is alive in well in some parts of the Arab world." Emanuel checked his watch.

"Exactly my point," Lia said hotly. "You put it on TV . . ."

"Best at Ramadan . . ." Emanuel went for irony.

". . . and people believe it."

"That's the point."

"Shit." Isabel looked at the dashboard clock. They had to get going. "What are we going to do? Woodrow, Woody," she called out and ran up the block. If the children weren't there, she would have collapsed into a full fit-to-be-tied attack of nerves. Her adored Woody. Since Prague she had more or less managed to keep the golems, ghosts, and ghouls at bay. Now they tightened around her. Drawn out like wood's grain. Limb by limb. Hollow by hollow as minutes passed without a sighting of her beloved dog. She worried the amber beads around her neck and ran back to the car.

Uri slid into the back seat of the car. He whimpered. "They've eaten him, I know it. He's never not here."

"Shh, shh." Lia slipped in beside him. "Woody's too smart to be caught by anyone. And besides, why go after his puny body when there are so many fat Golden Retrievers around?"

"Lia," Isabel snapped and continued to scan the horizon of her quiet street for the small white with brown spots body of her favorite Jack Russell Terrier in the world. Where was he? Trapped in her terrors, she began to shake. She was going to lose it. It was the body, it had a mind of its own.

"I hear him." Lia called out suddenly. "Woody, Woody."

"Woody, Woody, come here boy." Isabel screamed. "Woodrow?!"

"It's coming from back here."

Emanuel went calmly to the back of the car and opened the boot. The little dog jumped out, shook himself once, then once more, and walked back and forth behind the car. Emanuel scooped him up and brought him to Isabel. But Woody turned his head away.

"How did he get in there?" she asked.

Woody squirmed out of Emanuel's arms and jumped into the backseat with the children.

"Well, let's see," Lia said when they were all belted and Emanuel backed the car out of the driveway. Woody head's was on the boy's lap. His legs tucked next to the girl's. "Probably in his excitement he jumped in, and someone, most likely MOM, closed the trunk and voilà, a lost Woody."

"But why didn't he cry?" Uri stroked the dog's back.

"Probably thought these stupid humans will figure it out. Then he began to make noise when our not figuring it out went on for too long," Lia said.

"I'm so sorry Woodrow." Isabel turned around to pat his head. But he ignored her. Pissed off and proud of it.

2

By the time they arrived at the base, nearly all the shady spots were taken in the sparsely planted visitor's grove. It was early November and still very hot in the desert at noon. Yael waited by the base gate, tired but happy to see her family. They found a bit of shade and laid out their large woven mat.

Yael dove into lunch. After they ate she put her head on Isabel's lap and closed her eyes. Isabel caressed her forehead. Tucked in loose hair strands. Her dark thick Toledo hair was pulled back in a tight pony tail. Isabel ran her finger along the perimeter of Yael's ear. Small trace holes remained of her once many earrings. The nose ring too had come out. Army regulations. Isabel stroked her adored second born. Her femininity oddly framed in the masculine army uniform.

Something was up. There was tension in the lines of Yael's mouth, in her creased forehead. In her voice. Two days earlier Isabel called to ask if Yael wanted her to bring something extra special. Beyond the usual special. She said no. The usual and Woody. Make sure to bring Woody. His body was stretched out on her chest now. His head over her heart. She rubbed the soft fur behind his ears.

Isabel hadn't given the request much thought. Fact was she hadn't given Yael any special thought these past few weeks. The pressure of writing piling up coupled with the effort of keeping the demons down left little space in her mind. Isabel assumed Yael was living her normal army routine. But something had changed and Isabel had been remote. Guilt tore at her. She braced herself.

Lia strummed bassa nova chords on her guitar. She picked out some of their favorite Beatles songs. Isabel hummed along and kept watching Yael.

"I'll make coffee." Emanuel took out a small camping stove. He screwed on the fuel canister. Uri helped him measure the water and gauge the coffee. They squatted and waited for the water to boil. With a long stick Uri slowly stirred the fine coffee grounds in the bubbling water.

Yael opened her eyes and looked directly into Isabel's. "I'm being transferred."

"And?" Isabel did not take her eyes off of Yael's dark ones. She forced herself to sound calm, stalk of wheat in a hurricane that she suddenly was.

"That's all. I'm needed for more important work."

"Where?"

"Nablus."

"Noooo," Isabel deliberately held out the 'o.' "I don't allow it." Her voice rose. Control quickly lost. Not this. Not now. Not any time. "I'm calling your commander tomorrow. I'll go to his commander. You're not going to risk your life over there. Not for those people. No way." Shit. No tears. She had to be firm. Be strong.

"I'll be providing logistical assistance to soldiers, Mom. Nothing to do with settlers."

"I don't care. Our soldiers shouldn't be there. I want you to stay in our country." She wiped her eyes.

"Mom," Yael sat up, taking Woody with her. She continued to hold him close to her heart. "I requested it. I'm bored here. I can contribute more there. There's real stuff going on there."

"Real stuff for sure. Real fighting, Yael. War." Isabel forced herself to speak calmly. "It's not like going to a pub on Friday night and dancing with great looking guys. There's shooting. Shooting at, being shot at."

"Mom, you know I love you and with all due respect, I know it's war. I'm a soldier."

"Why don't you teach karate or krav maga? Those are important skills for soldiers to know."

Yael and Lia laughed. Times like these reminded Isabel of how little she knew of this country. And its army. Even after all these years she got it wrong. Even after all these years she was an American outsider. All she really knew was what Alon used to tell her. What Emanuel explained. What Molly gleaned from her sons. What Lia went through. And now Yael. And that's it. Isabel had never been part of the system and didn't understand its ways.

"That Lia and I know karate means nothing to the army."

But that much Isabel already knew. When they were going through the draft process, she tried, behind their backs of course, to maneuver them into sports trainer's positions. But the army had other plans. Isabel had also learned the hard way that one can't rebel against army officers and bureaucracy as she had against parents, kibbutz life-by-committee, Alon, Emanuel, and a society that continued to try to dictate her professional and sexual life.

"I should have been in a support unit last year when we were in Lebanon. Felt like a fool sitting here in the desert. I am going to do it now." Yael kissed Woody's head and looked relieved now that she told Isabel.

Emanuel brought over the coffee in small glass cups. Uri brought a tin of Emanuel's mother's homemade *rugelach*. Hot sweet liquid slipped into Isabel's body caverns. She always considered herself lucky. Two girls, no combat. She was not ready for this to change. During last year's Second Lebanon War she felt waves of anguish and relief every day. Anguish at the devastating destruction of homes and lives, at Uri's terror every time they needed to run into their safe room because missiles were on the way to them. And relief that Lia had not been called up for reserve duty and Yael was stationed in the desert.

Isabel remembered one afternoon when she and Molly came upon a group of female soldiers in Daliat Al-Carmel. Isabel had come to shop for a rug. The soldiers shopped for everything. Low riding green belts and grey guns accessorized their uniforms. Some of the women so small the weapons traversed the entire length of their bodies.

"Soldiers or not, women are women." Molly laughed as the young combatants faced the alluring commercial strip.

Women in men's clothing. Women both soft and tough. Isabel lived with these women, was like them to some extent, but still, she didn't get it. Why would Yael choose to move closer to the zone of combat? Isabel looked into her daughter's eyes. The orders had gone out. Yael wasn't consulting Isabel, she was informing her.

"I'm proud of you," Lia said.

"What did I miss?" Emanuel sipped his coffee.

"I'm being transferred. Base near Nablus."

Isabel's breath stopped. Two young men from their town were killed there in the past year and a half. How did parents of sons get through it? How would she? Isabel clung to the hope that by the time Uri turned eighteen there would be peace. The mantra of every generation. Still, Isabel insisted to herself and to Molly it wasn't just a delusion but a legitimate hope.

"Well, you'll be busier than you are here, that's for certain." Emanuel poured more coffee into small glasses.

"That's the point." Yael laid back down on Isabel's lap. Purged. Relaxed. Woody tucked himself into her side. Lia asked Uri what he wanted to sing. He requested the usual. Older sister and the little boy sang together in sweet soprano:

Puff, the Magic Dragon, lived by the sea
And frolicked in the autumn mist
In a land called Honalee.
Little Jackie Paper loved that rascal Puff
And brought him strings and sealing wax and
other fancy stuff.

Isabel used all her inner resolve to look and act naturally. She stroked Yael's hair. American soldiers in Vietnam dubbed a particularly loud gunship, Puff the Magic Dragon. Their playmate. Isabel fought the panic. She remembered how Suri sat rigid and worried on shore when Alon took the children into the sea. Water was a world not understood by the orphaned child from the walled city of Kamenets-Podolski. But the Mediterranean had always been Alon's playground. Yael's transfer fit into a system Lia and Emanuel understood. They were calm while for Isabel another chasm of dread and chaos tore open. Yael joined in.

A dragon lives forever, but not so little boys
Painted wings and giant rings make way
for other toys.
One grey night it happened,
Jackie Paper came no more
And Puff that mighty dragon,
he ceased his fearless roar.

Tears had to wait. Terror expressed privately. Isabel knew from Molly, from all her friends whose sons did battle, that you were not allowed to show the terror while inside the love smoked. Was it any safer on the roads? Molly asked rhetorically and frequently, especially when Yiftach returned to base, especially when he came home from Lebanon. He never spoke about the Special Forces unit and Molly and Noam never asked. Yiftach came home for the weekend, stayed out late with friends, then slept and ate a lot. In the early morning hours Molly stole into his room and sat by his bed.

"He looks so young when he sleeps," she whispered to Isabel as she made coffee in the kitchen. Was she crying? "So young and doing war."

"Molly, you think the old men are going to endanger themselves?"

"I would actually like to see an army of fifty year old *alter kakers*." Her voice rose up shrill, flushed with the anger of the impotent. "Netanyahu rushing in from one direction, Abu Mazen from another, Nasrallah and Mashal from a third. Let's see how far they'd get before *kvetching* about their hemorrhoids and those stinking boots. They need to sit down a little and can someone bring them a cup of tea. You'd see how fast they'd figure it all out. Easy to send the young to die."

Isabel took Yael's hand. She wouldn't let go. Not now. Not ever. She could only imagine how hard it was for Molly to say good-bye to Yiftach at the bus stop. She kissed him briefly. Gave a tight short hug. Reminded him to call her when he arrived at base before phones were put away. Last year, during Yiftach's first year of service, Molly came home from that goodbye and fell into bed until her first patient showed up. If none were scheduled, she'd remain in bed until one of her younger children came home needing lunch. Molly mentioned her sister's kids in London who acted out before they went off to university. They made great messes in their rooms, lashed out easily, and incited battles with their parents.

"Soiling the nest syndrome my sister calls it," Molly said. "Making home inhospitable so it's easier to leave. Our kids do the opposite. They hold tight, to home, to us, just a moment longer. And we . . . we . . ."

And then there was that morning last winter when Molly had been beside herself with worry. "It's so cold. I don't think Yiftach's warm enough with that army blanket."

"So let's drive to the West Bank and bring him his down blanket from home."

"Ha, ha, Isabel. He's freezing his ass off in a tent."

"Molly, honey, Yiftach goes off on James Bond missions. And you're worried about his blanket?"

"One thing's got nothing to do with the other."

What to say to the maternal protest against powerlessness. Reason was not a factor. Yet wasn't this the most reasonable worry in the world?

"It's different with a son." Molly sighed. "You'll see when Uri's drafted. Though maybe, *tfuu tfuu tfuu*, we won't need such an army then. Anyway, the whole thing's harder for us." She stirred her coffee. "We're foreign born."

"But we already lived through Alon and Noam in Lebanon."

"Husbands are not children," Molly said. "It's not that our Israeli-born friends don't suffer." Molly laid the spoon down. "But they've lived through wars, they've served. They're better at compartmentalizing the fear. Better prepared. We're totally inexperienced, Isabel. For us a child in a combat unit is a fast lane to hell."

Isabel didn't really understand then. Now she did. Within minutes she did.

3

"And besides," Isabel repeated Molly's words aloud to herself and to Lia who helped unpack the bags in the kitchen after the long ride home from the desert, "is it any safer on the roads and streets? You can be looking for a dress in Haifa and get blown up. You can be having a coffee in Jerusalem and see God on the concave side of your sugar spoon."

"She'll be all right, Mom." Lia put the bag of uneaten fruit on the counter and walked over to hug her mother. She was Israeli born and better prepared. "Yael'll learn a lot."

"I don't want her to learn a lot." Isabel cried and buckled against Lia's tall strong body. "I'm so scared. It's as if I've already lost her. I can't stop feeling the bullets, the bombs. Lia, I can't let Yael go there."

"Shh, Mom, it'll be fine, please don't worry so much."

But Isabel was past being comforted. This news, like Uri's breakdown in Prague's Old Cemetery, cued the demons waiting in the wings. She sank to the kitchen floor and sobbed. Maybe Dave was right all along. How could she have come to this country at war, make children, and let them be sacrificed? Was the last laugh on her?

"Why is *Ema* crying?" Uri entered the kitchen.

"She's afraid because Yael's going to a more dangerous army base." Lia knelt beside Isabel and stroked her hair. "It's not as dangerous as it sounds. Please, believe me. I was also in combat with Dido."

Which was not exactly reassuring. During Lia's army service Isabel managed to convince herself that Lia spent her time training dogs to sniff explosive materials far from any battle. Isabel didn't know then that canine crews worked closely with combat soldiers. No one, especially not Lia, ever told her differently. Even when Dido was killed by a roadside bomb Isabel managed to remove Lia from the scene. After her discharge Lia told her that as the dog's handler she remained with Dido until meters from every operation. Including that last fatal one. Isabel was like the grandparents routinely lied to by their children and soldier grandchildren. Who was crazy enough to tell grandmothers that their eighteen-year-old grandchildren were in mortal danger? Stories of routine drills near the northern border quieted everyone. The grandparents liked what they heard and asked no further questions.

Isabel's stomach lurched. She was going to throw up.

"Don't be afraid, *Ema*." Uri jumped into a karate stance in front of her and knocked over a bag of food. "Yael will get them like this and like that and like this and like that." He demonstrated his moves and took a rolling pin from the drawer and waved it around like a sword. "She's going to kick some butt, yeah."

"It's not a game, Uri," Isabel rebuked him sharply. "Now put that away before you hurt something."

But he was seven years old and had already spun off into his own fantasy. Running through the house with Woody at his heels he made war cries and mimicked the sounds of explosions. Larger voices and images of the symphony of war scorched Isabel's brain. Ambulances,

95

sirens, police cars, intelligence units screeching to a halt. A bombed bus like a beached whale mutely mourned its demise. The heavy shoes of the clean-up squads. The screams of the burned. Whimpers of witnesses.

Uri yelled "Aaaaa" at the top of his lungs and charged into the garden. He leaped over two cats and pointed his imaginary gun at two others lounging in the sun. They didn't budge, impervious to the noise and activity of the child. Maybe he imagined himself a soldier like Molly's Yiftach, green and black paint obscuring his face as he crept into narrow alleys drawing out enemy fire.

Worn out from the early morning ordeal with Woody, from the drive, from saying good-bye to Yael, Isabel stood shakily. "Lia, can you take care of Uri and unpack the rest, please?"

"Of course, Mom. Go rest."

She climbed upstairs to bed and closed the shutters. She lay down and, though it was warm, pulled the blanket up to her chin. Woody barked loudly as he ran after Uri kicking up a storm in the yard. Jaim Benjamin told her that German soldiers routinely let their dogs loose when they patrolled the small Greek villages. The dogs didn't do more than frighten the peasants and luckily couldn't tell the difference between a weathered Greek farmer and a young Jewish boy who looked like his grandson after months of working in the rocky fields. Jaim wore local clothing and his hair long. And no villager informed on him. They had little motivation. This village, this band of a few families, hated the Teutonic intruders, as they hated the Ottomans before them. The Huns and Visigoths before them. The Romans before them. They wanted to be left alone to grow okra, cucumbers, and tomatoes and tend their goats and olive trees.

Isabel closed her eyes and slid entirely under the blanket. No more light. No more thoughts. No more anything. She focused on breath and started to count from one to ten. Slowly. Deeply. It didn't work. She broke down at six and thought of Sylvia Baum from Lublin. Ten years earlier Isabel had written her book. On the morning the Jewish community was summoned to gather in the main square, Sylvia's mother sent her and her three year old sister, Manya, to the neighbor's. At seven years old, Uri's age, Sylvia already knew it was dangerous for Christians to hide Jews. She knocked on F Pani Kowalów's door. "Please take my sister. She's so little. I'll manage on my own." She kissed Manya on the mouth. "You behave nicely and do whatever you're told." And began to walk away. But F Pani Kowalów would have none of it. She grabbed Sylvia and told her to come into the house. They'd manage. And they did. The family hid the two little girls for two years. Then they sent them to relatives in a village an hour away. They remained hidden in a barn until the war's end.

While Isabel wrote the book, Sylvia's bravery overwhelmed her. Willing to go into the world alone at seven in order to save her younger sister. Lia and Yael were thirteen and nine at the time. They were so vulnerable and seemed utterly unequipped to plunge into such extreme danger.

Now, lying in the dark cocoon of her bed, Isabel ached for Yael. She didn't want to let the body she created and loved more than life itself out of her bounds. And she thought not of Sylvia's bravery, but of Ruchel's, Sylvia and Manya's mother. What happened inside her when she told her daughters to walk to the end of the street, to climb the two front steps of F Pani Kowalów's house and not look back? How did one say good-bye to a child like that and go on? Ruchel didn't survive. She was gassed in a truck cum mobile gas chamber in Bełżec a week later. Her daughters were spared seeing her strip in front of them. *Here mothers are no longer mothers to their children.*

Maybe it wasn't that the Israeli-born were better trained for trauma. Maybe trauma trained everyone. There was nothing new under the sun.

Isabel lay in bed for three days. High fever. Muscles aches. Joint pain. A burning throat. Uri needed to go to school. Meals had to be cooked. And there was Schine's deadline. Lia ran the household. When Isabel's conscience couldn't abide the situation any longer she dragged herself out of bed.

Weak for another three days, she managed somehow. As her body strengthened, so too did her mind. By the end of the week she began to feel a semblance of normal, helped by knowing that after six days near Nablus, Yael would be back on base near Ashdod.

Isabel returned to her work rhythm. Six-thirty a.m. reveille. Seven-thirty out the door to bring Uri to school. Eight o'clock at her desk. One p.m. Uri home for lunch. Then the usual cat and mouse game between spending time with Uri and revising sentences until late afternoon when she officially stopped working, turned the computer off, and ran errands, saw friends, Zakhi, and shuttled Uri to and from after-school activities.

Ten days after visiting Yael in the desert, Isabel was fully recovered, strong enough to walk in the fields near town with Woody and Emanuel. November's sky spread out above them. The setting sun stained thin wisps of cloud pink, orange, smoky grey. Fields showed timid signs of green as they waited open-beaked for winter rains to calm the deep thirst brought on by six months of Middle Eastern heat. The three of them walked briskly, silently, amidst this beauty.

"I feel the earth move under my feet, I feel the sky tumbling down." Isabel sang and smiled at the serenity around her.

"I want us to live together," Emanuel said, as if continuing the verse.

They walked through a patch of thorns. Woody tread carefully.

"What do you think?" Emanuel nudged at her silence.

After quiet seconds of forever, she answered. "I can't."

"Why?" Emanuel looked straight ahead. A leaking irrigation pipe created a large puddle on the path. "Why can't you?"

"I just don't want to live with anyone again." Isabel walked quickly around the stagnant water.

"What about when you're older?" Emanuel stopped walking. "You won't always have children at home keeping you busy."

"I don't know how I'll feel when I'm really old," she answered irritated with his request, yet again. She stopped and turned to face him. "I'm talking about now, the foreseeable future."

"I don't understand you, Isabel." Emanuel's face tightened. "How you can turn away from what we have?"

"I'm not turning away."

"Capping is the same as turning away." He looked at her directly. "I want to build a full life with someone, not be a weekend boyfriend. I want more, more commitment, more time together, more love. And I want it to be with you, but if you don't, then fine, but that leaves me no choice but to end it." His cell phone rang. He fished it out of his pocket and shut it off without looking at the screen. "I want us to join lives, Isabel. Lia, Yael, and Uri are attached to me. You know I adore them. Eva and Anna feel the same about you. We can be one family."

Isabel looked away and started walking. Emanuel followed. Woody too. A sudden push up a steep incline provided the excuse to remain silent. They walked around a large pond. The sky's pink, blue, and purple echoed on the water. White cattle egrets skimmed the surface, producing small ripples. To the unsuspecting eye this pond was just lovely. Only locals knew it as part of the sewage treatment system used to irrigate the fields. A sign, small enough to be missed, warned that the waters were toxic. Do not approach.

"Look, a nutria." Isabel pointed at a small brown head that poked skyward out of the water. Woody looked too. Isabel caught his eye and bent down to give him a quick pat on the head. How she wished this conversation would go away.

"So?" Emanuel wasn't letting it go anywhere but here. He stared at her. His mouth set sadly. His hands crammed into his pockets.

"This has not been an easy time for me. You know that." Isabel started slowly and tentatively.

"Okay."

"It's even a bit insensitive to throw this at me right now."

"True but when's the right time? When you're immersed in the next book? Or when Yael's on her post-army trek in Peru or China? Or 'til the next national crisis . . ."

". . . only thing reliable around here . . ."

"There is no good time. There is only now. This is the absolutely right time. I love you, Issie. I want to take care of you. I know you love me. Let me help carry some of the load. Just a little. Let me love you some more."

She wanted to cry. How could she say no? But how could she say yes? She married at twenty-two and cherished the liberty she had now. She was not ready to say no to tumbling on the beach with a new man. To kissing for hours in a dark corner of a café. To pressing together electrically on a street corner. Of not thinking beyond the moment of soft lips finding each other and a long night ahead. She was not ready to close up shop. And then there was Zakhi. Or maybe there was mainly Zakhi. She was not ready to say no to him.

"Emanuel, I love you. Give me some time to work it out in my brain. I'm sinking in the tide of deadlines. And you know I'm good at constructing things. But I'm also good at wrecking them." Isabel looked up at the faint outline of the moon. "So much has been dredged up in me. Please be patient."

He took a deep breath. "Okay, but not much longer, Isabel. By the new year, end of December, when you're done with this round of professional obligations, tell me. That's enough time for you to sort out how you feel. But I want it to be clear, if we don't move in together, it's over."

"Is that an ultimatum?"

"I guess it is."

"That's not very nice." Her tone hardened and the hairs on the back of her neck rose. "I won't be threatened, or pressured," she blurted out with more force than she actually felt. A facade of toughness, a learned default from New York.

"So be it." Emanuel looked toward the mountain range in the west. "I'm tired of waiting at the table for scraps."

They continued walking. Emanuel pulled at dead stalks in the field and without a word sprinted away. Woody ran after him until he realized Isabel was not following. He short stopped and ran back to her, fast as he could, panting and confused. Isabel walked slowly between long rows of grape vines. The fruit had been picked in August and September. The rank and file vines were recently pruned, prepped for winter's hibernation. Skeletal they looked like anorexic golems or Christs on crosses.

Isabel took her time getting back home. Emanuel was leaning against the gate. She opened the front door. Emanuel hesitated but entered. They drank cold water by the kitchen sink immersed in aggravation and silence. The day darkened prematurely at five.

4

Her monthly massage with Mati could not have come at a better time. Emanuel's ambush opened up another front sapping her resistance. She drove quickly, desperate for the deep probing release, the state of well-being she always carried away from Mati's clinic. His old hands and thick fingers kneaded her upper back with patience and intent. The same deep press and roll he used with dough in the early morning hours of Friday. When they emerged from the oven, he delivered about a dozen *challah* breads to assorted relatives and friends. Isabel too sometimes. A diagnosis of high blood pressure brought on the baking. Doctor's orders. Isabel let out a long swallow of air as Mati's hands moved to her mid-back. Less tension there. It would not hurt as much.

"You've had a rough time of it." Mati worked along her spine. "You've got to find a healthy release. There's a price to pay for this level of strain."

"Maybe I should start baking."

"Ha. I can think of a few other past-times that would suit you more. Nothing like seeking out new pastures, Isabel. I personally don't have the energy anymore but you, well, at your age . . ."

Isabel laughed into the donut hole in the treatment bed. The entire town knew Mati spent the better part of his married life bedding other women. Since she never talked to Mati about her sex life he knew nothing about Zakhi. Or Jiri. Only Emanuel. In fact she knew Mati through Emanuel. Maybe on their own Mati's enormous hands felt that Isabel didn't entirely neglect the intrigue or the chase.

"Sex is a fantastic release," he said, leaving no doubt of his intended meaning. "Especially with a young lover."

Isabel smiled and thought of Zakhi. She didn't need Mati's encouragement. But his enthusiasm for sex, his assumption that sex was a gift people didn't take advantage of enough, strengthened her resolve to carry on.

"But don't fall in love." He worked the muscles of her lower back. "Don't get confused. Don't give over power."

Isabel stopped smiling. Luckily Mati couldn't see her face. She was already kind of in love with Zakhi, and hints of the terrible vulnerability Mati referred to waylaid her more and more, though Zakhi wasn't interested in power games and wouldn't hurt her intentionally. But objective circumstances might.

"Yesterday," Isabel spoke down towards the floor, "I was in Haifa with my friend Molly. We saw this group of beautiful soldiers at the bus stop. She told me I was daft for pointing them out cause they're our children's age. Like I don't know that. So what? I said. I'm not going to have sex with them. I'm just admiring them."

"You keep admiring." Mati laughed.

"When I came to the country at eighteen," Isabel continued, "I was overwhelmed by the sight of so many attractive men doing physical work and in fatigues. Who knew Jewish men could look like that? When Alon came back from reserve duty, all scruffy and tired in his uniform, I practically devoured him. Poor guy, home for some rest from combat in Lebanon and all I wanted was sex morning to night."

"Could be worse."

"Mati, honest, you're my guru. Doesn't Trumpeldor's statue look like a big fat dick from behind? Check it out. You'll see. What can I say? I'm just flowing along. The modern state put the *zayin* back into Zion and I like it." Isabel heard the bravado in her words, an effective cover against exposure, but also true unto itself. When she shared this same playful insight with Molly she retorted that when she came here as a tourist from Ireland it wasn't the men that got her attention but the hairdressers who actually knew what to do with her wild curly hair.

Mati laughed out loud. "That's my girl." He rubbed her fingers, hands, forearms, and upper arms hard between his fingers. A serious work-out. First the right hand. Then the left. The tenderness of certain pressure points hushed her.

"Emanuel wants us to live together," Isabel said suddenly. She hadn't intended on sharing this.

"And?"

"I said no."

"You've been saying no for a long time."

"This was a very clear no. As in now he knows."

102

"How did he respond?"

"Badly."

"Hmm." Mati's knuckles inched their way along her board-stiff neck. These cord-like muscles were indentured to holding up a head thick with concentration camps, publishing deadlines, Yael in the army, relentless domestic demands, Emanuel, paramours, and fabulous love for her children, her mother, her country. The pain of the blood opening contracted passageways was so intense she groaned. She wished Mati could lift her skull off its hinges, oil the vertebrae, stretch the muscles, and then refit the whole contraption. She breathed into the weight and press of his hands.

"What did he actually say?"

"He said it's been four years. Enough time to know that we love each other. That we're good together."

"Uhuh."

"I didn't answer. Anything I said would sound like some bullshit excuse. But the truth is it's not him. It's really not. Emanuel's great and there's love between us. And kindness, support. But . . ."

"Breathe deeply." Mati's hands lay hot and comforting on her neck.

"He gave me an ultimatum."

His hands returned to her shoulder blades. "Not good."

"I told him to give me time. That I couldn't answer just yet. Not in the state I'm in."

"Stall. Excellent tactic. He'll calm down."

"Or not. I'm not going to be bulldozed into anything."

"Stay strong." Mati moved to the adductor muscles. "Listen, I've been thinking about your suggestion." He spread her legs slightly to reach her inner thighs and sprinkled drops of aromatic oil on the skin. "Do you hear me? Hello, Isabel, anyone home?"

"Yes, my suggestion. You mean the book?" She opened her eyes and stared down at the floor. Black curls and blue waves rode the rug's burgundy sea. Occasionally a yellow stitch emerged. A late blooming sunflower in harvested fields. Mati's fingers worked flesh not far from her vagina. She focused on his words.

"It's the thing for me to do, now, at this point in my life." He kneaded the muscles.

She breathed into the ache. Several times Mati had asked her to write his family's story. But Isabel only did first person accounts for people who lived in Europe during the war. Mati and his family moved to Mandatory Palestine in 1936 when he was a child.

"I totally agree and I'll help you organize it."

"The bread brought me back." Mati's hands rested on her back for a moment. "My only memory of my grandmother Leeba. And of Zamość." He pressed hard into the gracilis muscles. Painful but ticklish too. "She wore a kerchief and dark housedresses. And what strong hands. Large as a man's. I remember how she made the dough give way on Friday mornings. The tranquility in that room. The focus and joy in her hands."

"Like a Vermeer." Isabel muttered.

"Yes," he paused. "And within ten years that whole lot of god's faithful murdered. Some by typhus and some by starvation. Some by bullets and some by beatings. Some by electricity and some by gas."

"Mati, you're a poet. Write the book."

"We survived because my parents decided to emigrate. Sheer heresy in those days. Messiah hadn't arrived and my father had the gall to take his family to the Holy Land." His voice softened. His hands sat on the backs of her knees.

"Yes," she said, not sure what she was saying yes to.

"I can count on you to help?" Mati worked the oil from her thighs down into her calves. His thick fingers ran like a pestle in a channel and it hurt. She held in a cry not wanting him to stop. "What problems you have here." She flinched as he plowed harder into her calves. "This is the gall bladder meridian. Seat of anger in the body. Isabel, you need to stretch and meditate, set time aside for deep relaxation. And more sex. You're carrying too much, young lady. Your body is a road map showing all the crashes."

Isabel let out an involuntary cry as Mati walked his hands back up towards her head. He worked his way deeply into her neck muscles again. The pain, though not unbearable, was intense. She could handle it. Because it was expected. Unlike Emanuel's flare-up in the fields.

Mati turned his attention to her head. She tried to clear her mind. His tough fingers moved hard and fast all over her scalp, stimulating the blood. Her hair messed into a tangle. She blocked out thoughts of Emanuel, of Schine, of Suri and Yael, even Zakhi was banished as she stared down into the table's donut hole of peace. Nothing interested her more at this moment than Mati's hands. They flowed from her head to her shoulders. And when she turned on her back, he laid quiet hands on her forehead. Then on her breastbone. Chakra of the heart.

Isabel was grateful Mati supported her resistance to moving in with Emanuel. Molly's response when Isabel called her later that evening was not so hospitable.

"You're being immature and a fool. Emanuel's right. Stop trying to recapture adolescence. Time has come to move into the next phase, or risk losing this wonderful man."

Isabel made a sour face and stopped loading the dishwasher. She went out to the porch, stood by the railing, and stared up at the stars. She wanted to rebut with equally tough words, express annoyance, indignation even. But her words relaxed as they emerged.

"Molly, you've been happily married for twenty-five years. You and Noam just work so well together. You don't know the frustrations I've lived with." Isabel sat on the swing despite the chill night air. Woody jumped up beside her.

"We all have frustrations. Life is about balance and compromise."

The gloves came off. "I know monogamy very well, Molly. Remember, I spent nearly twenty years living it." Isabel went back inside the house. Woody followed on her heels. She slammed the door behind her. "I'm more than capable of living that way. I'm just not willing to."

"Even Alon's built himself a new life with someone."

"Great example."

"And if you're saying no because of Zakhi then you're totally setting yourself up for heartache. Zakhi's bound to fall in love with someone his own age, Isabel. He'll want children and leave you. Don't be naïve."

"Okay, Molly. Got it." She was angry at being judged. Angry at being unsupported. Angry that Molly's words echoed her fears. Isabel called Suri.

"I don't understand what you're fighting, Isabel." Suri tried to be understanding. She was clearly exasperated as well. Not for the first time, probably not for the last, Isabel explained that their different marriages affected everything.

"You became a widow in your fifties, Suri. I divorced at forty."

"So? We're talking about moving on, rebuilding."

"We're from different generations," she demurred.

"I don't hear you mention the word love." Suri challenged her. "And for whatever it's worth, Lola and Zizi agree with me. They came back from Israel last summer so impressed with Emanuel. You're not behaving rationally. A solid man is not so easy to find. A solid man that loves you like Emanuel, even rarer. Hold on to him, Issie."

"I can't bring another man into the house and then separate. Too traumatic for the children."

"Who says separate? Why separate? The children love Emanuel. He's a good father to them."

"They already have a father. They don't need another," Isabel snapped, surprising herself. Any tension when she spoke to Suri made her uncomfortable. She softened her voice. "This is not about their needs. It's about mine. Maybe I just don't love Emanuel enough, if that's how you want to put it."

"You love Emanuel, honey, and you know he loves you very much. You're being stubborn and silly. Relationships are not simple affairs. And no relationship is perfect. Far from it. But it's the way the world is structured."

When Isabel hung up the phone she took Woody's leash out of the closet. Time for a walk. Time to think. For Suri the terms of a relationship were different. After decades of marriage to Dave, a volatile, moody, and profoundly dissatisfied man, she sought out one man to rebuild, for a second time, the life she lost in 1941. She didn't care if Hal read different books than her. She didn't care if he read books at all. It was not relevant to her that he didn't understand the European films she took them to. Or that he watched sports on TV most evenings. Hal knew how to take her arm on the street. He held her hand at the movies. He made sure she drank enough water and had her afternoon nap. Suri was content with a man who just accepted her the way she was, foibles, strengths, and all. A man with no hidden agenda, who didn't demand she change for him.

106

Isabel was different. Ever since her divorce, she sought out a variety of men. Sometimes for exploration and diversion. Sometimes, yes, Molly, she spoke to her good friend in her mind, sometimes just for pleasure. For the experience of it. And to escape pain.

"I can't risk being dissatisfied now," Isabel said to Woody when they hit the street.

Woody looked around briefly to see who Isabel was talking to before he understood it was him. He wasn't impressed and ran ahead to the neighbor's dog. Isabel rejected Suri's claim that the couple was the structure to hang on to. Yet this helped explain the censored stresses that lay under their family's surface, that continued even after Dave moved to California. These were the stresses that cackled along the cross-continental phone lines and appeared in sharp relief on those high school mornings when Isabel awoke to find Dave seated at the kitchen table with Suri, drinking black coffee and reading *The New York Times*. As if this were their usual routine.

Isabel called Woody and they crossed the dark playground filled with swings, slides, jungle gyms, rolling barrels. All still. Lonely round midnight. A group of teenagers filled a bench in a shadowed corner. They drank beer and smoked hookahs. She heard them laughing and assumed they were involved in their own private world. But just in case she moved from the tall dark bushes to the lit path to widen the arc between them. New York in her. Woody ran towards them. He knew a party when he heard one.

"Woody, here, now." Isabel meant business.

He rushed back, reluctant but obedient.

"Don't you do that again." She hissed at him, unnecessarily harsh, taking out her upset on him. He knew this too and his look withered her. She wanted to erase Molly's antagonism and Suri's insistence from her mind. The former reaction was unexpected. The latter so numbingly familiar it threatened deeper love.

As they made the last turn that looped them back to their street, Woody stopped at a tall ominous gate. A friend waited for him there. The nightly routine. The dogs wagged their tails and touched noses. The dog behind the gate whined loudly. He wanted out. Woody lifted his leg and peed against the cold metal then was off to the next dog friend a few houses down.

In high school Isabel didn't know how to explain to her friends that her parents were married and yet not really. In those days plenty of kids had divorced parents. Fathers with second families. Mothers with live-in boyfriends. But this did not jive with her parents' choices. They remained married but lived in two different homes. On two separate coasts. Suri's high cultured Manhattan life style. Dave's fast-tracked easy moneyed West Coast one. Yet when Dave was around, they went out to dinners and plays and never neglected expensive vacations together. They'd laugh and drink wine. Enjoyed each other's company. Maybe even had sex. All this upset Isabel because it confused her. In tenth grade she blurted out that their charade of harmony sickened her.

"Charade?" Suri asked.

"If you get along so well, then why only once in a while?"

"When you're older, you'll understand, Isabel."

So here she was, decades older, walking the dog at midnight under a star-filled sky, the somnolent streets dimly illuminated, small lights spilling from homes where people like her were still awake, and still she didn't understand. And she remained angry and confused. After that one time, she never again asked Suri to explain the strange goings on between her and Dave. Isabel's need to protect her fragile mother overrode her own need for clarity. When Isabel finished high school she also knew that Suri would never supply her with answers to these questions or any others. Suri and Dave lived within shadows and shielded themselves behind paradigms—wife, husband, family—and refused to talk about any of it. Not the problems. Not the complications. Not anyone's needs. Nothing that suggested emotion. Just form and structure maintained with great attention to detail.

Isabel never adjusted to Dave's erratic incursions into their lives and they contributed to her decision to move to Israel right after college. To get far away from the tricks. Dave blamed Suri for this decision, because he couldn't take any responsibility for it himself. But Isabel wanted authenticity. She wanted concrete realities, the lava flow of words that made up discussions, arguments, even tears. Alon and life on kibbutz answered this need for many years.

A year after Isabel left New York Dave died in a car crash on California's Highway One. Then there was nothing left to wonder about. Suri, no longer a quasi-abandoned woman, was now officially a widow. Isabel was pregnant with Lia at the time and immersed in the promise of her young life. The move across the globe, to kibbutz, to two small rooms, to Alon, to their baby, provided her with a simple and precise canvas. Here were clear and definable borders to know and thrive within. Until of course they suffocated her years later.

When they reached the house Woody ran to his water bowl in the yard. Isabel went into the kitchen and poured herself a large glass of wine. She took it and the newspaper and headed to the couch. Uri came crashing in.

"Ugh," she moaned when he landed on her.

He burrowed in. He both wanted her attention and to delay going back to bed. Isabel put a hand on his head. The other on his thigh. Her baby was quickly outgrowing her lap. She soaked in the bed's heat he'd brought with him.

"How come you woke up? It's time to sleep," she whispered.

"Don't want to."

She didn't have the fight in her and so closed her eyes and leaned into the weight of him. She couldn't contain the love she felt for this boy it was so enormous. Eight years ago, Alon convinced her to have Uri. He hoped a baby would shore up the flimsy banks of their marriage. He pointed to plenty of couples who spawned a second set of children as the first readied itself to leave the nest. Like Molly and Noam. An Israeli thing. Isabel's American friends, even Suri, asked why, when she stood on the precipice of freedom with teenage girls, did she agree to be restricted once again to the house, to sleepless nights, to short trips abroad, to grammar school?

And within months of his birth Isabel realized they were right. It had been a mistake. Not the child himself. Not for one second did she regret bringing forth this son whom she adored more than life itself. But she lamented not thinking enough for herself. A baby couldn't heal the rift between her and Alon, and meeting the constant demands of a newborn child only made this more obvious. Within the first year of Uri's life, Alon packed his bags and went back to kibbutz. The place where he had lived contentedly with the rest of his clan until Isabel forced them to move away.

To some extent Uri was lost in these seismic shifts. Fortunately for him, his sisters, Lia at sixteen and Yael at twelve, did not lose focus. Totally delighted, they dove into motherhood zealously. They bathed, dressed, cuddled, and played with him. In the early mornings they brought Uri to Isabel's bed to nurse.

"Got to go to bed." Isabel roused herself and carried Uri to his room. Woody jumped into the bed and nestled against the boy. Isabel sat beside them and watched Uri's beautiful face soften into sleep. She wanted to kiss his eyes, his cheeks, his sweet mouth but wouldn't risk waking him. Instead she rubbed Woody's grateful head and speculated about Dave's extroverted difficult nature. And Suri's understated rigidity. Dave left Suri. Simple as that. But this Isabel had always known. What occurred to her now was Suri's part in the equation. Something pushed Dave out and west. Possibly the same something that pushed Isabel out and east. Not just Dave's ornery stubbornness, but also Suri's impenetrable veneer that didn't allow for life's messes, nor for the intimacy that comes with working through them. Suri's almost bellicose *joie de vivre* kept those closest to her at arm's length. Once Dave. Isabel still.

＊

"I don't know how you tolerate Mati," Molly burst out the next afternoon as she planted a large metal can of olive oil in the middle of Isabel's kitchen. The olive harvest in the Galilee was in full swing. This year's crop was bountiful and the oil was good and inexpensive. Noam always knew which olive press to go to.

Uri was at a friend's. Lia was studying in her room. The weight of the day rolled off Isabel's shoulders. She made them a pot of lemon-grass tea and cut slices of poppy seed cake. The two women sat at the kitchen table.

"Let it be." Isabel pushed honey in Molly's direction.

"I know we have different standards of behavior when it comes to men," Molly didn't let it be. "But still."

"I don't need to hear this. Ok?" Isabel pulled her plate closer. "You think I'm screwing up with Emanuel. That I screw too many other men. Which basically means more than one. Now Mati?"

"Mati's massages are unconscionable, even abnormal. Practically illegal."

"What are you talking about? Sounds like some research control group."

"You know what I'm talking about," Molly didn't look Isabel in the face. "The way he touches. Where he touches." She mixed honey in her tea. "But, yes, men in general. I could never fool around like you."

"Fabulous then that you don't have to. I like my little gifts from the cosmos." Isabel's fork dropped loudly on the plate.

"I'm not judging you, Isabel. I'm saying I'm different."

"Well it sure sounds like judgment. And of course you're different. You're married. When I was married I was also different. I've already stated that many times for the record. You're comparing apples and cars."

"I think I'd be different even single."

"Maybe. To each her own." Isabel would not apologize. She would not let her sexual appetite and storylines be bowdlerized.

"I went to Mati once." Molly squinted her eyes. "No twice, and that was enough for me. Most women I know won't go back to him after the first time. He's lecherous with those *grober* fingers of his."

"No, he's not." Isabel laughed.

"Yes, he is. He touches improperly."

"Mati likes touching. He gets into the muscles. And I like being touched. No big deal."

"Working muscles so close to the vagina is sexual harassment. That's a big deal."

"It's only harassment if you see it that way." Isabel's finger pressed down on sticky-sweet poppy seeds and she licked it clean. Woody loved poppy seed cake and sat patiently by her feet, waiting. "Problem with women is that they've internalized the view of their bodies as objects of male desire. If they took possession of their sexuality, like men do, then a man touching them close to their pleasure centers would only give them greater pleasure, not a sense of trespass."

"Lovely," Molly sniggered. "The ultimate feminism. Calling sexual harassment sexual liberation. Mati giving women favors. I love that."

"Molly, think of this for a second, will you?" A large jay crossed the patio window. "Imagine a female masseuse, top in the field, who happened to concentrate some of her time on the inner thigh muscles. Maybe sometimes, unintentionally, her hand brushed against the penis. Imagine if she spent time working the muscles around the balls since that's an important center of energy, often blocked . . ."

". . . first chakra, mula banda, blahblahblah, heard all this before . . ." Woody suddenly jumped into Molly's lap. Her piece of cake remained intact on her plate. "Oohh . . ." Molly was not a great fan of dogs.

"Down, Woody." Isabel held a small piece of cake in her hand by the floor. The dog was on it immediately. "And usually ignored for precisely the reason that it's too close to the genitals. But the line outside this woman's door would stretch all the way from our town past the stinking oil refineries in the Bay."

"So? Men always want their dicks touched."

Woody watched closely from the floor. Isabel could tell he wanted to jump back on Molly's lap. Not because of her. Because of the untouched cake.

"That's not the point. Men don't see their bodies as an object trespassed by women. They see themselves as possessors of their bodies, of their sexuality. If someone's willing to pleasure them a little, so be it. No big deal. And kind of wonderful."

Molly looked at her watch. "I've got to get home. Noam's probably on his way back from the airport. Short business trip."

"You know, Mati just doesn't offend me. He's my friend. And if I didn't like it, I would tell him to move his hands and he would."

Molly stood up brusquely. "I'm not sure you know what you're talking about. Sex is also about power. It punishes. It can be used as a weapon. There's a whole history of male abuse of the female body. Patriarchy 101. Speak to you later, love." Molly laid a gentle hand on Isabel's shoulder and dashed out. Her cake remained untouched. Isabel put the plate on the floor. Woody vacuumed it up in seconds.

The Waters

1

Isabel parked her car near Uri's school. How was she going to work sentences into life, prune and bolster them, animate and subdue words? Her nerves were shot this morning. She had stopped by the construction site after dropping Uri off at school to say a quick hello to Zakhi who was in a full blown rage.

She walked into the cavernous house and heard Zakhi yelling. "If you're not here by eleven, don't bother coming back, you hear. You're off the job." Silence. "I'm going to fry that jerk." Isabel watched Zakhi smack his hand against the wall. He turned and saw Isabel. "I'm going to fire his sorry ass." He looked untethered. "I've lost all patience for truant contractors and their tales." No smile, no morning peck on the cheek. He was too busy, too anxious. Isabel understood and felt bad for him, and knew there was nothing she could do. "Catch-22 of construction. At this stage where can I find another stone contractor with time available, exactly now when I need him most? And if I could find him, by the time he comes to take measurements, cuts and polishes the stone, by the time he completes the stairs, another month'll pass. And then I'll be screwed entirely. Sticking with Sucrat there's a good chance, even

113

with his bullshit and delays, that the ground floor'll be completed within ten days."

"Cut his check," Isabel said. "That bombshell at the end is your ultimate comfort."

Zakhi managed a smile. "Say the word and you have a job with me, Ms. Toledo." They watched the tiling crew carry boxes of bathroom tile into the house. Nebulous clouds like floats in Macy's Thanksgiving Day Parade drifted overhead. Forecast was for light rain. Isabel wouldn't tell Zakhi this. She knew that if the house was not buttoned up soon, all hell would break loose. Damage to materials, repairs, threats, and recriminations. Tempers pushed off the charts. And Zakhi couldn't close the house until most of the stone was in. Oh Sucrat, you who knew nothing must at least know this.

Zakhi dialed Sucrat. "Where the hell are you now? On your way?" Zakhi screamed. He paced back and forth. "Your guys showed up with stone for the front door saddle. They're so young they can barely carry it. I don't care if it's your son or your brother. You need to be here doing the work and supervising others. You know how many trades are on hold because of you?" Zakhi listened for a moment and closed the phone.

"Maybe we'll get together tomorrow?" Isabel smiled mischievously.

Zakhi nodded. He was too furious to talk. Isabel walked to her car and waved a quick good-bye.

As she drove to Uri's school Isabel wondered if something else, something not related to the site, was a trip wire for Zakhi. Sure, the rains were coming and, sure, Sucrat was infuriating, but she had seen Zakhi handle other hard situations with aplomb. There was something in his eyes. Or in the way he was both focused and distracted simultaneously. Thinking about their interaction she realized he hadn't really looked directly at her. He was holding something back.

Isabel parked and crossed the school playground. She entered the gymnasium carrying her family's four gas mask kits by their long plastic straps. Three adult size, one toddler. She wanted to crawl under a tree and cry. Simply cry. Give up the work, the pressure, and all her responsibilities. The time had come, the big let-down, she was sure of it. The something Zakhi wasn't telling her was this.

How foolish to have become so accustomed to him. How ridiculous to need him when needing was not part of the program. Inside the gymnasium, behind two long folding tables, stacks of rectangular boxes with gas masks were arranged according to age. The largest group was for adults, twelve and up. A smaller section was for children, three to twelve. An even smaller one was for toddlers. And at the very end of the hall were large plastic tents for infants. She had one of those when Uri was born.

Last week Isabel received notice to bring the family's gas masks to this ad hoc army depot in exchange for new ones. The filters, syringes, and sarin gas antidote were approaching their expiration dates. A long line of people moved slowly. Isabel stood in the back. She knew this gym well. Uri's class had their special musical performances and assemblies here. And their regular sports classes moved in here when it rained. The walls were covered with brightly colored posters of photographs from school events. A yellow satin banner wished all the children good health and good studies for the upcoming year. Right next to the stacks of military gear, a large papier-mâché sculpture of Spider Man looked ready to spring.

The line moved slowly. Two women in front of Isabel talked about Iraq using chemical warfare during their war with Iran. She turned away but their words were too close to ignore and besides in typical Israeli fashion they spoke loudly.

"They didn't use it against us."

"They better not even try."

"Let's not think about it."

Yes, please let's not think about it, Isabel thought because if she did . . . Her shoulders crumbled forward. It was getting harder to breathe. She felt faint, put the masks on the floor, and knelt down as if to tie her sneaker lace.

"You're next." The voice of the woman behind her crashed like a wave over her back.

Isabel stood gently, took up the box straps, and walked slowly as if contending with the resistance of waves in the sea.

She dumped the four boxes on the table.

"Identity card?" the soldier asked mechanically and used a scanner to read the barcode on each box.

Isabel fished the card out of her wallet. The soldier took it and consulted a laptop computer. Isabel looked around. A school hall filled with noisy people, columns of boxes, and soldiers standing around looking bored. The soldier behind the table opened the toddler gas mask box. She took out the large astronaut-like helmet, looked it over, and returned it to the box.

"Your child is seven. This is only good until three." She stared accusatorily at Isabel.

"I only got notice now."

"You don't need a notice to exchange the toddler mask for a child's. If something had happened he would have been without a mask," she said snidely, frustrated with Isabel's negligence. After what felt like a dramatic pause, she called out, "Three adult, one child three to twelve." When the other soldier brought over the boxes, she scanned their barcodes and pushed them across the table to Isabel. "Don't wait until he's 15 to change the next one to adult. As soon as he's 12 call the Home Front office and they'll tell you where to go. And here." She frowned and slid a brochure across the table as well.

"Thanks."

Isabel turned away. Four cardboard boxes bumped against her body. She hurried through the gym and playground. She didn't want Uri to see her. She hated when he asked about the gas. She would hide these boxes in their security room when she got home.

She threw the masks into the boot and looked at the brochure in her hand. Instructions for war. *When coming under attack, bring everyone into the security room and close the doors and window, including the metal shutter. Turn on a battery operated radio. Make sure there's water and a bucket in the security room at all times.* The security room. She had had one since it became part of the country's construction code after the First Gulf War. 1991. Thick concrete walls, metal shutters, a window and door with special seals designed to take an indirect rocket strike and supposedly able to delay seepage of gas or chemicals delivered by missile head.

During the First Gulf War, Alon and Isabel lived on kibbutz. No one had a security room then. Every time a siren sounded, every time a scud missile came crashing in from Iraq, they grabbed the girls and ran to the public bomb shelter a few lanes away. The scuds always came in the middle of the night. Maximizing terror. Saddam Hussein at play.

During the Second Gulf War, they lived in town. 2003. When the civil defense authorities told them to prepare the security rooms, they did. Water, canned goods, batteries, candles, matches, battery operated radio, blankets, buckets with covers, games, books, flashlight, television. And up-to-date gas masks.

Isabel returned home and for twenty minutes she played with the letters on the computer keyboard. Her mind dense like a brick. Nothing cogent appeared on the screen. She went to the kitchen and cooked pasta for Uri's lunch. She leafed through an interior design magazine Suri sent from the States. Like Zakhi, Suri wanted Isabel to consider retooling and thought design an excellent direction. Isabel cut up a tomato and cucumber salad. She made fruit salad. She took Woody for a walk in the *wadi*.

They passed a herd of goats, their dogs, their shepherd. A rain drop landed on her shoulder. She looked up. An enormous grey rain cloud passed overhead. Zakhi on site was probably fit to be tied. Another drop landed. Then another. And then a downpour. Woody and Isabel ran through the trees back to the house. By the time they reached the front door they were totally wet. Then just as abruptly as it began the rain stopped and the sun appeared. In Israel rain came one cloud at a time.

2

Isabel sat on a large flat rock and tried to relax into the beauty of the greens dipping in the valley below. Olive, Jade, Nile. A series of large clouds drifted over the Carmel Mountains. This past week she had finally managed to write another chapter of Jaim Benjamin's book and to celebrate she was taking Woody to Bet She'arim but first they stopped at the statue of Alexander Zaid. To take in the glorious view. The *yoreh*, the first rain of the winter season, had fallen a week earlier. A collective sigh of relief could be heard throughout the Galilee. Rain. Farmers depended on it. The government counted on it. Religious Jews prayed for it. And the average individual simply welcomed the switch from summer to winter. But since that first downpour there had been nothing but sunshine and blue skies until this morning's bank of steel-grey clouds. A greeting card from the rains to come. Fretfulness, a premonition of disaster, filled Isabel. Like the Winkler house, she was open and susceptible. Every day felt critical. The rains—not one cloud's worth followed by sun, but cloud after cloud of precipitation—would soon be upon them. A sunny afternoon would evolve into a night of thunderstorms.

Isabel tried not to think of Schine's pressure and stared at the natural finery laid out before her. She breathed deeply and reached for serenity. Another chapter done. But it wasn't enough. Winter signaled Schine's deadline. The bucolic landscape before her became quickly overlaid with a transparency of words: *pages, Isabel, I need pages, pages.*

Sitting cross-legged on the large flat rock, Isabel considered that no matter a calling to bring hidden stories into the light, that it just might not be worth it. Or not worth it anymore. Worth was not the right word anyway. She was not up to it anymore. Yes that was it. She was worn out and withered in the bright light of Schine's unyielding rush. He called every few days to remind her that she had to deliver Jaim's manuscript by the end of December. Five weeks away. Like she didn't know.

Cattle grazed in the field below. A black and white border collie ran energetically around their legs, herding them back into the group. He barked at the more stubborn cows and made sure the calves didn't wander far. He helped move the group east, where the herder, like Isabel, sat on a large flat rock under slowly drifting clouds.

In Bet She'arim, Woody cavorted with a large black Labrador. Round and round the dogs ran in circles on the lawn by the caves of the great rabbis and their families. Isabel sat on a bench some meters away and watched, relieved to be outdoors and not in front of her screen, happy to watch Woody at play, a constant source of entertainment and companionship.

She sighed deeply. On purpose. To calm herself. Jaim Benjamin's was by no means the only difficult book. They had all been difficult, each in their own way. Hana Stern's tale of being taken in, then sexually abused, by a group of Jewish Partisans. Zusya Feinstein who hid with his brother in a total of four haylofts for over three years. While the farm animals satisfied themselves with hay and slops, the boys sucked on straw and pulp from the pages of a book they had found in the woods when farmers thought it too dangerous to bring human food into the barns.

And Harry Roth's, truly the hardest to date. Forty years after the war, Harry was as enraged at his brother Saul for being a *Sonderkommando* as if it had transpired the week before. Miraculously they both survived Treblinka, but never spoke again. Harry told her about Saul and then commanded her sonorously not to mention him in the book. When she told Harry that the men who did this awful work didn't exactly volunteer, he thundered: "There's always choice. That is what makes us human, even in hell." And when she mentioned regret and forgiveness, he came back with, "People who were there don't have that privilege."

Woody and his new friend ran over to Isabel. She took doggie treats from her jacket pocket that they grabbed, swallowed, before rushing away to continue their tumble. Over the years Isabel constructed a space inside herself of attuned neutrality, a default empathy, from which she embarked on book after book. Roth's hatred of his brother heaved a stone into that space, practically blocking access. It was a grave journey into his mind and Isabel almost cancelled the contract. The paragraphs and chapters of Roth's life before the German army rolled into his small Polish town were assembled alongside the *basso profundo* of his final inexorable judgment. And even though he lost everyone in his family but Saul, Harry insisted on treating Saul like Amalek. "*Yemach shemo*," Harry echoed God's commandment to the Israelites to wipe out the memory of Amalek. So why did he told her about Saul in the first place?

Isabel looked up at the hillside. Thirteen minutes from her house to the caves. God did the same when he instructed Israel to destroy the memory of the Amalek nation. But he sealed their longevity with this command since the memory of the Amalekites would survive as long as the Bible was read. But Harry would have none of it. Not a word. Not a name. As if Saul never existed except in his memory and now in Isabel's as well. *Yemach shemo.*

Jaim Benjamin's book was weighing in as the most difficult since then. Not because she had to imagine existence in the grey zone of moral choices. Or reconstruct scenes of sexual abuse in a Ukrainian forest and then blank the screen. Or describe hunger that gnawed at the bones of boys. No, this story was hard to move inside of because Jaim reminded her of Dave. And Dave refused to speak to Isabel after she moved to Israel. *Yemach shema.*

"May I sit?" a young woman about Lia's age stood next to the bench.
"Of course."
The young woman smiled, pushed her long hair back from her face, and took out a Hebrew primer. Woody came bounding over. Someone new to charm!
"Don't be afraid," Isabel said. "He's harmless."
"He's adorable." The young woman pet Woody's head and laughed when he jumped up on the bench to sit beside her.
"You're from Spain?" Isabel heard her accent.
"Yes, Barcelona."
"Welcome."
"Thank you. And you, from here?"
"Yes and no. Originally from New York."
"New York. I have family there."
"It's a big place." Suddenly Isabel didn't feel like talking. Or not about anything deeper than the weather.
"I'm learning Hebrew at Haifa University."
Woody bounded off the bench in the direction of the caves. His Golden friend had gone in and Isabel watched him hesitate by the entrance. Woody never went into a cave by himself. He didn't even like going in with her. Would he now? Woody paused, raised his head to sniff the air, and ran from the cave, across the lawn in search of new friends.
Isabel turned and smiled at her. She had to get a hold of herself.
"Hebrew's not an easy language," the young woman said.
"No, it's not."
"Do you know Spanish?"
Isabel definitely didn't like the direction this conversation was taking. She was going to get up and find herself another bench.

"A little."

"So many Spanish speakers in New York, I thought you might have learned."

"I've picked up some words."

"And do you know Ladino?" the young woman asked.

Shit. No. Isabel shifted on the bench. She wanted to bound off like Woody but was stuck. She was human. Socialized to be polite.

"Also a little. Some words here and there."

"But that's not spoken in New York, right? Maybe by the older people in the Sephardi community?"

"Yeah, they speak it, I think."

"In Jerusalem I am learning Ladino with a special teacher. I love it. Spanish and Hebrew as one." She paused. "Both identities come together."

Oh fuck. Here it was. Hounded by the cosmos. Why?

"I am Jewish," the young woman said proudly. "I just found out two years ago. My uncle told us. Conversos. For hundreds of years."

"The Jews of Barcelona."

"Yes. A large community. The great Ramban lived there. But in 1391 Jews were accused of spreading plague. Those who weren't killed, converted. Like my family."

"Fascinating. Wow, I've really got to go." Isabel stood up shakily. "Lots of luck in your studies."

And she literally ran away. Rude and frantic.

3

Isabel called Zakhi after a sequestered week in the house. The result was good writing days. But she missed him. Texting back and forth was not enough. He didn't answer. She called throughout lunch with Uri and while she worked through a pile of ironing. How many times did she call all together? Six? Seven? It was not like him not to call back. Or to text to say he couldn't talk.

Later in the afternoon Isabel drove Uri to a friend and convinced herself that either Zakhi was with another woman or had a work accident. Jealousy coupled with fear. She sat at the main intersection of town, listening to his phone ring, ring, ring. She pressed redial again and again and again. Anxiety swelled as she drove to the Winkler site blind to the trees and rich blue of the sky. Her head stuffed with gauze she steeled herself to see Zakhi cold to the touch, electrocuted. Or maybe another woman there with him, walking through the rooms, impressed with his knowledge, his skills, his infectious charm. But only Moshe and two of his men were at the house, plastering the northern façade in a lovely shade of yellow. Isabel stood back and admired it and managed to talk normally.

"It's beautiful, Moshe."

"Yeah."

"Zakhi around?"

"No."

"Was he earlier?"

"Yeah."

"And now?"

"Don't know. He left early."

"You know why?"

Moshe hesitated. One of the workers said, "He got a phone call from his sister."

"Sister?"

"Yeah." Moshe gave the guy a look. "His brother died in the middle of the night."

"I'm sorry to hear that." Why was Moshe being so stubborn? He knew Zakhi and she were friends. "Funeral's today?"

"Guess so."

"Was already," the worker said.

She tried to smile at him, to thank him, but was too flustered. Moshe gave her a 'don't ask any more questions' look. He threw a large gob of yellow plaster against the wall and spread it flat with a metal float.

Isabel knew very little about Zakhi's family. What he said was usually not good. He left home at fifteen and enrolled himself in boarding school. Then the army. When he turned his back on religion, his family turned their back on him.

Without thinking twice Isabel drove to Haifa, to the religious section in Hadar; the public death notices would guide her to the family's apartment. Isabel struggled to keep her mind on the road. Here was the highway turn off to Haifa. She held her attention on the here and now for as long as she could and then her mind wandered, refusing to be reined in. She thought of Zakhi laying her down last winter in an ancient wine press in the woods. She remembered the beauty and pleasure she felt being half naked with him in a stone basin used thousands of years earlier to collect freshly pressed grape juice. She smiled to herself and then sunk into another memory of Zakhi's arms around her. This one of the morning they met two years ago. A patina of loss settled on the images.

Isabel had been on her way to Metulla. Yael and her friend Mica had spent a couple of nights there with Mica's grandparents. It was the beginning of June. By that point in their senior year of high school the kids worked exclusively on the end of year party and performance. They slept late at each other's houses and did not go to school except to rehearse. All state wide exams were behind them. Teachers accepted that no real academic work was done after Passover. Molly and Isabel shared a theory that this was the last bit of coddling. A June graduation could lead to a July or August draft date. Six weeks of basic training, an eight week course, give or take some weeks, and by November or December these young people, especially the boys, could be under fire. In combat. Killed and killing. She dropped Uri off at kindergarten and called Yael en route to tell her the ETA.

"Mom, Mica's uncle wants to take us ice skating at the Canada Center. Can you come in the afternoon?"

Isabel was already in the car and didn't appreciate the last minute change of plans.

"Sure, no problem. Three o'clock okay?"

"Perfect. Love you. You're the best."

Of course she indulged them. It was Yael and Mica's last few weeks of adolescence. Mica had a July draft date.

Isabel decided not to go home but to take herself on an outing since a brilliant sense of freedom wafted through her days. She hadn't yet begun writing the new book about Wanda Farber's life. With blue eyes and light brown straight hair, Wanda spent the war passing as Christian within two blocks of the Warsaw Ghetto. Every day she walked by the brick wall separating ghetto from Aryan side. Out of the corner of her eye she scoured the crowds for her mother, her father, her older sister, her younger brother. Once she thought she saw her mother and had to pinch herself hard in the thigh to not shout out. Wanda had seen it all. The overcrowding. The transports. The uprising. The decimation. Her scenes, her words, gestated in Isabel who was in the process of rereading the transcripts. It would take another week or so before she began to set down sentences.

Isabel decided to go to the Museum of Photography at Tel Hai. It was all the way north in the western Galilee and she hadn't been there in years. At Yishai Junction a good looking man with a clean shaven head drove a black car next to her. They waited at the light to make a left. Isabel noticed him because she could actually feel him staring at her. She wasn't sure why. Her hair in a messy pony tail was not particularly clean. She wore baggy house clothes. Even her sunglasses were old and scratched. Uri had stashed her new ones. He had a collection of sunglasses in some secret place and wore them around the house pretending to be a Hollywood starlet from the 1930s. The glorious androgyny of children.

The man's smile was rapacious but sexy. He had large white straight teeth. Isabel did not smile back and pressed down hard on the gas when the light turned green. A road block after Hamovil Junction stopped the flow of traffic. Police searched for illegal weapons. Maybe even bombs. The cars inched forward. Isabel turned her head. The same man with the foxy grin drove alongside her and again he stared at her. This time a reluctant smile peeped out on her face. At Golani Junction his car abutted hers. He was still smiling. Always smiling. This time Isabel gave him a genuine smile. At their fourth stop together, his car next to hers, she laughed along with him. Then they played tag. First he overtook her car. Then she overtook his. At Goma Junction, he rolled down his window.

"Coffee?"

Isabel nodded yes. It was ten in the morning. She had nowhere to be until three. He was attractive, young, playful and no longer seemed predatory. She followed him to a gas station café. They drank coffee.

Shared a plate of humus. He told her he was an electrician going to upgrade the electricity on his friend's farm near Kiryat Shmona. He learned that she ghostwrote for a living, had three children, and was going to pick up one of them in Metulla.

He leaned in towards her. "The Banias are not far from here. Lots of water this year. Beautiful. I'll show you, if you have time."

Of course she had time. She left her car at the gas station and they drove in his through fields and orchards. He parked in a small clearing in a grove of enormous eucalyptus and birch trees. This spot was not an obvious path to anywhere, but Zakhi seemed to know where to go. Which didn't surprise her. Lots of Israelis did. Lia and Yael knew of such places from years of school trips and youth movement hikes. And many men during their army service navigated great parts of the country on foot. It would be an exaggeration to say they knew it like the back of their hands, but considering the pint sized country and amount of outdoor activity, they knew it very well.

As they walked down a steep incline, Zakhi took her hand. The sound of moving water was nearby.

"Heavy winter rains and all that snow on the Golan Heights," he said. "I told you. Lots of water this year."

"Swelling Israel's miniature system of rivers and streams." Her words were clunky. "People come from all over the country to see the water." She felt so self-conscious. What was she doing with this strange man?

Zakhi didn't respond. They walked further into the growth. He held back thorny bushes for her to pass safely. The closer they walked to the stream, the more their shoes sunk into soft moist earth. And then they were there.

It didn't matter that she'd been raised with the large blue reservoirs of New York State. The sight of water in Israel, the fleeting plenitude it brought forth, always moved her. A precious commodity. A force in history. Abraham took his wife Sarah down into the exile of Egypt for the Nile guaranteed a year round supply of water. In the land promised to Abraham by his god there was drought. Three generations later Jacob's sons went down into Egypt again in search of water and food. And after twenty generations, or four hundred years of slavery, it took the strong hand of their god to create the exodus and bring them out. Jacob's descendants eventually wandered north to the Promised Land and its unreliable water supply.

One day she would write about this. Not historically. Poetically. The messianic line traced to water. Elchanan and Naomi leaving Bethlehem for Moab also because of local drought. When Naomi returned home ten years later with neither husband nor sons, but with Ruth, her Moabite daughter-in-law, she could because the water had also returned. And it was during the barley harvest made possible by strong winter rains that Ruth and Naomi's kinsman Boaz made merry. One fertility begat another and when they married, Naomi's status as a surrogate mother of sons was restored. For Ruth and Boaz begat Obed and Obed and his unnamed wife begat Jesse. And Jesse and his unnamed wife begat David. How Isabel loved all these unnamed women and their wombs. And then David became the second king of Israel. It was written that the messiah would come from David whose ancestor was a convert to the tribe. All because of the water.

"It's dry here." Zakhi pointed to a hospitable canopy of shade under a poplar. The mid-morning sun was already hot upon them.

Isabel sat and watched the water move quickly in wide and narrow flutes. The current was strong. Sporadic patches of sunlight sprinkled the surface with light blue and clean hope. A turtle slid off a low hanging tree branch into the bank's dark shadows.

"It's so lovely." She turned to Zakhi.

"Uhuh," he leaned over, covering her mouth with his. This was the time for lips, for tongues, for hands, for ears. For music: trees as rustling snares, birds as winds and chimes, water as bass. Zakhi's tongue left her mouth and trailed the cleft between her breasts. He worked his cool hands into the front of her shirt then unbuttoned it for more skin. He pulled her bra down to the sides pushing breasts and nipples up toward his mouth. He licked and sucked, then kissed her mouth some more. Her hands found his pants and opened them. Like a compass his penis pointed up at her and within seconds they were completely naked beneath the trees. He inside of her, moving slowly in circles, she holding tight to his smooth large body. He was gorgeous.

The smell of green, the sound of water, the damp spray, the feel of a stranger, put Isabel over. She moved her legs from his hips to his shoulders and ground herself against him. Being naked outdoors, the press of another's skin, the slip of sweat, the taste of mouth, the canopy of leaves, the calm offhand eye of the sky, all a fabulous correction to the compression of her days. She succumbed to it all.

"I . . ." became a moan swallowing words. The beautiful man, his hands, his mouth, his teeth. The sun streaming through thin skeins of weed. To be naked outdoors. The water, the buzzing bugs. "I . . . aaee," Isabel cried, "a bee . . ." and jerked herself to one side to avoid being stung in her privates.

Zakhi laughed. He turned her around and swatted at the bee. "I'm on watch now." He entered again and knocked her inside over and over and over. Anyone home, oh yes there certainly was. Zakhi picked up speed and velocity. When they finished, first her and then him, they lay among the reeds on the bank of the swelled river. He pressed his body against hers, tucked her into his arms, and she stroked his olive skin.

"Are you Yemenite or Sephardi?" she asked.

"Ashkenazi. Dark Russian. Sometimes called Black Poles."

"Stubborn traces of ancient Israel."

"Yes."

They lay quietly. Birds sang high in the tree tops. Turtles swam from bank to bank. Dragonflies hovered over the water's surface. Isabel looked up at the cloudless sky.

"The emancipation of woman is *only* an invention of the Jewish intellect."

Zakhi turned to look at her.

"Hitler said that in one of his speeches." Isabel paused. "It's that *only* that's so interesting."

"Sex and the Holocaust. I like it," Zakhi stared at her and laughed. "I get it. I'm over there half the time too. But when I'm here, I find this much more interesting." He put her hand on him.

"Much better." She laughed, happy to be distracted, happy to be taken out of her mind. She stroked the soft dark skin of his belly.

Their tumbling resumed. Round and around. First her on top. Then him. Then her again. She evaporated. Became part of the clouds. All molecules one. She brothered the wind. Brothered the sky. Brothered the birds, the leaves, the branches. Brothered the man.

*

Isabel hands clutched the wheel. She was immersed in the pleasures of Zakhi's body, in the memory of meeting him, and forgot she was driving until a passing truck's growl woke her. She turned on to Geulah Street. It was already evening and cooler. Sidewalks filled with children and adults. Many of the men wore black suits and hats. Some wore long black frocks. Married women wore scarves or wigs and young girls wore long braids down their backs. The number of baby carriages was staggering. Not for them population explosion warnings and planetary sustainability.

Isabel drove up the street and saw a black-bordered bereavement notice posted on a tree. She slowed down and read: Amos Kandel. Died that night. Funeral at noon. *Shiva* at his parents' home. A car horn blared behind her. She stared at the notice and kept driving. She really had no business being here.

"I ran away from their black and white world," Zakhi had said to her many times. "There's little room for color. What's new or different is unkosher and forbidden."

And what was unclear was also feared. And demonized. His parents named him Zakhariah because God promised to remember and redeem Israel after great peril. They named him Zakhariah to remember those who didn't make it out of Europe. She pulled over to stare at another death notice. That was part of the bond that she and he shared. And despite the slyly encroaching dependence on him, Isabel knew she didn't belong with or to Zakhi. Just as he didn't belong with or to her. She pulled her eyes from the black printed words and pulled out into traffic and out of this neighborhood filled with people who were her people and yet were not. A mistake to have come.

Isabel drove straight home. She missed Zakhi but at least he was alive and well. And not with another woman. This week she would share him with his family as they sat *shiva*.

4

"I don't want to take the job," Isabel said to Emanuel when they cleared the dinner dishes. Isabel had received a phone call earlier that day from Yehudit Klein, who had read Itka's book in the Czech translation and liked it very much. Would Isabel be willing to ghostwrite her life? "I told her I wouldn't be free for a while. She said she wasn't in a rush. The story's waited sixty years it can wait a few more months."

"Haven't you done enough?" Emanuel asked when she came back downstairs after putting Uri to sleep. "Aren't you tired of atrocity, Isabel?"

"In fact I am."

And when they went into bed, Emanuel continued, sensing her sudden openness to the discussion and maybe even to real change. "There's so many other kinds of books you can write, Issie. Or some other field entirely. The time has come. It's over. Look to the future."

It's over. Look to the future. Dave used those exact words to hammer down her interests and ambitions. Isabel's default rebel kicked in.

"It's not over for the people who lived it and whose stories deserve to be told," she pounced. This for Emanuel in real time and for Suri and Dave in her mind. "It's not over for any citizen of the world who still wants to know and understand what and how and when. It's not over for the living victims and perpetrators of genocide."

Isabel turned her back to Emanuel and went to sleep.

In the morning, she took Uri to school and stopped at the vegetable market on her way home. Of course Emanuel's words had merit. Atrocity was not a paradigm for living. But still, the past could not be willed away. It did not simply disappear because one decided not to think about it.

Right now, force of habit and an overwhelming sense of responsibility made her consider saying yes to Yehudit Klein. Though she hadn't committed yet and could breathe easy for a while. She filled her shopping cart with fruits and vegetables and paid absentmindedly. On the drive home she felt bad about her coldness with Emanuel the night before. Even this morning she got out of bed and left the house without kissing him good morning, making him coffee, or leaving a note. Three of her usual morning activities. Of course he was looking out for her best interests and he was right a lot of the time. But he wasn't right all of the time. And she wouldn't agree to live with him.

When she got home she stomped up the stairs to the second floor. She needed the book on Greek landscape that she left on her night stand. Emanuel sat on the bed.

"Oh. I thought you'd left for work," she said surprised.

He was dressed in black jeans, a black buttoned down shirt, black western boots, and held a riding crop in his hand. Isabel remained at the door waiting for some cue or clue. Why was he still here? Since when did he go riding on a weekday? And why did he look so stern? Not a word passed between them. It took another moment for Isabel to realize Emanuel was in character. She took a step back from the doorway. She was in no mood to be part of anyone's fantasy, sexual or otherwise. She had too much work to do that morning. But she couldn't keep saying no to Emanuel, especially since it seemed he was trying to feed her sexual appetite. Shit. Was this part of his campaign to procure her yes?

Isabel waited for his next move. Emanuel stood. She watched the boots and hips approach. She saw a red armband then a black swastika inside a white circle. She swallowed hard, slid down the wall, and closed her eyes. No, not the Nazi and the Jew. Sexploitation films, pulp fiction, pornographic web sites where Jews fuck Nazis in the ass and Nazis rape Jews, males and females alike, were abhorrent to her. Molly said that in the 1950s and 60s soft porn Stalag books were wildly popular among Israeli teenagers. Two taboos combined: the Holocaust and sex. Probably Emanuel devoured them too. But this was not a winning combination for Isabel. She didn't need to mime out the nightmares via sex. They were real enough in her mind.

Emanuel pulled her up by the hand and gently positioned her on the bed. He straddled her body, trailed the riding crop along her neck, and his tongue followed suit. Isabel moaned and tried to roll away, a dream from the night before suddenly upon her.

She was a teenager. Some younger children were in her charge. They crouched low in a dark corner of a shed in a peasant family's apple grove as German soldiers marched through the property searching for hidden Jews. The children huddled against her. She put her hands over their mouths even though they were terrified and quiet, so quiet that they held their breath as much as they could. Cacophonous orders to open the doors passed through the shed's thin wooden walls like bullets. *Türen öffnen!* Isabel woke up shaking.

Emanuel held her tightly between his knees and used the crop to lift her shirt. With a sudden radical movement, Isabel brought one knee up against his hip, let out a deep grunt, and thrust her pelvis skywards. She snapped her body over throwing Emanuel off of her. He lay on his back stunned. Isabel jumped off the bed.

"What the . . ." Emanuel asked startled. "That was pretty impressive, Issie."

"No, Emanuel." Isabel walked to the window and held back tears. Thin horizontal sun bands penetrated the shutters. Slits of light in Birkenau's huts. Slivers of dawn in a shed's wooden walls. "I can't, I . . ."

"Shh, shh." He came over and hugged her from behind. She let him lead her back to bed. She let him undress her. She knew he was trying to be more exciting for her. To surprise her. But that's not what she needed from him. She loved his steadiness, his dependability. She needed him to always love her while sparing her the roller coaster ride of his own emotions. For she knew he had them. She saw the love in his eyes towards her, towards his daughters, towards her children, and even towards Woody. And she knew he muted his lows. Molly said Emanuel was a prime example of a mature man. Even when he was buffeted to distant shores by passing emotion he held steady. He was anchored. Like his mathematics. He sought simplicity and elegance and most of all solutions. And, Molly would add, he was offering Isabel the chance to ride with him on this steady sea. Molly was right. She should climb on board. She should but didn't know if she could make it last.

With a quick yank, Emanuel pulled her pants off. He was smiling broadly and watching her face. He wanted to please her. He wanted to be her playmate, her soulmate, her go-to-man. And she loved this man. She could not deny this but she didn't want only him. She stared into his eyes. They were frisky. She could see how much he wanted to get into a role he thought would turn her on. Poor Emanuel, trying so hard and still managing to get it wrong. But she loved him and wanted him. Inside. She wanted the comfort of his strong body. Fuck Schine's deadlines. Fuck the man instead.

Isabel wrapped her legs around Emanuel's black pants. He let the Nazi armband fall to the floor and lowered himself to her. The pants' rough material chafed her inner thighs. Emanuel moved slowly. Back and forth. Isabel gave way to his rhythm. He watched, waited for her to shift from first to second to the third gear of pleasure. Then he picked up the pace and repositioned her legs on his upper back and touched the place precisely where her orgasm began. He pushed and rubbed against it. When her wave launched he beat against her shore with sharp jabs. Rolling hips. Delight spread from her epicenter and rose to claim her entire body and clear her mind. A string connected the tip of Emanuel's penis to the tip of her vagina. Love passed through the small space of air between their hovering lips. Isabel abandoned herself to joy and began to cry.

Emanuel always made sure she orgasmed first. Zakhi and Jiri did that, too. Sign of a man who appreciated a woman's body and sexuality, Zakhi said. Isabel didn't have a theory. She just knew that men who tended to their partner's gratification first were irresistible. Men who came "wham bam thank you ma'am or maybe just wham bam," as Martha Gellhorn described sex with Hemingway, were useless to women. No, worse, they were toxic.

Isabel held on to Emanuel. She drifted under his caresses in a cocoon of quiet. He kissed her collarbone and shoulders. She held tighter. Why not say yes to Emanuel, to this? After a few minutes Emanuel moved out of the embrace. Isabel watched him undress. He took off each item of clothing and folded it neatly on the back of the chair and walked back to the bed. Isabel didn't notice until he stood before her that the riding crop remained in his hand. He held it out. Level with his keen penis.

"Take the crop."

Isabel didn't want to. She would touch his body instead.

"Please," he said quietly.

She took it reluctantly. Emanuel lay down on his stomach.

"I'm not going to hit you with this thing."

He laughed. Turned on his back to face her. "Put the black shirt on now. And the boots." Isabel didn't move. "Now," he commanded.

Maybe Emanuel wanted this scene also for himself. He was not a child of a survivor but a nephew of many. His maternal grandparents were Zionists and left Poland in the mid-30s with their three youngest. All the other children remained in Europe. Emanuel's mother lost five siblings and ten nieces and nephews. For her the war was an open wound. And if for the mother, then for the child as well.

The black shirt hung down past Isabel's thighs. The boots came up past her knees. Walking was difficult. Only a thin belt of naked leg showed. She stood over Emanuel menacingly. If he wanted a spectacle, he would get one. She tapped his hip lightly with the crop. "Let's see your cock's reaction to the beating you're about to get."

A small smile opened on Emanuel's face. Thwack. Isabel brought the riding crop down hard by his head. He jumped. "I forgot you're trained in martial arts, my dear. Try not to leave marks."

"Quiet Jew." She brought the crop down again, centimeters from his thigh. Emanuel flinched involuntarily. She trailed the crop along his body, from his Adam's apple down the middle of his chest past his navel. There it rested. Then down through his pubic hair to his penis. She caressed his penis with the crop. Up one side, down another, and laid it horizontally at the base of the shaft above his balls. Pressing down lightly on his scrotum she took him into her mouth. Emanuel moaned. She pressed the crop down a little harder. It was uncomfortable and wonderful for him at the same time. He moaned louder. Abruptly she pulled away. "Stop making noise. *Jude.*" Isabel brought the crop down by his head.

"Oh," he groaned with interrupted pleasure, fear, and delight.

She bent low towards the floor, picked up the arm band, and put it on. Her arm with a Nazi swastika went up and down, up and down. Three four times and the riding crop cracking against the bed. Not that close to Emanuel. Not so far away either. Her arm mesmerized her. Disembodied. Homeless. Possessed of power. Liable to abuse.

A perpetrator. After so many years living inside victims' voices, she was a perpetrator. Seeing the situation from the other half of the universe.

And suddenly, like a thunderclap in a cartoon, eureka, a totally intuitive moment, Isabel understood Molly's antipathy to Mati. Limbs abusing power. Sex used as a weapon. What Emanuel was teasing her with now. What she was teasing back. What they felt titillated by, but what she really couldn't do. For them it was just play. A few bed whacks and shudders.

But Molly. Molly was touched against her will. Isabel didn't know how she knew but she was certain she was right and felt sick. She started to move away from the bed, stricken by the thought of Molly being hurt, but Emanuel took her arms and pulled her down to the bed. He held her arms flat against his chest, her face right on his groin. Isabel suppressed a wave of nausea but she knew the script and had to do right by the Jew. She took Emanuel's delirious cock in her mouth, pressed her tongue around the head that pushed up and orgasmed. She swallowed his thin semen. Faint, Isabel wriggled out of Emanuel's hold. In the bathroom she rinsed her face and chest and drank large gulps of water. Her body shook with grief. Emanuel found her sobbing over the sink.

"Come here." He held out his arms and hugged her. Kissed her forehead. "I'm sorry, sweetheart. I just thought . . ."

"I know. It's okay," Isabel muffled into his chest, "According to Hitler, anti-Semitism was a legal form of pornography. Even he admitted anti-Semitism was a kind of perversion."

"Shh, Isabel, shh."

"An allowance for fetish."

"Shh." Emanuel stroked her back. Ran his hands along her buttocks. Held her closer and brought her under the hot water of the shower. He soaped her body carefully from crown to toes. The water washed over her. Amniotic. Hypnotic. A balm for a fretful soul.

"I love you." Emanuel paused at the front door and kissed her lightly on the mouth. Time for good-bye. For work. He to teach at the university, she to bully sentences at her desk.

Alone by her computer Isabel stared out the window. A patch of migrating birds passed. She wondered about pornography. Was crawling into the skins of other people a form of pornography? Was this what Suri objected to? Was her experiencing the Holocaust from the inside a kind of degeneracy? Was her attachment to Zakhi and Jiri and who knows who else might pop up on the horizon also perverse or maybe just self-destructive? Isabel loved Emanuel but she didn't want to live with him. It felt burdensome. Treacherous even. Alone was better. Alone was reliable. Safe. Fast moving. Untethered. It was not lonely nor wanting. Alone was one small bag, her child and dog, and she was off.

*

Isabel opened Jaim Benjamin's file on her desktop and read sentences from the day before. Immediately she knew she would have a hard time penetrating the story. She couldn't think clearly. Her mind was like a spin art flinging thoughts everywhere. She called Molly.

"I'm coming over."

They sat together on a porch swing under Molly's birch tree.

"I want to ask you a question. You don't need to answer."

"Okay."

"Your reaction to Mati. Why so strong?"

"Mati of the illegal immoral probing fingers?"

"Yes."

Above them silver leaves rustled in the wind like cards being shuffled.

"Your relationship to your body, to sex is different than mine," Molly said as they pushed back and forth on the swing.

"But why so judgmental?"

She didn't answer.

"Molly, something happened, right?" Isabel stopped pushing at the ground. She looked at her best friend, wondering about the therapist who wouldn't disclose trauma. The shoemaker going barefoot again.

"I . . ." Molly looked down at the grass. Her spine curled. Her face crumbled.

"Forget it, you don't have to tell me anything. I'm sorry for being so nosy. You know how I like to have answers . . ."

"'Cause Suri never talks . . ."

"Yes, but it's fine, really. Let's drop it." Isabel took Molly's hand. She couldn't stand hurting her. Why press her to speak when she preferred to remain cloistered. Isabel's default mode, the one learned early on with Suri, kicked in. Her desire to know easily eclipsed by the need to protect.

"Everyone has their battles," Molly said. "And I think you have battle fatigue. I am truly concerned about you."

"I'm not fighting. I'm scribing."

"Fighting your own demons."

"Aren't we all?"

"Yes. You're right." Molly got off the swing and stood with her back against the wide white trunk of the tree. She looked at Isabel. "One evening, in Dublin, it was still early, still light, I was on my way home from visiting a friend." She stretched her arms up toward the canopy of leaves. "I love this tree." She looked up at it and looked back down at Isabel. "I was grabbed from behind and dragged to a construction site. A young man, about my age I guess, raped and beat me with a piece of wood. He hit me so much and so hard I thought I was going to die." Her voice tapered off.

"Oh Molly." Isabel left the swing and stood next to her. She took Molly's hand.

"At the hospital I had to have a tetanus shot. So many nails in the wood." Molly placed her hand on top of Isabel's who placed hers on top of Molly's. A stack of hands. A *rujumb*. "I was seventeen years old and virgin."

"Who have you told?"

"Only Noam. And my mother."

"Thirty years and only your husband and mother know?"

"And now you."

"And now me."

Isabel didn't tell Molly that she had this intuitive flash after her strange sex with Emanuel. The Nazi costume brought it out. Molly would laugh at Isabel's assumption of associative serendipitous insight, having no tolerance for mysticism or for anything that smacked of the recent vogue in spiritualism. She worked strictly from her brain. From reason. An Irish *Litvak*.

"It took years of love and patience, but Noam helped me feel good about my body and sex. Lots of love and patience. Sorry for being so mean about Mati. Guess I'm still a bit queasy."

"Don't worry about it." Isabel's stomach wound up in knots.

"Are you going to ask Suri?"

"I've been asking Suri for decades."

"Yes, but specifically."

"Specifically?"

"About being raped."

"You think?" How had Isabel had never considered that?

"May explain her silence. Her stubbornness. Who knows what she had to do to keep her little sisters alive in Siberia."

The shame. The guilt. The angst of sexual trauma. Of course.

"When I'm in New York I'll ask."

"Ask without expectations."

"It will be good for her to talk about it."

"Don't decide what's good for her. Open the door. Don't force her through." Molly looked down at her watch. "My two o'clock's about to arrive." They peeled one layer of hand off the other and hugged each other tightly. "Flow with Suri, Isabel. Words in a stream encourage more."

Isabel called Zakhi when she got home. He was still not taking calls. Three days earlier he sent her a text message that he was in mourning and said he'd call when the seven days of *shiva* were up. At her desk Isabel went straight to Jaim Benjamin's manuscript. Hard to believe but there were only twenty or so pages to go. Close enough to feel the end. Smell it. Surf her way into it. She dialed Zakhi again. The seven days were over and he hadn't called. But she needed to talk to him. Knowing he might be only minutes away drove her crazy.

"Enough." Isabel leaped up and kicked at a pile of papers. Woody looked up at her, thinking 'What now?' she assumed. She took out her phone as if it were a gun with a loaded cylinder. She pressed Zakhi's number again and listened to the ring ring ring ring ring. "I said enough," she yelled into the room. "Enough." She cried. She missed Zakhi. She missed Suri. She wanted Yael to be home. She wished Lia were here to comfort her. She even missed Alon. And then she realized that she wanted Emanuel. He was the one who held her the best, the most consistently, the hug with the most promise of all. The one who always took care of her. Isabel scooped up Woody in her arms and cried some more. He was accustomed to his mother's crazy ways and waited for it to be over. She kissed Woody on the head and set him back down on the floor.

"Thank you, boy."

He laid down again. This time he faced her, to keep an eye on her. No more surprises. She laughed to herself and faced the screen. Moved the mouse. Text showed up.

When the war was declared over, Jaim Benjamin came down from the mountains. He returned to Florina. Just one of two Jews who did. Jaim's neighbors welcomed him with food, with clothing, but they were wary. Strangers had moved into the Benjamin house. Jaim went into his bedroom and slept for days. On Sunday morning, when the entire village went to church, including the family that occupied his home, he went into the yard. Under a particular olive tree his father had buried some money, his *tefillin*, and jewelry. By the time the family returned for lunch, Jaim was gone.

Isabel's phone rang.

"Zakhi."

"Told you I'd resurrect after seven days."

"I'm so sorry about your brother."

"Yeah, it's rough. Luckily he only has three children. They had fertility issues. Imagine if he left a wife and twelve behind."

"Zakhi."

"What's up?"

"Finally getting some serious mileage on these pages. End's in sight."

"You should sound happier than you do."

She recounted her conversation with Molly.

He sighed. "The Baal Shem Tov said that light—אור—and secret—רז—each add up to 207."

"A secret revealed brings light into the world?" she asked.

"Exactly."

They were quiet.

"Any free time today?"

"Winkler house in ten?" Isabel closed Jaim Benjamin's file and stepped away from the desk.

138

"I'm already here. Make it five."

"I'm on it."

Isabel drove and thought of Zakhi's revealed secret. The world of the ultra-Orthodox that spawned, rejected, and re-embraced him in mourning. She drove quickly for she didn't have much time before Uri came home from school.

The Arts

1

It was night. The sky and the airplane cabin were dark. Yesterday Molly told Isabel that sometimes people did not expect others to act on their ultimatums. Declaring them out loud made their expectations clearer—to themselves and to others. It clarified limits. Isabel didn't believe Emanuel capable of such shallowness. If he said their relationship would be over if they didn't move in together, he meant it. Her heart stung at the thought of losing him though. She loved his soft humor. His intelligent disciplined mind. His handsome face and grey curls. His excellent coffee. The way he tickled her inner arm at the movies. She enjoyed their love making. Sweetness and comfort moved between them as they folded into one another. He inside of her. She inside of him. Skin, lips, tongues. It was not the wild unabridged passion she had with Zakhi. Or the soul-freeing sex she felt with Jiri. It was lovely and reliable and safe. But could she give up other men for it? If orgasms were a little death, Isabel pulled the thin airline blanket to her chin, then monogamy was somnambulism. The extremes of ardor corralled to a *parve* middle ground where the field shifted from meritocracy to mediocrity. From revelation to predictability. Orgasms on an assembly line. She despaired at this shut-off valve and feared her own inevitable mutiny.

Emanuel had driven her to the Haifa train station. The riding crop scene settled over them like a yellow dust. Every movement left a trace. Fortunately Emanuel had gone to a conference in London immediately after that morning and Isabel became super busy prepping for this trip. But now, after ten days of strained silence, he wanted to give and she was willing to accept this peace offering. More than that. She wanted to receive. She wanted to love and be loved by him.

"I wish I were coming with you." Emanuel leaned against the station turnstile.

"I know, but I'm going for such a short time."

This trip to New York was part of Isabel's policy of sitting with clients close to a book's completion. A chance to solicit a last round of comments and revisions, preventing unpleasant surprises after the manuscript was handed over to Schine.

"In three years we've only gone away twice, Issie. That time in Eilat and once to Tel Aviv. Never abroad." He wasn't rebuking her, only reiterating facts that spoke for themselves. The gauntlet thrown down at her feet a few weeks ago shadowed his words.

"We never have enough time." Isabel glanced at her watch. The train was due in five minutes.

"Let's make the time."

"Okay."

He opened his arms to her. "I know you need to focus on your work now." They held one another and their bodies spoke their own language. Calm swept away tension. Isabel leaned into the love. Still the day fast approached when she might have to make it concrete once again to Emanuel that she wouldn't not go all the way. A long trip to Thailand or Italy, yes. Coming home from that trip to the same house, no. They gave each other a full kiss. She turned one last time before going down to the platform. Emanuel smiled and waved good-bye.

Somewhere over the Atlantic, Isabel managed to push Emanuel's ticking bomb out of her mind. She stared at the soundless movie on the screen and decided to approach Suri by telling her that she was quitting ghosting. Jaim Benjamin's her last book. Not that this was necessarily true. It was only a consideration at this point, albeit a serious one. Serious enough to use to navigate around Suri's blockade. If Suri believed Isabel then maybe she would open up about Siberia. She would have no reason to fear that her life story would make its way to the pages of a book.

Hours later, Isabel having slept some and watched a romantic comedy that ended just as the couple was about to slide into their happily ever after, the plane began its descent into New York. A bitter taste coated Isabel's throat. She thought of Zakhi putting in extra hours at the Winkler site. Making up for the seven days he sat on a low stool at his parents' house, mourning the brother who wouldn't speak to him for ten years. Amos, the brother who just died, was on the side of the excommunicators. Contact with apostates considered a bad influence on the children. It was Aaron, the eldest of the eight children, who always called Zakhi, who believed in staying in touch, in maintaining a bridge. Zakhi knew Aaron continued to hope that he'd repent and return to the fold.

"Aaron was acting on my parents' behalf," Zakhi told Isabel when they met at the Winkler site after the *shiva*. "No one came out and said it, but by the way my father talked to me, touched me, it was clear that on the one hand there's pressure to disown me publicly, but on the other, he knows everything Aaron knows about me. At night when we were alone, after everyone went home or to sleep, we talked in the kitchen. My father held my hand the whole time. Asked real meaningful questions about my life. Like I was seven years old again when he used to ask about what I learned in school. Same keen interest."

"He loves you."

"He does," Zakhi said. "But not enough to stand up to his rabbi, or his community. Especially since we're Cohens."

"Different standards?"

"And rules."

"You're not allowed to go into cemeteries, right?"

"And not allowed to marry divorcees."

*

"Maybe I should learn the art of demolition." Isabel whispered to herself and pressed her face against the airplane window's cold plastic. The east coast's silhouette lengthened below. When the city came into view, she felt the rooftops pull towards the sky. The plane flew in low and turned round to Kennedy. The tall buildings, the lights of this other home, worked their charm. Gone were the goat herds, the groves of olive and pomegranate trees. A run of excitement, the pleasures of the urbane, ran through Isabel. Broadway, Central Park West, Riverside. Soon. She leaned further into the window, towards the asphalt, the concrete. Towards the rhythms of the metropolis.

Suri sent a car service. Just past midnight she and Isabel sat together in her small kitchen drinking jasmine tea. Hal was in Buffalo visiting his family. A serendipitous *bonne chance* to be alone with Suri. But was it really just chance? Zakhi believed that everything happened for a reason. Emanuel said there are patterns to circumstances, but he wasn't sure if there was meaning to these patterns. Alon didn't think about these things. Maybe he was happiest of them all.

Isabel stretched her arms above her head. Eleven hour plane rides wreaked havoc on the spine. She stood and walked to the kitchen window. Lights edged the Hudson. As a child she had paid a great deal of attention to the seasons on this wide river, the closest and certainly largest experience of nature in her urban life. White-grey ice floes locked the waters in the coldest weeks of winter. Slate patches spread along the surface on less cold days. And in summer, the river turned a lighter blue, not cerulean or beryl like the Mediterranean, Dead, Red, and Galilee Seas she now lived with, but a lovely sapphire. And in autumn and spring, on days of sunshine, the waters of the Hudson were royal and navy blue.

Suri asked about Lia and her studies. About Asaf. About Yael's transfer. About Uri's school and the pony. About Emanuel, his work, his daughters. Tired and nervous, Isabel felt like a spy in her mother's house. The pressure of the conversation she intended to initiate weighed heavily on her. Her responses were laconic.

"Has anything changed since your talk with Emanuel?" Suri took

143

a sip of tea. "If he doesn't hold the key to your heart, Issie, then it may not be fair to keep him waiting. He's in love with you."

"I'm exhausted, Suri." Isabel looked down the hallway. The catch-up talk was over for now. Under the best of circumstances she had little patience for what Molly called the current events reports: synopses of everyday life handed over in succinct paragraphs. The price paid when people who loved one another lived far apart. "I want to talk about everything, Emanuel too, but right now, I'm beat."

"'Night, lovely." Suri kissed her on the brow. "Your bed's made up."

Isabel watched her mother's back retreat down the hallway to her room. Shorter, thinner, a slight drag in her stride. Suri, in her late seventies, aging prematurely. The war taking its toll. Or maybe it was just the late hour. Why did everything have to be the war? And then Isabel grimaced comically to herself. She sounded just like Suri.

She went into the unlit living room. Entering a childhood home was like wading through a viscous liquid. Distinct, familiar, yet bewildering. Layers of obsolescence and the present-day converged. She turned on a table lamp. The dark green sofa stood where it always did. The hanging lamp from India with colorful bits of glass was in the corner. Here were the Persian rugs Isabel loved. Their deep warm hues always a comfort. And the Barcelona chair Dave bought right before she was born. But what's this? A new flat screen television and upholstered recliner? Whoa. Isabel stopped in front of these set pieces. Hal. Concessions to Hal after decades of a small television banished to the maid's room at the back of the apartment. So Suri was capable of change. Good.

Usually it didn't take Isabel more than a few hours to find her place in this cross-section of time, objects, and stories. But this visit was different. This visit was about unveiling, not dressing over. It was about speech, not the status quo. It was about change. More change. Isabel closed the light switch. The living room went dark and she walked down the hall to her old room and stood on the threshold. The remnants of her childhood had long given way to a simple elegant guestroom. Only the bed, the one Jiri came into last time she visited New York, remained from years past. Isabel stood by the window to look at the river again. Guilt overwhelmed her.

For Suri, Isabel's arsenal of questions would be a kind of trespass.

Isabel undressed, brushed her teeth, went into bed. Nervous, self-conscious, but also rebellious. Even a little proud of herself. Finally rebellious after decades of compliance. The need to protect her beautiful vulnerable mother finally giving way to Isabel's own needs, questions, her own pain. Isabel would ask. Let Suri say no, again and again, Isabel would persist and ask. And ask some more. No more stonewalling. At forty-six years of age Isabel was more than ready to return home to Israel with answers.

Molly had tried to lower Isabel's sights before the trip.

"Silence is commonplace for many Europeans. Not only that generation. Not just those who suffered the war. The culture of disclosure, of talk shows, of public therapy, is not natural to them."

To this day, she told Isabel, many of her Dublin friends remained suspicious of too much talk. They poked fun at Molly, said it made perfect sense that she entered the field of psychoanalysis, as one friend put it, that *loquacious Jewish science.* Molly illustrated her point with a joke. Two Irish men sit next to each other at a pub. They don't talk. After 3 hours and many pints, one asks the other how he's doing. His mate answers: Did we come here to drink or to talk?

Under the covers in her childhood bed, Isabel's inner censure uncoiled and she sought solace in the shadows on the walls and ceiling. Back home, pitch black Galilee nights filled her house. But in New York, the glut of street lights made nocturnal art in darkened rooms. As a child she told herself little dramas about the shadows. This often helped her sleep.

A constructivist shadow filled one section of the ceiling. She stared at the intersecting geometrical shapes, a large oval and various bands and rectangles, and thought of home. Seven in the morning there. Lia would be preparing herself tea and sandwiches for her and Uri to take to school. Uri would be stirring in bed as Lia came in for a second time to wake him. He was cozy under the down blanket and didn't want to wake up. Woody, curled into the pocket of his stomach, didn't feel like budging either. Isabel smiled to herself imagining those two. How school stretched endlessly for a boy of seven. Hanukah, and the vacation that would release him from such long spells of sitting at a desk, was just a few weeks away. And then there was Yael. No doubt she was already awake and in motion. Where, doing what, Isabel didn't know. And why was the greatest mystery of all.

After this inventory Isabel thought of Emanuel's soft good-bye at the train station. He was swimming or running at this early hour. Or maybe at his desk. She smiled thinking of his handsome face, his shy smile. And Zakhi was probably on his way to a construction site, or maybe in bed with a woman, his muscular arm draped over her curved hip. Isabel twisted her head towards the window, overtired from an entire night spent flying. It would be difficult to wind down. She didn't want to read. She didn't want to watch television since it only stimulated her. So she drifted, like she did when she was a child, over the elm tree's shadows in the far corner of the room. Her thoughts wandered until they faded near the wall's crown molding. A moment of peace.

The tree shadows swayed with wind coming off the river. Lately she had been thinking about writing a different kind of book to wean herself off the ghosts. It would be about the Holocaust but not personal stories. A concept book dealing with a particular phenomenon: Hollywood and the American government during the war. Twenty years of research had yielded gobs of reprehensible and compelling facts. Finally a non-fiction book openly authored by Isabel Toledo.

Some people counted sheep. Others counted down from one hundred to tease sleep. Isabel recounted facts. One. After the release of Borzage's *The Mortal Storm*, Goebbels banned the screening of all MGM pictures in German territories. 1940. He vowed to boycott Hollywood studios that portrayed Nazis negatively. Which meant realistically, from an Allied point of view. In those years, over ten percent of the American movie market fell in German-controlled European countries and Goebbels meant business. Two. Most American producers and studios took Goebbels' cue and avoided stories about the German war machine. Their eyes remained fixed on the bottom line. This included Jewish heads of studios.

Isabel turned on her left side to face the wall and tucked the thick blanket between her knees. Three. The American government was also not interested in cultivating antagonism with the powerful German leader and made it difficult for Chaplin to distribute *The Great Dictator*. 1940. Their policy was to leave Hitler alone. His continent. His business.

Four. Senator Gerald Nye, Republican from North Dakota, accused certain Hollywood personalities of goading America into war with Germany. He wouldn't come out and say it was mainly the Jews, but everyone knew who ran Hollywood. Still, in 1941 the non-Jewish Charlie Chaplin was subpoenaed to appear before a Senate Sub-Committee investigating whether Hollywood was in fact introducing pro-war propaganda into its films. Nye considered *The Great Dictator*'s final "Look up, Hannah" soliloquy a provocation. It's anti-fascist message was delivered by a Jew, a *nebbish* barber from the ghetto, who had the nerve to openly express his dream of a gentler more humane world. Five. Nye didn't know that Chaplin named his young Jewish heroine Hannah after his own mother. In real life this vulnerable woman was abandoned first by her husband, then by an unkind world, and finally by her sanity. Even twelve years after her death, Chaplin was trying to make it okay for his mother. Look up, Hannah, there was still hope. Isabel could totally relate.

Six. The big change came once the United States officially entered the war. After Pearl Harbor, Hollywood, with the government's encouragement, threw itself into the war effort. *Casablanca*. 1942. *Spitfire*. 1942. *We Dive at Dawn*. 1943. The boundary between politics and art so easy to spot, like a fresh pink scar. Isabel sat up in bed. She punched the pillow into a ball and laid back down again. The tree shadows danced. They bent and dipped while the Hudson kicked up a blast, a warning shot of the long winter ahead. It was early December and it felt like snow was on the way.

Seven. One of Isabel's favorite Hollywood-Holocaust morsels involved music. Forty-seven years after Irving Berlin, née Israel Beline, left Mohilev in Russia as a child of five, he wrote the song "White Christmas." Again 1940. A prolific year. America's popular music industry was rife with European Jewish composers who had fled the continent. Max Steiner won three Academy Awards and twenty-two nominations for *Gone with the Wind*, *Casablanca*, *The Caine Mutiny*, et al. Fredrick Loewe scored *Brigadoon* and *My Fair Lady*.

Irving Berlin was no slouch compared. *Holiday Inn* came out in 1942. Bing Crosby sang "White Christmas" as thousands of American troops were conscripted into the European and South Pacific theaters of war. Berlin who considered his song an amusing little number, a satirical throwaway, was surprised when it captured the longings of both the fighting and civilian public for a peaceful, family, and community-centered world. "White Christmas" became an enormous hit then and remained America's most recorded song. The iconic American Christmas carol.

Isabel turned on her back and relaxed into the ludicrous. Her eyelids no heavier.

"Eight. Irving Berlin," she spoke out to the shadow boxes hovering over her, "a Russian Jew, fled the cold snowy land of his birth. There, white Christmas time was also pogrom time, second to Easter, best time of year to kill Jews. Nine. Or maybe this is still part of eight? Berlin won an Academy Award for 'White Christmas.' 1942." Isabel closed her eyes. This was where it got better. Really better.

Nine. During those same exact months that Berlin became America's top pop troubadour, his religious compatriots in *Deutschland* became real-time victims of a populist xenophobia.

"Paradox a rubber dinghy to cling to once the ship's hull dips below the water's surface," Isabel spoke out to the room's darkness and continued to trace and address the shadows that twisted turned, dipped, and blew. Feeling no tide of sleep plowing in from the horizon, Isabel got out of bed and stood by the window.

"The Jews in Berlin, in all of German-occupied Europe, also listened to the radio a lot during those months. Not for music, not for nostalgia, or comfort or pleasure. Certainly not for white Christmas crooning." The windowpane was cold. "They listened obsessively because their lives depended on sorting through the maelstrom of rumors and instructions that came with the Final Solution." The river was black and the sky filled with low lying clouds. Riverside had emptied of traffic.

Ten. The Czech composer and conductor, Hans Krása, declined conducting posts in Paris and Chicago. He could have gotten out of Europe and made his way to good steady work in Hollywood. But instead of mixing cocktails with Berlin and Brecht in L.A., he ran Terezin's *Freizeitgestaltung*: Administration of Free Time

Activities Committee. His *Brundibar* passed the censor because it was a children's operetta in which the children defeat evil and save their sick mother. Itka and many Terezin prisoners were filled with treasured hope when they saw it. Eleven. Towards the end of the war, under Krása's artistic directorship, the Red Cross filmed *Brundibar*. A German showcase to the world that Czechoslovakia's Jews were being cared for in the ghetto. After the filming Krása was deported to Auschwitz and murdered. October 1944.

Isabel sat on the narrow window sill and stared down at Riverside. A bus without passengers quickly took a curve. A taxi stopped crookedly by the curb and a couple spilled out drunk with alcohol and desire. They kissed deeply, pushed up one against the other, stumbled and disappeared into a building. The glass was very cold against Isabel's skin. She wondered where sleep was. Wondered about the white snow.

2

The following morning Isabel went down into the subway and, as usual whenever she was in a crowded space in the States or Europe, felt the absence of security guards checking bags and surveying the crowd for strange behavior. How easy it would be to set off a bomb in this city. She could almost hear the cell phone ring seconds to detonation. Afterwards surveillance cameras would retrace the scene. They would see the man in a bulky coat. But that wouldn't help the murdered, the maimed, and traumatized.

These thoughts and fears rose in her as she sat in the train car and watched a man across from her in an especially bulky coat. She stared at his hands. If they began to play with his cell phone, she'd run. But he dozed. One hand in a coat pocket. The other held the phone passively on his thigh. Her stop came. She got off the platform as fast as she could and bounded up the stairs to the avenue. On her way to Jaim Benjamin's on 11th Street, and in honor of her children, Isabel paused in front of a donut shop. When the children came to New York and woke up super early courtesy of jet lag, they always raced to the donut shop on Broadway two blocks from Suri's. A lot of time was spent in front of the grid of color and sugar appliqués: frosted, sprinkled, butternut, jelly, crème, glazed, crullers. They bought a baker's dozen and on their way back to Riverside started eating. On her own, Isabel passed on the donut ritual but remained in front of the plate glass window for a few seconds to feel connected to her children on the other side of the planet.

Jaim and Isabel sat at his small round dining room table.

"Lovely flowers," she said nervously, admiring the orange lilies and eucalyptus leaves in a vase next to her. A month ago Jaim asked her not to send any more pages. I trust you, he wrote. Finish the entire manuscript and then we'll sit. And here she was.

"Mr. Schine told me you worked punctually." Jaim placed a cup of coffee on the table. He pushed the sugar bowl towards her. He looked fit and full of vigor for his eighty years. His grey hair was thick. His lined olive face handsome and alert. No hint of depression this morning. "Let's begin."

Isabel plunged into the manuscript with him working page after page for the first four chapters. Jaim had very few comments.

"Here, help yourself." He put a plate of brioche on the table. "They're from the bakery on Bleecker." He paused. "Isabel, I have a question not related to the book."

"Hmm." Crumbs of flaky brioche crust stuck to her fingertips and mouth. Much better than a donut. She knew what was coming. At some point all her clients asked how a nice girl like her got into this line of work.

"I know I asked this when you interviewed me last time, but maybe not so directly. Maybe I was too sensitive, too shy. I feel closer to you now. I can be more honest, I hope that's okay."

"Sure, please." She spread blueberry jam on the remaining piece of brioche.

"How come you're so involved with the Holocaust and not with the Spanish Diaspora? You're a Toledo after all."

Isabel put the brioche back on the plate. Not the question she expected. Not the question she wanted to hear.

"You see," Jaim continued. "If I were a writer, I would write a book linking the Inquisition to the Holocaust."

Isabel said nothing.

"Have you considered, how strange it is, absurd even, that the small Jewish community in Spain and Portugal wasn't shipped off to the camps despite Franco's alliance with Hitler?"

Should she tell him about her high school years and the ache for Spain? How she came to favor, as one did a lame leg, the Holocaust of the twentieth century? Because it was more recent. Because she helped make emotional reparations for fifteen individuals and their families. Because she earned money writing these books. Because of Suri. And Dave Toledo, the absent father, the link to Spain, was no longer.

"Franco had Jewish roots." Isabel responded out of politeness, her silence making more of a statement than she was willing to own. Emotions sequestered. "King Ferdinand too. His grandmother was Jewish and when her bones were exhumed and burned by the Inquisitors he said nothing. Even the King was afraid of the Church."

"Is that why Franco restored synagogues in Toledo?"

"Could be." Her Spanish side bled through despite her resistance.

Jaim pushed his chair back and stood up. He walked around the table. "After the war I heard that Jews who proved Spanish ancestry got transit visas from Spain to Portugal to America." He faced away from her. "Had we known we could have made it. My family. My brothers, little sister, maybe alive still." He paused. "I think you should write about this."

Isabel felt she had landed in a game of hot potato but instead of a small handy object a large meteorite had fallen into her lap. And it burned.

"You know, Isabel Toledo, in Spain, in Toledo, Seville, Cordoba, Barcelona, and I could go on, like in Germany, a Christian with Jewish ancestors was often persecuted. One-twentieth in the blood lines was enough for the Inquisitors to take an interest in you. Imprison you. Torture you. Murder you. The Nazis stopped doing their math at one-fourth." Jaim paused.

Isabel stared at the orange-rich lilies and the restful silver-green eucalyptus. "The facile reduction from a name to a number," she said feeling heat rise in her. The shifting shape of the present tense.

"I want to take you someplace." Jaim walked to the front door and she followed. "Close by."

They walked east on 11th Street and crossed Sixth. The avenue was so congested Isabel pulled into herself. Years ago she had lost her tolerance for this kind of urban density. Walking among the pack of people crossing from one sidewalk to another she quieted herself imagining the fields around her home. She and Jaim Benjamin continued east towards Washington Square Park. Suddenly he stopped next to a low dark brick wall.

"Look."

Isabel peered through a wrought iron gate and saw a very small triangular cemetery. Weathered letters and numbers on timeworn gravestones were spotted with moss, fungi, pigeon droppings, and dead leaves.

"Hebrew." She turned to Jaim.

He pointed to the plaque by the gate and read out loud: "The Second Cemetery of the Spanish Portuguese Synagogue Shearith Israel. In the City of New York. 1805–1829." He looked up at Isabel. "The first one's all the way downtown. In Chinatown. This is the second. There's another on 21st Street."

"Shearith Israel on 70th and Central Park West?" she asked.

"Right near where you grew up. The Spanish-Portuguese Synagogue. First Jewish congregation in North America. 1654."

"We never went there. Never went to any synagogue." Isabel scanned the graves as best she could through the small iron gate.

"No Toledos here." Jaim was ready for her. "But the footprints of your ancestors are all over this city. And it's this easy to find."

"I've passed this place hundreds of times and never saw it. Never knew it existed."

"I know. I'll see you tomorrow."

And when Jaim Benjamin walked back towards his apartment, Isabel remained staring into this hole-in-the-wall cemetery. Heaps of people walked by, oblivious to the dead buried in their midst. How had she missed it all these years? She had to see the one on 21st Street. Were Toledos buried there?

The Third Cemetery of the Spanish-Portuguese Synagogue Shearith Israel in the City of New York, 1829–1851, also occupied a quiet plot of land that was practically invisible. A little larger than its 11th Street counterpart, it was sandwiched between tall brick buildings with a small sign at the top of a graceful black iron gate identifying it. Only when Isabel began to hang on to the bars, trying to make out the Hebrew and English on the headstones in the back, did some passersby pause to wonder what she was looking at. Like her they saw a flagstone path, a few trees, crooked tombstones of varying heights, tall grass, and pieces of litter swept into the open space by the wind. The footprints of your ancestors are all over this city, Jaim had said, but there were no Toledos in here either. Had she begun to think in clichés? This was almost as bad as being haunted by golems and ghouls. If she were like her grandmother Bella she would spit three times over her left shoulder to ward off the evil eye. Instead Isabel shuddered in the cool air and turned away from the dead.

Isabel needed to walk. She headed north. Suri's apartment's was sixty blocks away. In city terms, a piece of cake. She passed through Chelsea, Herald and Times Square, Clinton, then hit Carnegie. Pounding the pavement, street after street, block after block, crosswalk upon crosswalk, was her habitual way of moving back into the city of her childhood.

Autumn cool gave way overnight to winter chill. She walked briskly and looked up at buildings, those familiar and those renovated. Oyster-white clouds floated against the sky's flat iron blue. The skyline of the urban stride: with Dave on the way to Radio City Music Hall, with Suri as they walked from B. Altman's up Fifth Avenue to Sak's then east to Bloomingdale's. This was the horizon of her adolescent saunter through the Village. West to east and west again to catch the Seventh Avenue line home, giddy with the city's magnetism and the careless joy of being young and mobile.

When she reached the glorious sanctuary of Central Park West she breathed deeply. A few blocks up she saw a group of men carrying big boxes down the steps of a grand institutional building with arched doorways and Neo-Classical columns. She paused. It was Shearith Israel. Of course it was.

Jaim Benjamin's exhortation pestered her. Isabel crossed the street, squeezed past the movers, and entered the synagogue's prayer hall. She sat quietly in a back row taking the space in slowly. This was her first time inside even though she grew up only a few streets away. The windows caught her attention first. Tall Romanesque arches filled with pale yellow stained glass. Three arches on each of the four walls. Twelve windows for the twelve tribes of Israel, like in Prague's Altneuschule.

"Tiffany," a mover said passing by.

"What?"

"Tiffany, you know the fancy glass maker. Windows are his." He waited for Isabel to make a sign that she understood. She smiled and nodded. He nodded back.

Louis Comfort Tiffany. Isabel thought of his full name. Did his windows bring comfort to the small community of Sephardic Jews in a not always hospitable New World? The raised dais from which the Torah was read stood in the center of the room. Sephardic custom. Isabel rose from her seat in the back and moved closer to it. Did Dave ever venture inside? Did his parents pray here? Was Suri ever here? Dave's presence was so strong suddenly that Isabel expected to see him smirking in one of the pews. But aside from Isabel and the movers, the sanctuary was empty.

Dave and Isabel sat together in a synagogue once. On another island. Lifetimes ago. She was twelve years old and they had flown down to St. Thomas for Christmas. Suri browsed through the duty-free designer shops and Isabel complained of boredom. Dave suggested they explore and not far from Charlotte Amalie they stumbled upon the Congregation of Blessing and Peace and Loving Deeds. A bronze plaque said it was founded in 1796.

"Nine Sephardic families established this place," Dave read out loud.

Isabel said nothing. Dave never talked about Jews or religion. She never heard him show interest in Spanish Jews, except to mention occasionally the families and friends in the New York community he grew up with. But even then, this common history was a passing footnote. Nothing important enough to linger over.

"After that, more Jews arrived from England, France, and

other Caribbean islands. This is the oldest synagogue building in continuous use under the American flag."

Isabel couldn't believe he was excited by this. Her father the proud Jew? As a survivor, Jewish pride was naturally Suri's domain. Though she too made great efforts to keep a low profile on the divine. Once Suri told Isabel that god was passé. This was after Isabel moaned that her Jewish friends went to Hebrew school and were preparing for bar and bat-mitzvas that year. She also wanted a big party. Suri told her she had no problem with the party. She could have a party. She could have a European tour to mark her coming of age. She could go on an African safari. Just leave god out of it. God had nothing to do with her being alive and making it to age twelve. Isabel dropped the subject. No party, no world tour, certainly no Hebrew School.

Dave and Isabel sat on a bench facing the dais in the middle of the room. Soft white sand covered the synagogue floor.

"It's the beaches creeping in." Isabel slipped her feet out of her sandals and dug her toes into the cool sand.

"No," Dave said. "It's a reference to Egypt. From the bondage of Europe to the freedom of the New World." Dave's love for America equaled his loathing for the Old Worlds of Europe and the Fertile Crescent.

Isabel spied a brochure on the dais and got up to retrieve it. "The sand covering the synagogue floor pays homage to the trials of the New Christians during the Inquisition." She read out loud from the pulpit. "They would gather in Spanish and Portuguese cellars to say their Hebrew prayers. Sand on the floor muffled their footsteps and voices." She closed the pamphlet and looked at Dave. He was even more enthusiastic. Like before a basketball game at Madison Square Garden. Or when he described California to her and Suri. He had already begun to spend a lot of time there. Doing business, Suri said.

"Why don't we have a spontaneous bat-mitzva celebration for you, Isabel? You're twelve. Perfect timing."

Isabel was surprised. A little appalled. Suri would hate the idea. Where was all this Jewish interest coming from suddenly?

"If we do it here," Dave nearly shouted out, "it will tie you to the Toledos. Our family came to the New World with the Dutch in the 1700s. We're originally from Spain, not Ohio, I remind curious Americans. We crossed through France into Holland after the Expulsion. Boarding Dutch ships, we were among the early seventeenth-century European settlers in Brazil, then Curaçao, before moving to the United States in the nineteenth century."

This was the longest family history lesson she had ever heard from Dave. Isabel knew few cousins on his side. His parents died soon after her birth. Dave had no siblings and kept in touch sporadically with his extended family. If it weren't for his name, his dark features, and his one remaining childhood friend, Leon Herrera, Isabel might not have even known he was not Ashkenazi. But eventually she learned from Suri that for generations these Spanish Jews married only within their community. By the time Dave chose as his wife a Polish Yiddish-speaking Holocaust survivor, the days of radical shunning for marrying out were long past.

Sitting in the empty Shearith Israel Synagogue on Central Park West thirty-four years later, Isabel didn't remember her specific reaction to Dave's lively suggestion of a bat-mitzva on St. Thomas. But it was along the lines of a curt no. At the seditious and remote age of twelve, the last thing that interested her was someone else getting religious at her expense. If Dave wanted a Jewish experience let him go pray by himself.

Isabel sat near the dark mahogany *bima*. Through the middle set of doors, New York's sky darkened with clouds. She should get home. Suri was probably wondering what was keeping her. But Isabel lingered. A moment more. A *shearith*. Remnants of memory were all that remained.

Isabel's last conversation with Dave took place not far from where she now sat, in the American Museum of Natural History. She had graduated from Barnard four months earlier with a B.A. in Modern European History and had decided to move to Israel, to kibbutz, to Alon whom she had met and fallen in love with. At twenty-two, Isabel didn't need Dave's blessing. But she wanted it.

They had come to the museum, a neutral space, to try and talk about her life. In the Hall of Ocean Life, Suri and Dave sat next to one another on a wood bench. Isabel walked around the replica of a ninety-four foot female Blue Whale suspended overhead and waited for words that never came. Every time she circled past her parents she saw they were lost in their own thoughts. The mass of the whale, three school bus lengths, dwarfed all other creatures in the room, including Dave, though he seemed not to notice. He held himself aloft and aloof and wouldn't look at his wife or daughter.

After ten minutes or so, Isabel went into the Hall of North American Mammals. Dave and Suri got up from the bench and followed. A room of dioramas. Beautifully rendered backdrops. Stuffed animals, replicas of flora and water sources, figures of Native Americans. Animals in their natural habitat.

"Native Americans are to White America as Jews are to Poles," Isabel addressed Dave ignoring his don't talk to me body language. They stared at a stuffed doe and fawn posed to drink water from a stream. A mannequin dressed as an indigenous man stood behind a tall shrub watching them. His bow at rest.

"Enough, Issie," Dave said but still would not look at her. "You don't have to go and politicize everything. It takes all the pleasure out of life."

"You've never been to Poland," she said, relieved that he responded, upset that he was contrary as usual. Why did she expect anything else?

"And I don't want to go to Poland. America's perfect for me."

"On the sophisticated streets of old Krakow," Isabel's voice quickly became shrill, "young musicians play Klezmer tunes. Tourist shops sell dolls of Hasidic men holding enormous gold *kopecks* against their breasts."

Suri stood quietly. She looked intently through the glass at the painted backgrounds, the stuffed dead animals, the life-sized human dolls.

"So?" Dave asked.

"So?" Rage at injustice, at invisibility, at Dave's terse dismissal of what was important to her, filled her. Isabel raised her voice despite the quiet in the hall. "Now that all the Jews are dead, we're charming. Tourist-worthy. Just like Native Americans. Romanticized in these dioramas since they're no longer an economic or political threat to the white man."

"I still don't understand why this upsets you so much." Dave moved to the next diorama with bison on a Wyoming plain. His voice rose to match hers. "The world's cynical. Nothing new under the sun. *Enough* with the horrors, with the past. It's a sinking ship, Issie. Move forward or be left behind. The future's a blank screen. Write your own script."

"It's not that simple." Isabel glared at him.

"Oh yes it is." He faced her. "Moving to Israel is a return to the ghetto."

"Israel's not a relic, Dave. It's alive, it's now, it's dynamic, it's . . ."

"Dangerous." He turned away triumphant. Israel had just become embroiled in Lebanon and it was clear to so many, except the powers that be in Israel's government, that this military operation was not a good idea.

Isabel began to cry. Suri took her in her arms, stroked her head and back. She gave her semi-estranged husband a sad look. He glared at them.

"Dave, you don't know what it's like to be stateless and at the mercy of history," Suri said quietly. She looked at a squaw with a papoose strapped to her back. The woman gathered berries from a bush on a steep cliff of the Hudson Palisades. "I wanted to go to Palestine too, but in 1945 the British didn't allow the refugees in."

Dave's shoulders drooped. Suri never spoke from the moral high ground of a Holocaust survivor. But now that she had, what could he say? For Suri history was real enough. She couldn't choose, no matter how hard she wished, to not be part of the script of Germany's incursion into Kamenets-Podolski. The blank screen of her future would forever contain terrible scenes from her past.

Isabel held her mother tighter and hated Dave then—for resisting her, for hurting Suri. And she wasn't sorry when he left New York after a few days. Only Suri accompanied Isabel to the airport three weeks later when she flew to Israel, to Alon, her suitcases and heart bulging with love and hope, pride and longing. One year later, almost to the day, Dave had a massive heart attack and crashed the car he was driving on Highway One. A hotel reservation in Monterey never reached. A young woman in the car beside him died as well. Isabel was pregnant with Lia and didn't travel back for the funeral.

3

Isabel left the synagogue and its backward crawl. She texted Suri not to worry, that she was walking the city and loving it. She headed north along the park, walking out of her childhood neighborhood into the nineties and continuing into the low hundreds. The cold crisp air sparred with car exhaust. Isabel took long slow breaths anyway, as she did in the fields by her home. She cut west on 104th Street, passed her old apartment on Broadway, and then went uptown again through the Columbia-Barnard campus. She continued down the hill to Manhattan Valley, stopped to look at 125th Street filled with people shopping and going places, and pushed up the long incline into West Harlem, moving from her college to her high school neighborhood. On the corner of 133rd street she stopped to catch her breath. Suddenly an image of Mr. Melamed, her plastic arts teacher in eleventh grade, came to her. She hadn't thought of him in decades.

"Real walk down memory lane today," Isabel said snidely and out loud. She was not comfortable inside herself. And not just today.

It was Mr. Melamed who one late winter afternoon started everything. Not fair to blame him. He thought he was helping and Isabel didn't have to take the bait he set out before her. The sun had come in to the art room that afternoon at a low sharp angle. The class worked intently on a still life. It was quiet and concentrated. Mr. Melamed placed an open art book beside the drawing Isabel was working on. She looked away from her drawing to the open page. She didn't recognize the artist. A woman's portrait, the Virgin Mary she assumed by the white halo around her hooded head. And then she knew, simply knew because of the resemblance: olive skin, dark heavy lidded eyes, high cheek bones, narrow chin, and prominent nose. A Spanish woman. A Spanish Jew. Isabel stared at the face and looked for words to give the hurt a context: *Mater Dolorosa* the painter called his woman in the painting, a face so close to Isabel's own, a face from the Toledo line, a face lost to murder, conversion, exile.

"*Anusim*," Mr. Melamed said. "The ones who disappeared. Converts from Judaism to Christianity. El Greco liked to paint them when he lived in Toledo."

That painting flung Isabel from one ghetto to another. From Toledo to Kamenets-Podolski. From Spain to Spanish Harlem. She knew then that she was trapped inside a name that reeked of the geometry of horror. Queen Isabella of Castile on one side. Bella and her German and Ukrainian thugs on the other. 1492/1942.

Once Isabel passed 135th Street, her high school neighborhood, her body knew where it wanted to go. One block after another, twenty passed quickly, and then she stood by the main gates of the museum complex on 155th Street and Broadway, once known as the Acropolis of the Heights. A cultural oasis that had none of the draw that went along with a downtown address. The Hispanic Society of America was still here. It had not moved downtown as had a number of the other museums and prestigious institutions that were once housed inside these gates. But Isabel had come for it specifically and peered in tentatively through the bars. Then, as if easing herself into a large body of water, Isabel passed through the main gates and entered the complex slowly. Here were the elegant McKim, Mead, and White buildings. Here the water fountain, dry as usual on this ordinary day, but turned on once a year when the American Academy of Letters presented its awards.

El Cid was still high on his horse in the middle of the dry fountain carrying the unfurled flag of Valencia. Beneath him small statues of naked men guarded their genitalia with swords and shields. Petite deer pranced among them. *El Cid Campeador.* Born Christian Rodrigo Diaz, he fought for King Alfonso VI of Castile against the Moors. Then he became *Al Sayyid*, the Lord, and fought for the Moors against Alfonso. Then he fought for himself until he conquered Valencia and named himself King. A hybrid, a soldier of fortune. The Lord Champion. 1000.

All knowledge connected to this place flooded Isabel's mind. She hadn't visited in decades but it was totally familiar to her. She nodded at the guard sitting inside the entrance to The Hispanic Society. A stack of brochures beside him. The usual hush and hollowness inhabited the building as she climbed toward El Greco's Jews, letting her hand trail along the yellow and blue geometric tiles lining the walls of the circular staircase. She stopped at the top, looked around the second floor, and made note that except for a young guard at a small table by the balcony railing, she was alone in the museum. Just as it had been in high school. The guard looked up, smiled briefly, and returned to her cell phone.

Isabel went left as if by rote. But with trepidation. She studied each painting on the wall before The Greek's, pausing in front of Luis de Morales's *Ecce Homo. 1560–1570. Behold the man*, Pontius Pilate called out when he presented Jesus to his fellow Jews. Hanging next to this painting was *Jesus and an Accuser*. Also by Morales. Jesus's eyes were closed. He had a soft reddish beard. His long nose had a bump in it. His accuser looked exactly like Alec Guinness playing Fagin in David Lean's *Oliver Twist*. 1948. Would ironies never desist? Three years after Allied forces stilled German ovens, anti-Semitic stereotypes were fodder for the British film industry. She would include that in her book. Yes, it wasn't just America.

As she did yesterday when she arrived to her childhood home, Isabel walked slowly and ambivalently toward El Greco's oils. Something known. A memory of comfort. A question of welcome. The paintings hung as she remembered them: *Saint Jude, Saint Dominic, Saint James the Great, Pietà, The Holy Family, The Penitent Saint Jerome*. The walls on which they hung were a freshly painted clementine orange. But unlike in high school, it was not the *Pietà* that captured her. Now *The Holy Family* drew her eye. Mary's face was not elongated and sallow. This Mary's hydrated cheeks and olive skin sang of life. Her large dark eyes shone. She looked like Isabel had come to look since adolescence. And the face of Joseph standing behind her holding their infant son was similar to Dave's. Behind them stormy clouds were basted onto a grey-blue sky. Surreal wallpaper to human myth.

Domenikos Theotocopoulos always signed his paintings in Greek characters. He lived for nearly forty years in Toledo, a city once as famous for its Jews as it was for marzipan. By the time El Greco moved there to paint the altarpieces for the Church of Santo Domingo el Antiguo, most Jews were New Christians. 1577. Within two years he completed nine paintings, launching the successful stage of his career. Why did El Greco chose to live among these people? Why did he fill his religious portraits with them?

They were known as *conversos*, those who converted. *Anusim*, those who disappeared. *Marranos*, pigs who managed to wiggle their filthy ways around the scrupulous Inquisitors. What was it about these very same people that inspired Rembrandt to paint them when he lived in Amsterdam's Jordaan district one hundred years later? Same people. Same destiny. Christian Europe's dark minority had fled Spain and Portugal and in Flanders were free to live openly as Jews.

The day after Mr. Melamed told Isabel about the El Greco paintings that hung on the walls of The Hispanic Society twenty blocks north of their school, she walked north to see them. She went dozens of times after that and immersed herself in Spain of the Middle Ages, the Golden Age, and beyond. She studied the lives of Jews from Castile, Seville, Granada, Cordoba, and Toledo. She read documents from the Inquisition and sentences handed down from the *Autos General de Fé* in Toledo: Don Pedro Diaz, alias Henriquez, Portuguese, money changer of Madrid, burned alive; Joan Berrio, bigamist, 200 lashes, nine years exile, seven in the galleys; Ana de Cazzeza of Madridejos, sorcerer and trickster, sentenced to wear the dunce's cap, lashes, and exiled; Jacinto Vasquez Arauso, relapsed to Judaism, burned; Isabel Ruiz Gutiezzer, relapsed to Judaism, burned. Isabel tried sharing all this with Dave on his rare visits to New York but he would cut her off.

"Such old news, Issie," he'd say. "Let's go to the movies."

Isabel sat on a low wood bench in the museum and stared at the Holy Family. Here was a Mary full of love and awe for the naked baby her body had produced. Here was a mother whose beauty and subdued libidinal energy were enlivened by her fat healthy child. Isabel had spent hours focused on the mourning Marys, on the suffering Marys, a reflection of her adolescent state of mind no doubt. But right next to them hung a joyful contented *Madre*. Here she was, Isabel's *doppelgänger*, captured in oil paint, 1580–1585, provoking Isabel to take up Jaim Benjamin's challenge. To take on Spain. Bring Emanuel fully into her life. Celebrate life. Isabel's head fell heavy into her hands. Her eyes closed.

"Are you enjoying yourself?" The guard startled her.

Isabel raised her head slowly. How boring for the young guard who spent hours alone in a museum with few visitors.

"Yes, very much." Isabel shifted on the bench.

"If you're interested, in the library downstairs you can see the first edition of *Don Quixote*. You know, like the Broadway show, *Man of La Mancha*."

"I know," she said even though she didn't. About the musical, yes, of course, scored by Mitch Leigh, née Irwin Michnik. He won Songwriter's Hall of Fame Award for "The Impossible Dream." But the first edition manuscript of *Don Quixote*? No. Nothing. She had spent all her time on these benches and never stepped foot in the museum's library. Cervantes and his fictional historian narrator Cide Hamete Benengeli who translated the Arabic into Spanish and told the tale of a knight and his windmills in the waning days of Empire. A hero soft in the brain. An unthreatening critic. Rumor had it that Cervantes had Jew maybe even Moor in him. Rumor had it that the novel was not penned by Cervantes but by a Jew yet to be outed by the Inquisition. Why else have Don Quixote remain silent when Sancho Panza boasted of being free of Jewish or Moorish blood or when Dulcinea described her expert salting of pork? His compatriots championed their Christian credentials while Don Quixote said nothing.

And in the end, hearsay. Cervantes wrote the first modern novel about a knight whose quest for lost chivalry conjured a flying carpet of social criticisms and comedies. Martyr, idealist, satirist, fatalist, victim of his own mind, victim of the regime's unjust definitions of morality and vocation, Don Quixote, the anti-hero, maybe a New Christian, maybe not. Quixote, Cervantes' golem, like his compatriot Yosele fashioned by Rabbi Loewe in the Prague ghetto just twenty-five years earlier. 1580.

The guard, sensing their brief conversation was over, walked back to her chair. Isabel got up and went over to glass cases filled with green, blue, red, and yellow tiles. She scanned description cards listlessly and stopped when she read in faint print: *El Transito Synagogue, Toledo*.

Cuenca, the index card explained, were mosaic tiles constructed much more quickly than the traditional labor-intensive *aliceres*. The older method of mosaic art entailed making careful geometric cuts from large ceramic pieces. The small pieces were fitted together in the desired pattern, fixed securely with a bonding agent, and their sharp edges filed smooth. Finally the gaps between the small pieces were filled with a thick layer of grout. Five time consuming steps.

In the *cuenca* process another index card explained, a layer of plaster was spread on the entire surface and molded into a pattern of raised lines. The hollows were then filled with colored glazes and baked. Four quick steps.

Cuenca tiles developed at the end of the fifteenth century when the deadline of the Expulsion loomed before the Jews of Toledo and Seville. What choice did they have but to construct quickly. *Cuenca*, the matzah of tiles.

The Keys

1

Exhausted, Isabel took a bus down Broadway from the museum to Suri's apartment. She was also suffering antiphonal angst—the Holocaust in one corner, Spain in another. Desiccated, desperate for food, alcohol, and sex, she got to Suri's to find a note. *Home late. All Bartok program at Lincoln Center. Food on stove. Chilled wine in fridge.*

Isabel took a long bath. She ate and drank. She melted into the comfortable large cushions of the living room couch, closed her eyes, and waited for a sleep that didn't come. She went into her old room but couldn't face the bed. It mocked her need for sleep. She stared through the window at the black river, at the Boat Basin's sampling of lights. Isabel retreated from the window and sat on the bed. She jumped up and sat back down. Jumped up again and ripped off the sweatpants and flannel shirt she was wearing. She put on a dress, stockings, heels, necklace, drop earrings, and perfume. Out. She needed to go out. She left a note, *Don't wait up. Catch up with you in the morning*, and placed it on top of Suri's.

The cab took Isabel to the bar on Houston where she met Jiri months ago. Crowded, noisy, sex in the air like last time. Like she liked it. She found a seat by the bar.

"Extra dry vodka martini," Isabel told the bartender. "Olives."

She looked around. What would it be like to live in New York all the time? So many eager men. So many handsome ones. The bartender brought her the drink and smiled. He too was handsome. Very. Younger than Zakhi. No way. One young man was enough. Or at least one at a time. Isabel took a long sip. It went down smooth and sharp.

"Hi."

She looked to her right. A woman talked animatedly to her girl-friend. Not her. She twisted in her chair and looked left. A man about her age waited for a response.

"Hi."

"How are you this evening?"

He had a European accent. What were the chances of this happening again? Months later. Same bar, same Isabel, and a European.

"Okay, not great. You?" Where was he from?

"Better now that I'm talking to you." He had a very nice smile. "What happened to make your day just okay?"

She couldn't place the accent. "Too much to get into, believe me."

"Try me."

Dutch? Hungarian? Polish? Find someone else she chided herself. Find an American. Twist away. Show your back. But she couldn't. He's not *them*: soldier, police, concentration guard age. He was her age. Maybe a bit younger.

"Hmm?" he persisted.

"There's a lovely museum at the northern edge of Harlem that most people don't even know about. The Hispanic Society. Worth visiting. You live here or passing through?"

"Business. I guess that means passing through, though I seem to come here quite a lot."

He moved closer to her. He was very handsome and didn't take his light blue eyes off hers. Isabel could take him into the bathroom now. She could kiss him and feel if he was worth pursuing. She could fuck him in his hotel room. Get back to life. Get back at the ghosts. Choking her. Circling her.

"What kind of business?"

"Banking. And you?"

"Ghostwriting."

"For whom?" He didn't miss a beat. Didn't raise an eyebrow.

"Mostly old people. About ghosts."

"Ghosts?"

"In The Hispanic Society they have works by Velázquez and El Greco. Goya's too, And an incredible full room mural by Sorolla."

"I'll try and go. Would you like to go dancing?"

Isabel downed the rest of her drink. Dancing?

"Now?"

"Yes."

"Sure."

"Great." He put money down on the bar and helped her with her coat.

They waited curbside for a cab. He leaned down and kissed her on the mouth. Okay. Here they went. She leaned into him. He smelled good. His hands were on her ass. They felt good. A cab stopped. They climbed in. He named a club. The driver floored it.

"You have an accent," he said to Isabel.

"An accent? Me? I'm American. I'm from here, New York."

"Nevertheless, you have an accent." And he lunged at her again and stuck his tongue into her mouth. She opened it wider. His hands were on her breasts. Her hand was on his crotch. She needed another drink.

In the club, Isabel downed a martini and ordered another right away. The alcohol made everything softer, easier. The man with the light blue eyes and a well-cut jacket took her out into the middle of the dance floor. The music was loud. He pulled her close. They ground against one another half time to the beat. He kissed her neck. She softened some more.

She couldn't remember leaving the club. Or the cab to his hotel room. Suddenly they were there. He undressed her quickly. She was drunk. Energy sizzled between them.

"*Ja. Sie sind sehr schön. Sehr lecker.*"

"You're German."

"*Ja.*"

"I can't . . ." Isabel pushed away from him. Stumbled to the chair. Dizzy. Weak. She dropped her head between her knees. What was she doing? It wasn't working this time. And not because he was German. That was just the cosmos making sure she got the message.

"You okay?" he sat down on the floor beside her and took her hand.

"No."

"Water? You're very lovely." He stroked her leg to bring her back to a boil.

She was lost though. No return. She stood and started pulling on her clothes.

"I'm really sorry. I don't know your name."

"Walter." He brought her a glass of water.

A gentleman.

"Walter." Isabel drank the water and pulled on her coat. "I really am sorry. I'm usually good at this kind of thing, but something's . . . well . . . it's not something I can talk about."

"Can I see you tomorrow? Dinner?"

"I'm sorry, no. I'm busy and then I fly home."

"Home?"

"Israel."

"Oh. Okay. I've been there. Many times. Love Tel Aviv." He dressed quickly. "I'll get you a taxi."

He insisted she take his number as they waited for a cab in case she changed her mind about dinner tomorrow night. Or if she wanted to meet in Tel Aviv. He hugged her warmly. A lovely man. Should she try and stay? She looked at him and thought she could swim in those blue eyes of his. But then Zakhi appeared. And Emanuel. Especially Emanuel. Molly said Isabel used sex to ground down the pain of Suri's detachment and Dave's antipathy. *Boker tov*, as they said in Israel, good morning, meaning this was not news to Isabel. But now that her habitual refuge felt compromised she felt herself completely at a loss. What did it mean? Who was she suddenly? How come sex didn't veil the pain but had become its own source of discomfort and dislodging?

"Thank you, Walter, you've been very generous and kind," she said when he closed the cab door for her. She looked straight ahead as it drove off.

In the morning the apartment was empty again. Another note from Suri. She was at aqua aerobics. Isabel sat at the kitchen table with a large mug of coffee and *The New York Times* reading a front page piece on the Israeli army's buildup of troops on the Gaza border. A photograph of a tank making its way down a dirt road took up half the lower section. A far more interesting image than Hezbollah's small rocket launchers on the other side of the border. Tanks moved slowly. They were dramatic. They seemed to tell their own story. Though what happened when and why and how was always only part of the story. Scenes constantly splintered and slipped. Everyone claimed his perspective was right. And everyone was right of course. And wrong.

How wonderful if a newspaper could be laid out like a page of Talmud. The barest of facts in a small box in the middle: six rockets launched into Israel from houses near Gaza border. No injuries. Israeli tanks mobilized on border. Holding fire. Then all around this central box would be a patchwork of rectangles with different interpretations of these details. From far left to far right. From utterly secular to fundamentally religious. From Jewish, Muslim, Christian, Arab, Israeli, American, European, male, female points of view. From the historical to predictions of future implications. That tablet would invite discussion. That format would resist didacticism.

But it wouldn't happen. People were too wedded to their points of view to make room for others. Isabel turned the page. An unemployed factory worker let his semi-automatic rifle rip in a do-it-yourself chain store in the Midwest. Pieces of big stories—especially those with violence—made headlines. Sold papers.

Suri returned from exercise class with bagels, lox, cream cheese with chives, and olives.

Isabel set the table. "I went into the Spanish-Portuguese synagogue yesterday." She began *the* conversation.

"Beautiful space." Suri brought more coffee and the two women sat down. She watched Isabel spread a bagel with cheese. Food: the first rule of survival.

"You've been there?"

"Of course. Your father and I were married there."

"What?"

"You knew that."

"No, I didn't." Isabel put the knife down.

"It's no big deal, anyway. More important than a wedding is the marriage, and ours was not as luminous as the synagogue. Though we managed." Suri put her hand through her light brown hair. It was still thick and shiny and framed her shadowed grey eyes. Isabel's beautiful sad mother.

"Tell me."

"What?"

"About your marriage."

"Not now, Issie."

Isabel sulked into the steamed milk in her coffee mug.

Suri put her hand on Isabel's. "I'm enjoying myself too much and we have so little time together. Look, the sun's out. Such a beautiful morning, I feel warm all over. I don't want to go to a cold place, darling."

Isabel looked at the brown spots on Suri's hand and the fight in her melted. She fell back into her familiar posture: protect, protect, protect. This woman knew famine, terror, abandonment, and a whole host of unnamed horrors. Let it go, Isabel told herself, let her be.

"Okay, mama." Isabel brought Suri's hand to her lips. How she missed her sometimes, so much of their lives spent apart.

Suri took a long sip of coffee and when she put the cup back carefully on the saucer she smiled.

"But I still want to know something about Siberia, Suri," Isabel blurted out suddenly, surprising herself. She couldn't contain the split—part of her chanted *protect protect protect* while the other raged *tear down the barricades*. "Just a little more than the bare bones outline you've thrown my way over the years." And the words themselves, pushing to emerge, showed Isabel which side of the split was stronger.

She needed words. Plain simple words. She had always needed words. They made it concrete for her. The agony, the damage, history. And now more than ever she needed Suri's words to slam the brakes on using the Holocaust as her measuring stick in the world. Last night's bar scene rose in her gullet. She could no longer abide the dark freefall of these past few months, and her decades-long obsession.

"You can spend your life on morbidity, Isabel, that's your choice." Suri pushed away her plate. "An unfortunate choice in my opinion."

"It's not a matter of choice, or morbidity. I need to know."

Suri gave her an impatient wave of her hand. "All you need to know is right in front of your eyes. Look out the window. See the beauty and delight of each and every day." A person who at the age of eleven managed to keep two out of three younger siblings alive in Siberia was tough, if nothing else. But if she were tough enough to survive Siberia, Isabel told herself at that moment, she was tough enough to talk.

"Okay. Can you tell me if I was also named after a relative of Dave's? Not only after Bella?" Isabel leaned towards her. "Is Isabel also about the Inquisition, not just the Holocaust?"

Suri stood abruptly. "I wasn't paying homage to history, if that's what you mean." She brought the dishes to the sink. "I lost my mother as a child and named you after her. It's that simple."

"Is it?"

"Issie, honey, it's not enough that you immerse yourself in the nightmare with those books you write? *Gevalt*, are you going to start up again with Spain and the Inquisition? I thought you finished with that in high school. Life's too short to worry about the evils of history. There's so many of them." Suri started to put the food away.

Isabel got up from the table and walked to the window. On this sunny morning the Hudson was grey-blue.

"It's not just about the past and its pains, Suri." Boats rocked in the Boat Basin. Further upriver a tugboat pulled a large ship. "For me history has always been about the individual. I wrote Rosa Levi's story because I cared for her." She turned to face Suri. "Anyway, I'm thinking of giving up ghosting." She should have said this first before asking about Siberia. How had she forgotten about the strategy she concocted on the plane ride over?

"Excellent," Suri said.

"For whom? Not for those who still want to tell their stories."

"For you. Why don't you write stories or articles about life in Israel? Or take up painting again. You did such beautiful work in high school."

"Yeah."

"This news makes me happy."

Isabel looked back at the river. A bank of slate grey clouds collected. The water darkened. She faced Suri. "What happened in

Siberia, Suri, please tell me?" Isabel couldn't stop herself. The words erupted, the hurt seared. She was desperate to know.

Suri closed the dishwasher and stood slowly. "Now's not the time. Jaim Benjamin's expecting you, isn't he?" Suri turned to leave the kitchen.

"There's nothing to be ashamed of, Suri. Nothing I won't understand. Don't I have a right to know?"

Suri looked stunned. Isabel took two steps towards her mother.

"I don't think repression is the correct prescription for trauma. You're smart enough to understand what I mean. It's for your sake, mama, but also for mine. Please." Letting Suri retreat with her practiced facility would maroon Isabel once again.

"I should revisit the past for *your* sake?" Suri took two steps back. "I see now what they mean by the age of narcissism," and she walked out of the room.

Isabel was not accustomed to Suri being so sharp with her. She went back to the window. There was expanse—water, clouds, nature, release, relief. Her tears obscured the boats. Still she imagined the tugboat pulling straight. In a few minutes it would drop anchor in the river's mouth near the Statue of Liberty and the large vessel it pulled would disengage and set sail for Europe.

"The Holocaust is not a life, Isabel, it's death," Suri said gently. She had re-entered the kitchen and came over and put a soft hand on Isabel's back. "My grandfather was a rabbi. He advised his grandsons not to become doctors. Doctors spend their days with sick people, he said. Choose a profession where you see life and beauty every day." She leaned against Isabel. Her cheek against her back. "You're not even a doctor and yet you choose ugliness and sickness and death. I don't understand. Isn't it enough that I went through it?"

Isabel turned from the window and pulled Suri towards her and held her tight. How small Suri's body had become. A cub. A motherless child.

2

Two hours later Isabel sat with Jaim. He was in even better spirits than the day before. An uncommon reaction to a project's close. Most people experienced a down turn at the end of the project. The buoyancy of telling giving way to a re-experience of loss. Sometimes accompanied by a sudden self-consciousness: how would the book be received? What they never voiced, but Isabel imagined they asked themselves, was whether she had done a good enough job. These fits of insecurity passed with the book's publication. For inevitably, from family and friends, the feedback was positive. Jaim Benjamin's reaction though was jubilation. He was not at all concerned about peoples' responses.

"Talking about it has done me a world of good. There it is," he pointed to the stack of manuscript pages. "I don't have to hold it any longer. I'm free."

"What section would you like to go over?"

"Nothing. Good the way it is."

"No language that grated on your nerves? Maybe I got something wrong?"

"It's wonderful. *Gracias escritora.*"

"You're welcome."

Isabel was relieved. She could go home now to do a final gleaning through the rows of sentences then send the book to Schine. She looked forward to a respite from his *pages, Isabel, I need pages, pages.* Until the next book.

"Did you know, Isabel, *niña,* according to rabbinical order, since the Inquisition Jews have been forbidden to step foot on Spanish soil?"

She shook her head no. What next?

"In 1968, the Spanish Justice Minister, Antonio Oriol, presented the official annulment of Ferdinand and Isabella's Expulsion Decree to Samuel Toledano, President of the Federation of Spanish Jewish Communities."

"In 1968 the movie version of *The Fixer* came out. Malamud's version of the Beiliss blood-libel trial," Isabel said reflexively not sure Jaim could follow her, though she wasn't sure she could follow herself. Just another coincidence. Seemed she was compiling an addendum to her book on Hollywood and the Holocaust. Coincidences meant nothing, they meant everything.

Jaim gave her a strange look and continued. "In response, after what I like to think of as a twenty-four year sigh, in 1992, the 500 year anniversary of the actual Expulsion order, the Chief Rabbis of Israel revoked the ban."

"So now I can go to Spain?" They laughed. "Imagine," her words slowed down, "a comparable ban on Germany, Austria, Poland, France, Croatia, Greece, the Ukraine, Belgium, Belarus, Czech Republic, Slovakia, Latvia, Lithuania, Holland, Norway, Italy, Hungary, and the rest. A 500 hundred year boycott of the continent. Starting now. Europe dead to the Jews."

"Imagine." Jaim got up from the table and removed a small object from the top drawer of a small bureau. "Here." Jaim unfolded the cloth covering a large black metal key with an ornate curlicue head. "Take it."

Isabel placed the key in her palm. Her fingers curled around it. She knew without being told that it belonged to Jaim Benjamin's ancestral home in Andalucia.

"It's been passed from father to son for over 500 years. I want you to have it now. Go to Seville, Isabel, open the door."

Isabel closed her eyes and tried not to see a narrow cobbled street. A small wood door in a high stone wall.

"Please, whenever you can, even if it takes years. And afterwards, when you've turned the lock, give the key to my son. And he will give it to his."

"Why not let Marc do it himself?" Isabel opened her eyes. Jaim looked sad.

"Because Marc's a doctor, not a writer. I want you to be there, I want you to feel it. You need to remember that you too were there, you, Isabel Toledo, there, just look at you. Then write what was done."

"I don't know." Her spirit bent low. She didn't want the key or the mission.

"My name is Jaim." He put his hand gently on her forearm. It burned. "The Spanish version of Chaim, though we haven't lived in Spain for hundreds of years. I speak Ladino and pray as we prayed in Spain. When my family was sent to Auschwitz, they spoke to Jews from Rhodes, Salonica, and the Peloponnesia in Ladino. In Auschwitz, Isabel, songs of Spain."

Isabel left Jaim and started to walk. Again. Her head swirled. A faint outline of a sidewalk appeared in front of her. Mechanically her feet pressed down on concrete and asphalt, one block after another. Street numbers dropped. She looked up and saw she had passed Soho and was already in Tribeca.

The temperature dropped too. A snow flurry began. She should take a bus, a train, a cab, and go somewhere. Where? Back to Suri's. Or a museum, bookstore, someplace warm. Indoors until her meeting later in the day with Schine. She walked past last night's bar. It lacked all charm in daylight. She continued to steer herself downtown. The cold penetrated her coat as she waited at a curb for the light to turn green. She tightened the scarf around her neck and buried her hands in her pockets. A man covered his gyro cart with thick clear plastic. The smell of burning flesh turned her stomach and she sprinted through the red light. Burnt flesh. White ash. White flakes. She ran for a whole block. Breathing heavily she stopped in front of a brick wall covered in a black and blue graffiti tag. NED. It was beautiful. And then she saw a red swastika in the upper right corner. No control, no finesse. A red gash demanding attention. Clearly not Ned's hand. She didn't move. Maybe it was meant as just geometry. Maybe a Hindu reference. No. It was pivoted, rested on the tip of one leg. Nazi swastikas in New York?

Isabel forced herself to keep walking, head tucked into the small collar of her coat, feet crunching on the slowly accumulating snow. She didn't look up. She didn't want to note or be noticed. Two blocks later she stopped for a red light and quite unexpectedly saw the Herrera Print Shop sign. Leon Herrera. Dave's boyhood friend. Their parents grew up together. And their grandparents before that. Part of the old Sephardic community of New York. Early Saturday mornings Dave and Isabel would drive down to Tribeca, to Leon's printing business. The streets were empty. Sidewalks quiet. The West Side Highway clear except for them gliding along in Dave's silver Cadillac. At Leon's, as the men talked, Isabel played with a stack of stock and a manual print block. Setting her own text that ran no more than two or three lines: *I love Suri. I love Dave. Leon's our friend.* Even as a child Isabel called her parents by their first names.

Suri had not mentioned Leon in years. Isabel assumed, actually she assumed nothing. But here she was, and here he was. She rang the bell.

"It's Isabel, Isabel Toledo," she said to the intercom. The door buzzed immediately and there was Leon waiting for her with open arms and a huge smile.

"What are you doing out in this snow? I think there's going to be a storm." Leon ushered her in. He insisted on making her a cup of tea and wanted all her news. He knew a little about her life in Israel from another member of the childhood group. He told her about his three children. Two sons in the business. His daughter a high school English teacher. Seven grandchildren all together. His wife was well. In a few days they were off to Florida for three months.

"How's Suri? It's been years since I've seen her."

"Good. She's good. She's with Hal, you know. He's good to her. Leon, sorry for being so abrupt, I don't have much time, but what can you tell me about Suri and Dave? About their marriage?" It was not easy for Isabel to ask, but maybe she was supposed to find Leon. For answers. Today. Now. On this trip. Another coincidence with meaning, no meaning.

He smiled paternally. "Not much. But I think Dave felt driven out by Suri's silence. By her war. She's always so cheerful, so lovely, you know how she is. But she never talked about her childhood. Maybe that came between them." Leon sat back in his chair.

"Did Dave ever talk to you about it?"

"No, not really."

"So he's like her in some ways."

"You're an only child, Isabel. It doesn't take a genius to figure out there was distance between them. And then he moved away."

She went over to the large paned windows. The mighty Hudson

was bullet grey and choppy. The storm approached. Could it be this? Sexual coldness? Caused by rape? Maybe Suri's reserve was not about rape. Maybe it was just the accumulation of too much trauma. A simple numbers game. Too many childhood years without a protective love between herself and a staggeringly cruel world. Too much responsibility. Too much guilt about Shiya who died.

"Why didn't Dave share his family's history with me?" Isabel tried another tack.

"You know that Isabel's been a name in the Toledo family for 400 hundred years? Isabel Toledo made the crossing from Holland to Curacao."

"I know almost nothing about the Toledos."

"Odd."

"Dave was allergic to history. Global and apparently personal too."

Leon looked uncomfortable. But Isabel pressed on. "Did Suri know that Isabel Toledo is a name stretching back to Spain?"

"I'm not sure she cared to know. Suri's . . ."

"At some point Dave gave up trying to make it all right for her?" It was rude to interrupt him but there was little time for formalities.

"I think so. Maybe. I'm not sure, Isabel. I never talked to Dave about Suri. And she's a very private person. Anyway, we're not a generation of shrinks like yours. We just accept the cut and the scab."

He came over and put his arms around her.

"Thank you, Leon," Isabel whispered and sunk into his paternal embrace, somehow able to hold back a deluge of loss.

We just accept the cut and the scab, Isabel repeated over and over in her mind as she continued southward. Snow fell all around her. One block after another. Flat bed of concrete. Curb. Step down. Asphalt street. Curb. Step up. Flat bed of concrete. Step after step. Curb down. Asphalt. Curb up. The flakes became so thick she could barely see two blocks ahead. She shook from the cold and pulled her scarf over her head. Her gloves were not warm enough and she dug her hands deeper into her pockets. She was not used to the East Coast's cold anymore. She breathed heavily and the frosty air hurt her lungs.

"Accepting the cut and the scab destroyed their marriage," Isabel said out loud. Precisely what she did not do by moving to Israel, the new skin that grew around the scab. And ghostwriting was a deliberate reopening of the cut, a draining of pus and allowing the wound to heal properly so the system—mind, body, soul—did not become septic.

Isabel walked towards Battery Park. The streets were increasingly empty and the sky a screen of old fashioned television fuzz. She saw silhouettes of buildings behind white floating particles. Then the ghost outlines of the Towers, like Klezmer music on an old Krakow street, rose before her. All that remained. Memories. Imprints in the air. In Poland, in Prague, in Lisbon and Toledo. Without being told, Isabel's body always knew when it found itself on the streets of former European ghettos. Josefov. Jew Town. Juderia. And now, on the soil of the new world, she felt it again. Contours of containment. Violence. Injury. And soon enough right before her the buildings that should have been there but were not.

Since Yamasaki's towers were laid low Isabel had avoided coming this far downtown. She had enough sites of terrorism back home. But here she was on the Family Viewing Platform awed by the size and scale of the Freedom Tower's construction project. 200-foot-tall cranes filled the pit. A cluster of tractors, some with shovels, some with cups, some with spikes, moved back and forth like dancing bugs. Candy striped concrete mixers rolled in by the dozen. Crews of thousands were employed. Heavy equipment was contracted by the year. Materials ordered by the millions of feet and cube. Documentation, construction and contractual, filled bookcases, filled rooms.

Snow gathered into a soft blanket on her body. Isabel could almost see the Towers' shapes for she remembered them as one would a personality. Though a palimpsest of disjointed events broke the narrative thread of her life, buried beneath it all, seeping upward as teeth pushed forward in a mouth, was the plot line of a New York childhood.

She took a long shallow breath of cold air. And this plotline included the Twin Towers. When Windows on the World opened in 1976, Dave took her and Suri there for lunch. At sixteen not only was Isabel bored by any outing with the parents when she could be with friends in Central Park or the East Village, but she was too nauseous to eat. The steel, designed not to resist air currents on the

106th floor, swayed up to eight inches in high winds. The steel was also designed to withstand the impact of a small airplane which its designers thought could happen accidentally. No one anticipated the shock and heat of two enormous jet planes with loaded fuel tanks crashing into the structures. Yet when this happened twenty-five years later the steel sheered.

Isabel remembered the day. The hour. The minute that it happened. Four p.m. local time. She had gone to pick up Yael from a friend on the other side of town. The friend's mother held a cell phone against her ear. "I don't believe what my husband's saying," she turned to Isabel. "A plane crashed into the Twins." They rushed to turn on the television and watched the second plane fly into the South Tower. It took Isabel two days to get through to Suri.

She remembered how clean up began as soon as the earth cooled. In Israel too one day's terrorist site was tomorrow's regular bus stop. All traces of terror wiped away with alarming speed and efficiency. And the land where the Towers once stood worth so much that of course construction commenced as soon as possible. Landlords, insurance companies, tenants, all focused and proud to be part of the reclamation of the air space of lower Manhattan. Only the smaller reconstructions experienced delays. Fallout from emotional and psychological landscapes not so easily cleaned up. Parents who never returned home. Parents frozen in bereavement for incinerated children. Spouses and mates clutching threads of last words. Friends left hanging. Bosses, colleagues, employers, employees vanished without graves. Reduced to white bone and ash.

Isabel plunged her hand into her handbag and wrapped her fingers around Jaim Benjamin's key. Keys from Spain. Keys from Poland. Keys from Germany. Keys from Russia, Ukraine, Paris, Rome. Keys from Palestine. Keys of refugees all over the world. Isabel closed her eyes. How much easier to destroy than to build. She tightened her grip on Jaim Benjamin's key from Seville. At this moment thousands of people in and around New York City were in possession of keys to apartments, offices, mailboxes, personal safes, closets, desks, elevator shafts, electrical boxes, plumbing stations, sprinkler systems, fire boxes, boiler rooms, cars, vans, motorcycles, bicycle locks, trucks and fork lifts that no longer existed. Relics of the phantom towers.

The Stairs

1

When Isabel got home from the airport she found Alon, Lia, and Uri cooking dinner.

"Hope it's okay." Alon opened the door. "Uri was with me all day. I missed Lia so I came into the house when I brought him home. We got to talking. She asked me to stay for dinner."

"No problem. Everything okay at home?" Isabel usually didn't ask Alon about his relationship. It wasn't a tender issue any more, no, that was long over. Still she was not especially interested in hearing about Hila, the divorcee with two children and a dog, whose kibbutz apartment Alon moved into two months after he left their home here in town.

Molly pointed out that Isabel had basically told Alon to pack his things and leave. That Isabel had no right to dictate to him how long he needed to wait until he began a new relationship. Not true, Isabel countered. In fact it was Alon who huffed and puffed his way out of their home. Isabel wanted to go to marriage counselling. She wanted to give it more time. Uri was a baby. And while Isabel might not have had a right to tell him when to start a new live-in relationship, she certainly could have an opinion about it, especially since their children spent time in his new domicile. But that was years ago and everyone had mellowed since.

"Everything's fine. Hila and the kids are in Zurich visiting family."

"Nice."

"Dad, Mom," Lia called out. "Chow time."

"You go on," Isabel said. "I want to shower first."

It was a little surreal when she came downstairs and there they were. The happy family. But hell why not. Alon and Isabel had such great love once. And she loved him still in so many ways. And the children, yes, for their sake, a lot.

"I want to take Uri to the desert over the Hanukah break." Alon made himself a sandwich thick with avocado.

"Sure, but only after the class party. That's happening here."

"Here?" Uri asked astonished.

"Yes, I told Idit. You'd like that?"

"I love that!" Uri beamed.

The doorbell rang. Uri ran for the door and returned with Emanuel. Isabel didn't recall telling him to come now. But she must have. He didn't usually come on his own. The men were polite, just a little awkward with one another.

"I'm going to the desert over Hanukah," Uri announced.

"Anna and Eva will be here then. Maybe we'll join you."

"With Alon," Isabel added.

"So?" Alon asked. "Be great for us all to go. You too Isabel. Get you away from your desk."

"We'll see. Meantime all I'm thinking about is my bed. I didn't sleep on the plane."

"I'm off." Alon gave Lia a big hug and kiss. He gave Uri a big hug and kiss. He gave Isabel a small kiss on the cheek and shook Emanuel's hand. He sailed out of the house they had built together. But they were over that. Old news.

"It was strange with Alon," Isabel said to Emanuel when they were in bed. She wanted to sleep so much but wanted to feel connected to him too. The time in New York was good for them. She had missed him.

He hugged her. Kissed her hair. "I missed you. And yes it was a bit strange with Alon."

"I didn't know he'd be here . . . I missed you, too." Isabel couldn't control her eyes closing. Her body sank into sleep.

*

"Beautiful, huh?"

"I love them." Isabel fingered the cherry wood front doors of the Winkler house. "So smooth. What a gorgeous crimson grain."

"Crimson grain. Sexy description."

She laughed.

"Come upstairs. Something else to show you."

Isabel followed Zakhi into the Winklers' master bathroom. The elegant glass block wall was in and muted light filled the room. The porcelain white fixtures were in. Even the shower doors were waiting for their new owners.

"This steam apparatus was installed yesterday. System needs to be tested."

"Imagine your crew taking steam baths."

"Imagine us." Zakhi's white teeth sparkled.

She laughed some more, adoring that they were really just playmates. Love was for grown-ups. "Naughty boy." She wagged her finger at him.

He grinned greedily and trailed behind her as she walked the house to admire the finishes that had been completed since she last visited. Doors, windows, cabinets, fixtures. The house finally closed to the elements.

"Great ass," Zakhi said when she led the way into the living room.

"Great house. Looks pretty much done to me."

"Almost. Next week the painter comes in to lay a soft and final touch on it all."

"Get a load of these cabinets." Isabel opened the Scandinavian-style doors in the kitchen.

"Put in a couple days ago." Zakhi was proud of the work.

"Wow." She pulled out the pantry's stainless steel hardware.

"Retractable. State-of-the-art."

"This house is amazing." She spun the corner cupboard's carousal and watched it gently settle back into place.

"I missed you." Zakhi drew his arms around her.

"I missed you too."

He kissed her full on the mouth. "How'd it go with Jaim?"

"The book part, excellent."

"What other part was there? A date?"

Isabel looked at him. A crooked smile on her face. Was he serious?

"Sort of. He asked me to do something for him."

"It's none of my business, Isabel, but aren't you wasted on old men?"

"Stop it." She laughed and sat down on the Great Room's floor even though it was covered in dust, plaster, bits of wood. "Not everything's about sex."

"Not everything, you're right." Zakhi laid down beside her. "Just about everything."

"Jaim took me to these old cemeteries right there in the middle of Manhattan. Spanish Jews." She looked out through the large glass doors. Beyond the patio, the mountain framed the valley. Broccoli and tomatoes filled the fields. "He . . ."

". . . wants you to write about Spain."

"Yeah."

Zakhi rolled up from the floor and paced the room dramatically. "Your date with history, sweetheart. Listen carefully: *My heart is in the East and I am in the far West. How can I taste what I eat and how can I enjoy it? How will I fulfill my oaths and vows while Zion is in Edom's snare and I in Arabia's chains?*" He paused theatrically in front of the glass doors as if they were a painted backdrop. "Rabbi, poet Yehuda HaLevi finally made his way to Jerusalem from Toledo, if I remember correctly, in the 12th century. One legend has it he was trampled to death by a horseman outside the gates of the city. Another that his boat set sail from Alexandria and never made it to the Promised Land."

Zakhi strode around the room as if it were a stage. "Or maybe, dearest, you prefer Shlomo Ibn Gavirol from Malaga. Poet famous for his lamentations. Or Rambam, mighty Moses ben Maimon from Cordoba, physician, philosopher, genius. And let's not forget the lesser known but highly poetic Samuel Usque." He stopped moving and crouched next to Isabel. *Consolations for the Tribulations of Israel* written in Portuguese when he was already in exile in Italy, just about the time our favorite Kabbalists fled the Inquisitors and set up shop here in Tzfat. Sixteenth century *Altneu*-Age Judaism in the Galilee. *Oh Europe, O Spain hypocritical, cruel and lupine, raging wolves have been devouring my woolly flock within you . . .*"

"How do you know all this?" This clever sexy as hell *yeshiva-bocher* in construction clothes had her bewitched. As usual.

"Tisha B'Av's a general mourning fest, dear heart. You were not raised religious and don't know that a whole day is set aside for an all-out lamentation-slam. Not just for the holy Temples in holy Jerusalem. Those you know about. But for the blood libels of England, 12th century. The burning of Talmuds in France, 13th century. The brutal Crusades, 13th, 14th, and 15th centuries. And the Holocaust of the 20th century. Spain and the Expulsion, in the 16th, the loss of some of the greatest Jewish minds ever, is a live and pressing wound in the Orthodox cult of memory." He sat down beside her and took her arm in his, held it up, kissed it from fingertips to shoulder. "The Inquisition, the Expulsion, avoid it like the plague, Isabel."

"From Toledo."

"I know, double reason to tell your Spanish survivor to leave you alone."

Isabel stretched out on the dusty floor and stared at the high ceiling. "Jaim gave me the key to his family's house in Seville."

"Oh no." Zakhi paused. "I'll go with you if you want. To Rambam's house in Cordoba. Even to Toledo." He sounded serious.

"I didn't promise Jaim anything. I took the key and told him I'd think about it." She stood leaving an angel imprint on the floor. "But I dreamt about being in Spain last night. I was on a dark street."

"Which means?"

"Don't know. Should I go or avoid it like you said?"

"An uninterpreted dream is like a letter never opened." Zakhi stood and came to her.

Isabel put her palm against his smooth cheek. "Yes, rabbi."

"Yes." He leaned in closer.

Usually when rabbis' words fell off the tip of the same tongue that during sex went deep inside her, she turned on. But now they made her sad for they dragged a throbbing 'no' in their wake. She felt the perimeter fence of their relationship. Isabel stared back into Zakhi's face. "You can open my letter any time," she said keeping it light and playful. Those were the rules of the game.

Zakhi laughed and kissed her again.

"I've got to go. Almost at the deadline. The book will be off my desk real soon."

Isabel pulled away and blew Zakhi a kiss. She practically ran to the door to get away as fast as possible. She had nearly sunk there in the quicksand of desire.

2

Several days later Isabel proofread Jaim Benjamin's manuscript for the second to last time. She was so immersed in the book that she had little patience for anything else and climbed into bed at every opportunity. Not to read. Just to lie quietly and focus on oblivion.

The phone rang. She decided not to answer and not to check who was calling. But as soon as it stopped ringing, it started again. So she answered.

"Hey, want to drive into town for a bit?" Zakhi asked. "I'm going to look at an old house that needs renovating. Why don't you come along?"

"To prepare me for my career change?"

"Maybe."

Because she was within sight of the manuscript's finish line, she could afford a short break. "Sure."

Isabel put aside the pages and changed from house to street clothes. Half an hour later she walked up a stone path to a small square house near the center of town. The windows had green wood shutters in need of repair. A small porch overlooked a terraced front yard. Right away Isabel liked it. Early 1960s. Utilitarian. Simple clean lines. The owner and Zakhi sat on old metal chairs on the porch.

"Door's open," the owner called out in a thick South African accent. "Hi, I'm Harvey Grunwald. Was just telling Zakhi," he turned to Isabel when she joined them, "that I bought the place for my daughter. She's in Johannesburg now but I expect she'll arrive within the year."

He walked them through the house. "I want to add forty meters. My daughter has two small children. One hundred here are not enough."

Isabel paused to look at the high ceilings, the built-in cabinets, and crafted wood shelves in every room. "I love these sliding glass doors. And the trundle windows are great for cross-ventilation."

"Not common to see this much carpentry from the sixties," Zakhi added.

"I want a complete gut rehab," Harvey said. "Bring it down to its shell and start from scratch."

"It would be a shame to do away with it all." Isabel closed the living room doors and slid her hand along the etched glass panels. "There's a great deal of charm in these period details."

"These doors are collectibles." Zakhi nodded at her.

"So disassemble them carefully and call in the collectors. I want everything clean and modern and new. My daughter won't understand their charm. She'll see old and ugly."

"Shame." They walked into the bathroom. "Now this is old and ugly," Zakhi said. "Bathrooms and kitchens need a complete face-life, but the other rooms, I'm not so sure."

But Harvey was. Everything but the exterior walls was to be replaced. The additional forty meters he wanted on top. They walked outside to the yard.

"The ceiling here is concrete. The realtor said it wouldn't be a problem to replace the thin wood walls of the attic with concrete block and to add some windows."

"And lift the roof." Isabel looked up from the front steps.

"No," Harvey insisted. "I was told it wasn't necessary."

They stood together and stared at the pitched roof with its small dormer window in front.

"If your daughter and her family are unusually short and intend to remain so then yeah," Zakhi said. "Otherwise Isabel's right. They'll only be able to stand straight in the very middle of the space where the pitch is high."

"Okay. Lift the roof." Harvey saw the facts as they were.

They walked through the rooms of the house once more. "I need a little time to take it in. I'll let you know by the end of week." Zakhi wrote notes and numbers in his notebook.

"We're not in a rush. I just want you to give me a rough estimate of what can be done and how much it'll cost. I've built two houses in my life," he informed Zakhi warmly but boastfully. "One in Johannesburg and one in Ra'anana. Experience has taught me that architects design beautifully but know little about the true construction costs. I want some idea of financial scope before I even tell an architect what I want."

"I understand."

"I'm hoping my daughter and grandchildren will arrive by the Holidays. The children are little so the school year isn't a factor yet. Can it be ready by then?"

"September, October? Five months of construction more or less. Two months of planning. Renovation license should go quickly, or maybe we don't even need one if the exterior walls stand. We'll probably need approval to lift the roof. Meantime start working with an architect." Zakhi tucked his notebook under his arm. "Yeah, September, October is a reasonable finish date. But I need a week or so for a rough estimate."

Harvey handed Zakhi the keys. "Give me a ring when you're ready and I'll drive up."

*

Yael had been out of contact for days.

"A routine practice, but someplace where there's no reception. So don't even bother, Mom. I'll call you when I'm back on base."

Isabel didn't think about it, or not that much. She stopped trying to figure out when she was being lied to and anyway the truth only spiked her anxiety. Her knowing did absolutely nothing to alter world affairs or her daughter's fate in the big mess. But Isabel did listen more to the news. Casually she would ask people if something was afoot. And then, three days into Yael's cell phone blackout, on her way back from Molly's, the radio played some of the sad songs aired on Memorial Day and on Holocaust Remembrance Day, the songs played when something really bad happened, like a terrorist attack on a bus or in a mall, or a large number of soldiers killed. Isabel pulled to the side of the road and opened her cell phone to read the headlines. A major battle was taking place right now in Nablus. Isabel called Yael's cell phone. It remained stubbornly off. Of course. Isabel tried again and again anyway knowing it was not on and probably not even with Yael. Since phones could be tracked, even with the GPS off, they were left on base during certain operations.

Isabel called Yael every few minutes on her drive home and continued when she got home.

"Let's just eat supper, Mom." Lia was not impatient, she was too kind for that, but she was firm. "Their phones are closed or not with them. She'll call when she can."

Isabel didn't answer. And didn't listen. She continued dialing Yael's number until she put Uri to sleep, after she put him to sleep, while listening to the news every hour on the hour, and until she fell asleep at three a.m. In the morning there was a news bulletin that two Israelis soldiers and five Palestinians were killed. And more Palestinians wounded. The fighting in the narrow streets of the old part of the city was sporadic but was not abating. Isabel had no way of knowing if Yael was there, but she had no way of knowing she was not.

Two more days passed. Isabel lived inside a leviathan silence that swallowed whole persons, lives, worlds. Meantime the end of December approached, the witching hour when the strong winter rains would be upon them and Jaim's book would be sent to Schine. Isabel pushed Yael and all surplus blackness out of her mind. She went into town with Woody. Zakhi said she could stop by Harvey Grunwald's house and say hello. He was taking measurements and making calculations. She was in desperate need of distraction.

But when she arrived at the house Zakhi was not there. Woody and Isabel sat on the front porch and waited. Isabel looked out at the green ravine descending towards the sea and tried as hard as she could not to think of Yael in fatigues lying face down in some ditch, operating the device that kept her in contact with her troops.

To stop thinking, she stood up and paced the porch. Then she tried the front door. It was unlocked. She and Woody went inside and walked through the rooms. Indeed it would be a pity to tear out all the woodwork in the bedrooms. Zakhi told her the man who built the house, circa 1962, was a carpenter. Did all the work himself. Isabel went into the front bedroom and opened the closet. There was a place for blankets, for socks, for hanging and folded shirts. The kind of components common at IKEA these days. Only these were decades old, made of solid wood, and by hand.

She went into the back bedroom and opened its closet doors. There was a pole for hanging clothes on one side. Behind the second door were very shallow shelves. Isabel studied them. What could they be for? Linens? Papers? Woody jumped onto the lowest shelf and pushed against the back panel with his nose.

"Stop, Woodrow." What was he up to? Isabel stared at the panel some more then realized that this space was considerably shallower than the one on the other side of the closet. She stepped away for a better view. A definite misalignment. Error or design?

Her hands worked mechanically. They took out all the impractical narrow shelves. Her breath was so light it almost disappeared. When she pushed against the back panel it moved. Not much but it moved. She looked closer. There were no screws or pins or joints of any kind holding the panel in place. She pushed right, then left. Low then high. She pushed harder and angled the panel enough to grab a corner. Woody pushed too. Then she lifted the panel out altogether.

A space about one meter by one meter materialized beneath a staircase that sliced through the back portion of the house, connecting the yard to the attic. Woody jumped in. Isabel sat on her haunches and stared into the niche. Numbness crept into her limbs. Vertigo flooded her, the rabbit hole of history inviting her in.

She used the flashlight function on her cellphone to scan the interior. Snakes and scorpions filled ravines around town. They had no trouble making their way into homes, especially into their dark secreted spaces. But the little room, if it could be called that, was surprisingly free of dirt, dust, even insects. Woody sniffed incessantly. Isabel moved the light along the walls into all corners and seams. Shelves, built decrescendo following the line of the stairs above, were empty and clean. This room—it couldn't really be called that—one meter square—this space was ready and waiting.

Isabel didn't budge. "Woody, come out right now," she whispered firmly but he was too busy smelling to obey. "Woody, come out already," she whispered again unaware at first that she was whispering and when she noticed not understanding why. Woody ignored her. She turned her body sideways and slipped into the narrow opening. "Woodrow, out." She crouched low. The dog continued his investigations and didn't look up. Should she let him stay? Was he capable of being quiet like the dogs during the Exodus? In Europe parents either risked detection or left a crying child outside a hideaway. On a bed. Outside a church door. Among leaves of a forest.

A wave of revulsion came over her. The dog would stay. Where was Zakhi? He should have been here. He might have been taken and she couldn't afford to wait any longer for him. Already too much time had passed. No hesitations. Minimum delays. Every second critical to escape, to increase the chances of survival.

Isabel grabbed her bag and not without difficulty drew the closet doors inside and fitted the panel back into place. She sat down slowly, sank against the wall, closed her eyes, and stretched out her legs. Like magician's black velvet, in the darkness of her mind the space was less small. Under its supple texture she was anywhere. Woody laid beside her, his head against her thigh. Not because of the tightness of the box. He always preferred sitting close. She put a hand on him and waited for her eyes to adjust. But there was no light penetration to correct for. Black, black, black.

Isabel turned on the phone's flashlight and saw she had 40% battery left. She tried not to think of electric outlets meters away outside the closet. Of children who expected her home in the late afternoon. Of frantic publishers, survivors, home owners, lovers, house chores. The wide net of civilization she was both caught and sheltered within. She shut off the phone. The plastic rectangle's loud good-bye jingle filled the small amount of air. Simple contact with the outside world denied. The need to conserve resources already paramount if she were to last for days. And she had to. She had it easy all these years sitting at her desk, entering and exiting the pain whenever she felt like it. Moving from a railway car's suffocating interior to a hug from one of her children in her spacious kitchen. Slipping out of the stench of a concentration camp's latrine to sit in her fragrant garden. Turning away from witnessing a friend being murdered to having a sexual tryst in the afternoon. All so easy for Isabel Toledo. Isabel the voyeur.

"But I haven't prepared properly." She defended herself from the grand inquisitor perched in her soul reeking of bald despair. "I need to go home and get all the stuff in my security room stockpiled from the last Gulf War." Water, canned goods, batteries, candles, matches, battery operated radio, blankets, buckets with covers, games, books, flashlight, television. And gas masks. "That's what I need. Europe and Israel. Jews hiding from the gas." She sounded like one of her books.

Fingering Woodrow's velvet ear she wondered how her mind would react to living for years in this box. She would shit and pee in a pail. Listen 24/7 for sounds of the enemy. She would tell herself stories. If she could she would even write some down. She would sing. She had a great repertoire in her mind. And she would collect every memory of every person, place, and thing she'd ever loved, and would finger them thoroughly until there was nothing that didn't belong to her, that she couldn't touch. She brought her knees to her chest. Hugged them. The air was brittle and heavy. How did one breathe in such darkness, in a place that didn't exist?

Arid, like ash, like dust. A golem's remains in an attic with no access. A recess full of high strung eagerness and nightmares. Isabel licked her dry lips and riffled through her handbag. Wallet, pad, pens, date book, hair brush, box of gum, flash disk, Jaim Benjamin's key, water bottle, and finally a little cylinder of maroon lip color. She applied some to her mouth. Then she wiped her finger along its smooth top and wrote the letter *aleph* א on the left side of her forehead which wasn't easy. The letters must be legible. She swiped her finger on the lipstick again and wrote the letter *mem* מ then *taf* ת.

"EMeT," she said out loud. Woodrow, her faithful audience, adjusted his head slightly against her leg. "In the beginning when God spoke the universe into existence he sealed it with the first, middle, and last letters of the aleph-bet. *Aleph, mem, taf.* אמת." She closed her eyes. "Zakhi told me that." She gave Woody a squeeze. "*Aleph, mem, taf* spells truth. Molly says that God the writer revises plot lines every autumn. That Israel's a nation of neurotic readers and compulsive commentators." Isabel hoped Woody was paying attention and opened her eyes. Black. Black. Black. She breathed slowly. She couldn't be too careful with the oxygen. "On the Day of Judgment we ask the holy scrivener to write us down in the Book of Life," she lectured Woody. "*Chatima Tova* Jews say to one another. *May you be written in for the New Year.* A people who know ourselves through letters, words, signatures, seals."

Isabel put the lipstick back into the bag. The Hebrew letters on her forehead, like a third eye, chiseled a channel through her dark mind. She spread the fingers of one hand on Woody's belly. Her other dipped into the bag again, touched Jaim's key, and recoiled as if the key were a burning coal.

"I am the Holocaust's golem," she confessed not to Woody this time but to the world reverberating on the other side of the box spreading indifferently in five directions. "Sacred incantations, inscriptions, vigilance, and stealth." She dug into her bag again. With her left hand she turned on the cell phone and then its flashlight. With her right she took up pen and paper.

I have shelter in a windowless shack made of rough planks of wood on the outskirts of Tana a.k.a. Antananrivo, the 17th-century fortress city that reminds me of Kamenets-Podolski. High walls. Narrow lanes. Only here there are such beautiful tall trees. Someone says they are found only in Africa.

A shantytown of Jewish Polish refugees has sprung up right outside the city walls. We are the people the Poles wanted to ship off mainland Europe, before Hitler and his Solution. A national commission from Poland visited the 590,000 square kilometer island of Madagascar in 1937. A feasibility study. Would it be possible to re-settle Poland's three million Jews there? Major Lepecki said 40,000–60,000 could be sent to the island. Jewish commission members countered with a realistic 2,000. The local population of 25,000 French citizens protested the idea entirely. The indigenous Malagasy people weren't consulted at all. After France fell to Germany, the Third Reich decided to make this island the largest Jewish reservation in the world. Madagascar—a place where millions of Europe's Jews could be shipped and contained. Where they would no doubt die by the thousands from disease and deprivation. The prototype for the ghettos the Nazis eventually got around to setting up on the continent itself.

For the first week I barely leave the shack, afraid of the people around me, afraid of the bright sun, the hot sky. Afraid. Baby Sholem loses weight. Three-year-old Raizel stops talking. A man in the shack next to me brings a pail of water every day and some fruit. Bella, he says to me gently, you've got to consider coming out. We are beginning to organize ourselves. Food, better shelter, self-defense. We need your help.

Then he frightens me even more when he says the local French population threatens violence against us. To pacify them the Germans promised to halt more shipments of Jews, even while this answer to the Jewish question is being spread round. Speaking at a Nazi party meeting in Krakow, Germany's Governor-General of Occupied Poland, Hans Frank said, the Jews would "be shipped, piece by piece, man by man, woman by woman, girl by girl."

I manage to pull myself together. A girl of eleven, here with her father, stays with the babies for part of the day so I can work. I plant a kitchen garden. I'm used to hard physical labor. Strength returns to me from pushing my fingers in and through earth, pruning dead leaves, picking bugs off stalks. No matter the dirt is hard-packed and inhospitable. No matter the vegetables that come to life are dwarfed and tortured. It's life all the same. And the work exhausts me. And the exhaustion helps me sleep at night, a child on either breast, the three of us on a blanket on the ground, skinny, frightened. But together. And alive.

When I think of my other children in bitter Siberia, Suri in charge, I collapse with grief. When Raizel cries for Zizi, her twin, her lost limb, I fill with despair. I hold my babies closer and try not to think of my parents, my sisters, their children, my cousins, their children, my friends, their children, the Jews of Lublin, their children, the Jews of Lvov, their children, the Jews of Boyen, their children, the Jews of Warsaw, Krakow, Kielce, their children, the lost continent of Europe, each city a shadowy star on the map of my mind, filled with souls set adrift.

A few of the men begin to hatch plans of escape. They are convinced that whoever makes it to mainland Africa, not so far away—the

Mozambique Channel at its narrowest is 400 kilometers—can make their way north along the coast. Once in Egypt, they'll either take refuge with the Jews there, or continue north through the deserts, Sinai and Judea. With the help of Bedouins they'll slip around British checkpoints into Palestine.

Their talk arouses me beyond words. To bring Raizel and Sholem to the sands of Tel Aviv, to live in the stone lanes of Jerusalem, to work in the citrus orchards of Pardes Hana. It's too much. An offering of the Garden. I can get crazy just thinking of it. So I stop. It's too good to be true.

I'll wait out the war in Madagascar, the fourth largest island in the world. I'll till the hard soil and bless each day that there are no train stations from here going to Treblinka or Auschwitz. I'll sit with my children under the tall Baobab trees. The skinny branches at the top of their razor-thin trunks are like arms sheltering us. Trees like human beings helpless before cruelty. We'll learn French and Malagasy. We'll travel to the tropical coast of the island and learn the language of the lemurs. And in the end, when the madness ends, for it will end, everyone agrees, Hitler will be stopped once the Americans enter the fight, we will return to Kamenets-Podolski, to my medieval walled city on the western front of the Ukraine. I will gather my vagrant children. We will clean the house and weed the garden. Life will begin again. Everyone a little older, a little wiser. Maybe I will even remarry. I am still young and attractive enough. No doubt there will be many widowers after the war. Like me they will need to start again.

"Compare the Jews of Europe and the black masked lemurs of Madagascar," Isabel said to Woody and put her pen down. The dog ignored her. "From isolation to containment to endangerment. Both survived the onslaughts in the end. But just barely." Isabel closed the phone's flashlight and breathed deeply and slowly. She felt empty, but not in a peaceful meditative way. She felt sick empty. Drained of hope. Anguish in this black hole empty because the folly of trying to build bridges of sentences and paragraphs back to Europe was clearer than ever.

"I'm pathetic." Sorrow pressed down on her. "Suri can't be spared *being stateless and at the mercy of history.*" That sentence of hers from decades ago branded forever on Isabel's brain. "And putting Bella in Madagascar helps nothing. Absolutely nothing. Masturbation. Perversion."

Isabel dropped the notebook to the floor. So little air under the stairs. Failure taunted her. Tears followed. Her nose ran. Her throat was parched. Her legs stiff. And Woody was suddenly restless. But Isabel wouldn't budge. She took a tiny sip of water because supplies had to last. She spread her arms out and touched the ceiling, touched the walls. How did people live like this for years? How did they breathe and eat and think and hold on to courage knowing the odds of a happy ending were against them?

But what choice was there when soldiers and dogs hunted outside. But there was choice. There was always the choice to live. For one could also *surrender to easeful death, sweeter than to love.* Delbo reminded readers of that. *No more requiring the impossible from a heart at the end of its resources.*

Isabel lay down on the concrete floor. Her head on her arm. Her knees folded. Woody curled into the pocket of her stomach. She looked up at the slight shadow of the stairs that she imagined more than could actually see. She removed Jaim Benjamin's burning key from her bag and held it firmly in her hand. Her fingers traced the large teeth and intricate curlicues of the head. She brought the key to her mouth. Tasted the cold metal. She brought the key to her forehead as if to bring down a fever. She brought it to her heart to mend the break.

Suddenly there were footsteps. Loud heavy ones. Boots. Her heart stopped for a second then began to knock so hard against her chest it hurt. She sat up quickly to hear better. Did she imagine them? Woody lifted his head. The steps were real enough. A growl gathered in Woody's throat. Isabel quickly closed his snout with her hand. Not a whimper, not a growl. They were goners if he barked.

Her eyes struggled to hold on to the near insubstantial differentiations of light. As if for sense. Just to have something to hold on to. Her body quaked. Her bladder pressed to give way. Woodshed. Wardrobe. Potato pit. Barn. Poland. Czechoslovakia. Germany. France. Yugoslavia. Romania. Italy. Greece. Holland. Hungary. Belgium. Austria. Albania. Ukraine. Belarus. Latvia. Lithuania. Hungary. 1939. 1940. 1941. 1942. 1943. 1944. 1945.

Woody writhed to free himself. Isabel's grip on his snout tightened. He threw his head right, left, and pulled away from her. His short back legs anchored to the floor for leverage. There was tapping at the window. A fist banged against the front door. *Türen öffnen!* Isabel stopped breathing. Her lungs and heart made too much noise. With his paws Woody tried to move Isabel's hand from his face. She put her other hand on his throat, pushed him down on the concrete floor, then fixed him in place with her thigh. Not now Woodrow, she begged him in her mind, not now. They would find them. Pinned beneath her weight he grew impassive. Isabel stared at the stairs above her head. Someone was on them.

The footsteps stopped. She breathed just enough. Then the steps resumed. For the first time in decades she prayed to whatever cosmic universal force might be listening and begged to live for her children's sake. For Suri's. She remembered Yael and the fighting in Nablus. Her insides ran liquid and she peed her pants. She listened with all her might for boots on the stairs and floorboards. For flashlights clicking, rods pounding cushions, for closets turned inside out, for dogs that sniff out flesh. No. If Woody smelled another dog he would go crazy. Dizzy with fear she pushed down harder on Woody, hoping he would understand how critical their situation is. How he must be quiet.

Isabel's ears and eyes opened as wide as possible, antennae desperately tuned to notes of the death knell. And suddenly there they were. More footsteps on the other side of the wall. She was barely able to bear the tension. The anticipation of brutality. Better a bullet than a beating. Better a snapped neck than torture. Her body collapsed into itself. The pressure on Woody's small shape increased. Her breaths shortened. There was little air left.

And as suddenly as the footsteps came, they passed. Quiet. Then some more quiet except for her heart's painful throbbing. She waited. And then waited some more. Maybe the boots were waiting too. But finally she no choice. She was stiff and choking. Slowly, fearfully she unfolded her legs. Her lower back and hip hurt from the concrete floor. She sat up gradually, peeling herself off Woody. He laid still. She waited for him to move as well. He'd be shaky on his legs at first. But then would rise and stretch his spine slowly. Upward then downward facing dog.

But Woody didn't move. Isabel poked him gently in the ribs. Stillness. She touched his back. Nothing. Her stomach flip-flopped. Bile rose in her throat. What did she do? She was without ballast, a ship gone under in torrential seas. All panic and terror she retched on the floor. How could . . . she have . . . she brought her face close to Woody's. She saw nothing and only felt his immobility. Another wave of acid came up. She retched again.

She put her hands on Woody's stomach. To feel for breath. Again she brought her face close to his. A sign of life somewhere? Suddenly he let out a low growl, lifted his head slightly and snapped. Isabel threw herself back. Startled, scared. Woody's breath was slow and raspy but little by little he raised himself. His legs trembled so much they hardly supported him. He hobbled to a corner of the dark cube.

"I'm so sorry, Woodrow," she whispered. "Please don't be angry. I tried to save us."

Did she cause internal injuries? A collapsed lung? What did she do? Sometimes mothers suffocated their crying children trying to protect them. Poland. 1944. Nahariya. 1979.

"Woody, please, please forgive me, favorite Jack Russell in the world," Isabel cried quietly and moved closer to him. "Leon told me to accept the cut and the scab," she said with a slight melodic intonation, a golem's lullaby. "Enough running the gauntlet. You hear me, boy?" She smudged the א off her forehead. אמת became מת. What once grew from *truth* now lurched toward *death*.

"Woody, please, please come to me," Isabel begged wanting to check his body. She needed to know how badly he was hurt. But he would have nothing to do with her. Fear crashed around her. Yael's unit fighting house to house. Street to street. Her dread intensified. Something really bad was about to happen. Her whole system just knew it. Liquid ran from her eyes. From her nose. Her stomach cramped. *Now, right now she needed to know Yael was alright.*

She dumped the contents of her handbag on the floor and blindly reached for the cell phone. Her crying intensified waiting for the phone to turn on. Her hands shook. She couldn't see the buttons despite the back panel lighting. She was heaving and hyperventilating and managed to push the number four, Yael's speed-dial number. When the cellular phone company's pre-recorded message came on instead of the usual message in Yael's sing-along voice asking one and all to leave their name after the beep, Isabel plummeted. She lost her child. She lost everything. Like in Poland. Like in Germany. Like in Spain. *Wszystkie zostały utracone. Alles ist verloren. Todo está perdido.* Isabel slumped to the cold concrete floor, lost in a reverb of terror.

3

Later Zakhi told her how when he drove up he saw her car, but couldn't find her. He walked around the house, peered into the windows but there was no sign of Isabel. He looked in the backyard, under the clementine and loquat trees. He climbed the stairs and looked in the attic. He looked in all the rooms, in the cabinets, and decided she was in town getting them a coffee. After an hour of working on the construction budget, he began to worry.

"Suddenly I heard scratching and whimpering. I followed the sounds to the back bedroom. Then there's barking from behind a wall. Sounded like Woody. I followed it and opened the closet doors. I saw the narrow shelves stacked on one side and pried open the back panel. Woody jumped out and ran towards the front door."

Zakhi held her close. "I saw you lying on the floor. I thought you were dead. Wasn't easy squeezing through that narrow opening. But then I saw your chest move. I felt your pulse. Slow but regular. You fainted."

Isabel kept her eyes closed. The day light was strong even in December. Zakhi rocked her in his lap, kissed her hair. Children and dogs: not reliable companions in hiding.

"Was the man who built the house a survivor?" she asked faintly.

"Yes," Zakhi said. "Harvey told me he was. Very proud of his work too. Did everything himself. Said being a carpenter saved his life in Auschwitz."

"A functionary."

Zakhi handed her a bottle of water. "I don't understand this man. He builds a hiding place for himself, for his family, despite the fact that there's a State, and an army. In 1962!"

Isabel said slowly, "The cannibalistic vortex of history."

Suddenly her phone gave off a Received Message ring. Maybe Yael. Even bleary, she lurched towards her bag.

"I'll get it." Zakhi found the phone.

Isabel looked at it. From Yael.

Back. Talk later. Love you.

Isabel was too relieved to move or respond outwardly. Her finger, stained with maroon lipstick, caressed Yael's message on the little screen. Tears came. Woody ran back into the house and laid down beside her. He leaned into her. Apparently all was forgiven. She melted into Zakhi's chest and arms, into the reliable comfort of her little dog. Zakhi pulled her even closer and hummed, *Oyfn Veg Shteyt a Boym,* a lullaby Suri sometimes sang about a forlorn tree and a mother fussing over her child. As if a winter coat slipped off Isabel's shoulders and the heat of day was finally able to penetrate icy darkness, absence didn't tug at her anymore.

"The dead are entitled to their quiet too," Isabel whispered.

Zakhi stopped humming. They sat quietly in Harvey Grunwald's empty house. Then he cleared his throat. "My grandmother sang *Rozhinkes mit Mandlen* to me. Want to hear it?"

Isabel nodded, yes, very much. Zakhi's grandmother, Brayne, came from Boyen, a stone's throw from Kamenets-Podolski. Very few degrees of separation between them. A *landsman,* Suri would say. Those who share the same geography. When Zakhi began to sing, Isabel imagined Bella holding her close. Skin talcum soft, spotted as a leopard. Soothing terrors, softening the blows.

In dem beis hamikdosh
In a vinkle cheider
Zitst di almone bas-tzion aleyn.
Ihr ben yochidl Yidele vigt zi keseider
Un zingt im tzum shlofn a lideleh
Sheyn: Ay-lu-lu.

Unter Yidele's vigele
Shteyt a klor-vayse tsigele,
Dos tsigele iz geforn handlen

Dos vet zine dayn baruf
Rozhinkes mit mandlen,
Shlof-zhe Yidele shlof.

*

After a three-day melancholia spent in bed, Isabel resurfaced. She called Suri and told her what happened under the stairs. It was not easy, but she needed to tell her mother. Simple as that. The next morning at eight o'clock the doorbell rang.

Isabel opened the door. "What?" She could not believe her eyes when she saw Suri standing there. "Suri. Is everything . . ."

"I had to come. We need to talk."

Isabel hugged Suri and brought her into the house.

"*Savta!*" Uri ran from the kitchen and into Suri's arms.

"*Savta?*" Lia ran downstairs and joined the group hug.

Isabel still couldn't believe it. "Suri, is everything all right? Are you . . ."

"Everything's wonderful. I just missed you. Even at my age I can be spontaneous. Hal brought me to the airport yesterday morning, I got on a noon flight, and here I am."

Isabel was overwhelmed. Happily so. But nervous. Lia took Uri to school on her way to the Technion. Suri showered and Isabel made a fresh pot of coffee and waited. She knew Suri didn't just hop on a plane because she missed them. They had been living apart for twenty-four years and this was a first. Trips were usually planned well in advance. Intra-country tours mapped out. A stop in Europe, either coming or going, also a must.

"That's good." Suri came into the kitchen and took a seat across from Isabel at the table. Woody placed his two front paws on Suri's lap. He wanted up. "C'mon, boy."

That was also a first. Suri was no fan of pets and always maintained a polite distance from her daughter's menagerie. Woody jumped, gave Suri's face a quick lick as if he too couldn't believe this makeover, and curled up adorably in her lap before she changed her mind.

"So," Isabel said. "Hungry?"

"No."

"What's up?"

"Issie, what you told me . . . about you, about Woody . . . that hiding space. It affected me very badly." She looked directly into Isabel's eyes. Tears filled hers. Had Isabel ever seen Suri cry? "I called Zizi and Lola after you and I spoke. I hope it's okay but I had to share it with someone."

"No problem, Suri. I don't . . ." and stopped herself. Now was not the time to sting Suri by emphasizing that *she* didn't have a problem talking about pain.

"I realized after I spoke to them, after we discussed this terrible terrible," she choked, "liability you live with, that the time has come for me to tell you about the war."

Isabel breathed deeply and she took Suri's free hand in hers. She squeezed it. Suri's other hand rested on Woody's nape.

"In Siberia, we suffered terribly. Not just cold. Not just starvation. Not just deprivation. But four little children with no protectors. No one to place their body between us and other adults." She licked her lips and took a sip of coffee. "Shiya died one very cold night from hypothermia. We were in a wooden shack with a tin roof. We clung together as one body to keep ourselves as warm as we could. But in the morning, his face was blue, his gorgeous mouth blue. We didn't understand at first that he was dead. We were so young. I ran over to the barn and told the farmer. But before he came back with me to the shack, he threw me on the ground and raped me. And spit at me. He told me I killed my brother and would go to hell."

Suri held Isabel's hand tighter.

"You see, he had offered to let us all sleep inside the house by the stove if I had sex with him. He was old and fat and smelled of vodka. He hadn't washed in months. I was eleven years old. A virgin. Of course I said no. He said the shack was what we deserved. And only for one night."

Here it was. Molly was right. Only sexual shame could drive such silence. And guilt.

"I'm so sorry, Suri."

"There's more." Her hand slipped under Woody's warm belly. He adjusted himself. He liked this. "After that I understood the rules of the game. If Zizi and Lola and I were to survive, I'd have to let men have sex with me."

Isabel stopped breathing.

"After the first few times I learned not to be there at all. I went somewhere else in my mind. Usually to my mother in our kitchen. Or I focused on the warm stoves, the soup, the bread, and the promises I received that my sisters wouldn't be touched."

Isabel started to cry. Poor Suri. She couldn't take it. She wanted to kill each one of those motherfucking monsters. Twist their necks with her own hands. Gouge out their intestines.

"Three little girls on their own. I was so afraid. So lonely. After Zizi and Lola slept, I cried myself to sleep every night. I wanted my mother so badly I was willing to cut off my arm for her. Even a leg. Just to have her with us again.

"I felt she was alive. That kept me going. After the war, of course I looked for her in all the channels. All the offices and agencies. And then a neighbor from Kaments-Podolski found me in New York. He survived the death pits. He lay wounded under dead bodies for three days then crawled out and made his way east through the forests. He was eyewitness to Bella's murder. Raizel and Sholem had already been killed on the walk to the pits. Each baby thrown up in the air and shot for target practice."

Isabel went and sat on her knees next to Suri's chair. She wrapped her arms around her mother's waist. Suri kissed Isabel's head. Woody jumped off Suri's lap and Isabel climbed into it. They held each other and wept. Her poor poor mother. Her sweetest Suri in the world. What did they do to her?

"Shh," Suri said and hugged Isabel tighter. "I love you Isabel. With all my heart. When you were born, I was reborn. You were everything to me. You still are. You and your children are proof that life's still good. Please. Believe that. We can still live and love."

Isabel pressed into Suri and held her closer, closer, closer still. "I love you so much, mama."

The Lights

1

Suri, Lia, Uri, and Isabel spent the morning at Haifa's Festival of Festivals. Red, white, and green blinking lights decorated metal camels and plastic reindeer on rooftops and balconies. Garlands of colored lights lined doorframes and storefronts. Silver and gold tassels adorned lampposts and window bars. Synthetic perennially green fir trees dressed up shop windows and street corners. "We Wish You a Merry Christmas" and "O Christmas Tree" in English, "*Jraas Elieed*" and "*Lyelet Samt*" in Arabic rang out of portable stereo systems. Oud solos of "Deck the Halls" and "Joy to the World" filled *Wadi Nisnas*. This year Christmas, Hanukah, and Mawlid fell literally in the same week. To celebrate music, plays, poetry, and art from around the country with the theme of Black Coffee transformed its alleyways and narrow cobbled streets into an outdoor stage and gallery.

Uri ran from building-sized photographs to free-standing sculptures of coffee cups, from colorful murals to wall reliefs. When Isabel, Lia, and Suri caught up to him he pretended to be a museum docent.

"Here," he said in a high toned nasal voice, his arm akimbo, "we have a full size mural by Vafa'i Yassin," he read the name on a white plaque. "It covers the whole wall. Notice the colors. Blue and green swirls. Not exactly like the coffee you and I like to drink."

The women burst out laughing as he paused, waiting for their reaction. Isabel needed some revelry and accomplices. Jaim Benjamin's book was finally off her desk. Schine called from New York last night to congratulate her on a job well done. The manuscript was already being readied for printing. The cover art was being explored. A Purim publication indeed.

Just like that, just like that, a snap of the fingers, a corner turned. The carpenter's hidden cupboard, Suri's story, a hyper clarity had come over Isabel: she no longer need to shore up cracks and tuck away the vulnerabilities of history. Suri didn't need to revisit the killing grounds of her childhood. She didn't need to be rescued. Isabel could tie the salvage dinghy up to the dock and move on. She was through with the war. No more ghosting. She chose life.

Uri ran ahead and stopped next to an apartment building whose entire side was draped in white fabric. A haphazard coffee spill in its center. Under the enormous brownish blot, Osnat Bar-Or and Ofer Kahana included a date: October 2000.

"The start of the second intifada," Isabel said recalling the hostilities that erupted in Jerusalem's Old City over that Rosh HaShanah weekend. Violence and fear accompanied its spread from Qalqilyah to the Coastal Highway, from Nablus to the Galilee hills, to her town, to the villages of her neighbors.

"Coffee stains look like dry blood," Lia commented.

A lot of the art in the Festival showed the country's pain, its fragile seams. And even though Isabel wouldn't ask Suri any more questions, walking through the alleys of the *Wadi* and seeing art respond to trauma, Isabel knew, from deep inside, that in the long run, expression as a form of protest, as a way to tell the story, was a more powerful antidote to injustice and sorrow than silence. Isabel wondered if Suri saw it too. Isabel sighed and Lia linked her arms through her mother's and grandmother's.

They walked on. Outside a barber shop a quartet of old men played backgammon. The owner, the barber himself Isabel assumed from his light blue smock, gestured for her to come inside for a drink. She helped myself to water from the tall cooler and smiled at the subtle bite of anise. The barber had spiked the water with arak. He smiled mischievously. "Take some more."

"One glass is enough before noon." Isabel smiled back.

"But it's the holidays. More is permitted."

"No thanks," she laughed. "I'll ask my mother if she wants some."

"Certainly. Welcome."

Neither Suri nor Lia wanted arak spiked water but thanked the barber and gave him big smiles. They watched the men and their moves on the backgammon board. Someone produced a candy for Uri. Someone else asked him what play to make next. The child leaned against the man with the candy, studied the board, and gave advice as if these men were familiar beloved uncles. Only the promise of a ride on Lia's back pried him away.

"Before religious madness polluted the environment, Christianity, Islam, and Judaism prospered together in Spain, and most especially in Toledo. There was equilibrium, and harmony if only for a short but meaningful time. The *Convivencia*, Golden Age of Iberia," Isabel said as they walked away. Lia knew this already. Uri wasn't listening. Suri seemed resigned to her daughter's interests. No more writing. No more questions for her. But history would remain her passion.

They wandered away from the men and into an indoor gallery exhibiting the more delicate works of art. In two pieces, one featuring Bruce Lee in a montage of photo and paint, and the other, an inked drawing of a little girl, coffee and blood spills were once again indistinguishable. The cup in the little girl's hand exploded into invisibility leaving only a large hole in her abdomen with black coffee/blood spurting like a fountain in a city park on a hot summer day. They moved on to a painting showing used coffee grinds at the bottom of a cup waiting to be read.

"Like Rorschach," Suri said.

Isabel nodded in agreement. In between the dark grinds, in the light of untouched surfaces, amidst nooks, crannies, rivulets, and the moon-like shell of the demitasse, a message waited for those able to read it. In the Middle East those who could decipher this language were frequently consulted. Even revered. And hanging heavy and sharp like a sword over everyone's head, the question of what the future would bring remained fraught with endless hope and dread.

✳

Early the next morning while the children and Suri slept, Isabel left the house to meet Zakhi at the Winklers. He had called to tell her that all trades were off site except for the painter.

"The project's nearly finished and the key to the front door's burning in my pocket. House lights ritual time. When can you come?"

"Now," Isabel didn't miss a beat. "Get ready."

Isabel pulled up next to Zakhi's truck on the just laid stone driveway. Where one day grass would grow in between the flat stones, mud now sprouted dark, rich, and wet. Winter was upon them fast and furious. And though Christmas wasn't white in south-west Asia, neither was it warm and sunny. A grey sky anchored in thick clouds showed that the rains had most certainly arrived.

Isabel entered the Winkler house and paused to look around. The space reverberated with the beauty and the promise of the newly built. She waltzed into the kitchen. Zakhi was screwing light bulbs into fixtures. There were overhead ceiling spots, under cabinet spots, and interior cabinet spots behind glass doors. She leaned against the door jamb and watched him work. How she loved to watch this man work. When he was done with the fixtures, he took a light bulb attached to a short electric cord and plug and moved towards the cabinets. He pushed the plug into a countertop socket and the light bulb at the end lit up.

"יהי אור"—let there be light," Isabel pronounced solemnly.

Zakhi turned around to smile at her.

"Good morning, sweetheart."

"Excellent morning," she responded.

Zakhi moved from outlet to outlet. Each time the light bulb flashed on Isabel said let there be light. She moved in to the kitchen, closing the gap between her and Zakhi.

"Have you decided to do the Grunwald renovation?"

"In town? Yeah, sure."

"Did you tell Harvey about the hideout?"

"No."

"Are you going to?"

"Nope. Going to bury it between sheetrock walls."

Zakhi was so cool she could burst. "In hundreds of years archaeologists will wonder what 21st-century Jews in the Holy Land were up to."

"Exactly." Zakhi gathered his equipment.

"Think they'll read Europe's footprint here in the Middle East?" Isabel followed him into the dining room. "Jaim Benjamin told me even today Crypto-Jews in Mexico and New Mexico are afraid to come out."

"Wow, that's sad." Zakhi played with a switch of a ceiling fixture. A standard white plastic lead and weak bulb hung crookedly from the ceiling. He left the light on and moved to the future television corner.

"I've got some news for you," Zakhi spoke casually and grinned that sexy, rapacious, playful grin of his. "I have a girlfriend."

Isabel's smile contained a tsunami of anxiety which crested with the stifled questions: was it over between them? Who was this woman? Had he been seeing her for months? Isabel knew she had no right to ask or to know. She had no right to rights period. Her smile wouldn't tone down. Good thing. It kept the tears away.

"Wonderful." Isabel trailed after him. Her stomach bottomed out. Objects all around her smudged into undifferentiated images. She held her spine especially straight. She would not collapse inside. "Tell me about her."

Zakhi acted as if he hadn't heard. This deliberate casualness—telling Isabel in between switches and sockets—meant he was protecting her. Isabel stopped following and pressed herself against a wall. She waited for him to answer while the wall held her up.

"Zakhi, why are you telling me about a girlfriend as if she were a traffic report?"

He continued not to answer and didn't look at her either. He walked to the far side of the big room and tested another set of outlets.

"I'm happy for you. I want you to be loved and to love and to have it all." Isabel walked over to him while managing not to cry. He stared out the large plate glass window. The mountain range framed the valley's lime green and teal patches. Isabel put her hand on Zakhi's broad arm. "You haven't even told me her name."

"Keren." He turned to her. "She's great, you'll really like her. I know it."

"I'm sure of it. She good to you?"

Zakhi laughed. "Of course." He hugged her, put his face in her neck, and took a deep breath of her.

Isabel would always be grateful that Zakhi had come in to her life. That he taught her to play traffic tag at intersections. That he took her down to a place by the river and gave her back exuberance and joy, rebelliousness and licentiousness, all in one tumble. Zakhi had helped her contain the pain and had gracefully ignored the tyranny of time and numbers. Until now. Now it caught up with them. The tears broke out, unwelcome, unnerving, revealing.

"Shh." He held her close.

"I'm sorry. I guess, I just . . ."

"Shh." He kissed her hair and stroked her back.

A wrenching nausea in her stomach reminded her how the obsolescence of their relationship has been shadowing them all along.

"Come on." Zakhi disengaged from their tight hug. "We've got lots of rooms to check before getting down to business. It's been some time, Isabel Toledo, since I've seen you naked."

"What?"

"House lights ritual? You started it."

"I'm not . . ."

"Not what? Don't you remember, all lights tested and on, the last time the empty house is our playpen . . ."

"But . . . if you're in love, then I don't see how . . ."

"I didn't say I was in love. I said I had a girlfriend. Like you have a boyfriend."

"That's different." She was irritated. "Emanuel and I aren't going to have children together. There's no need to make a solid plan. We can continue to be together and still remain apart. But to really be with someone, married, I don't see how it fits. And anyway, Emanuel and I . . ."

"You've already married me off. Thanks, but no thanks." Zakhi laughed. "And about Emanuel . . . don't expect him to hang around forever under your conditions. You are one tough lady, Isabel Toledo. Don't know if I could handle your terms."

She retorted. "Choice is his. Or any man's."

"Not so easy if he loves you. And I think Emanuel does."

Isabel followed Zakhi upstairs to the second floor. "People choose their destinies in relationships."

"And I choose to play with you." Zakhi flipped on all the lights in the master bedroom. The ceiling fixture. The bedside sconces. "I want you now." He turned on the spots in the bathroom and walked in and out of all the other bedrooms, bathrooms, and walk-in closets on the second floor, turning on every single light in the house. Isabel followed closely.

"Zakhi . . ."

"Aren't you the one who says domesticity kills relationships?"

"I do."

"So let's just keep going our way. It works for us."

On this rainy grey day at the end of December, inside a spanking new house burning bright for all those in the valley to see, Zakhi Kandel took Isabel Toledo into the back bedroom. He laid his jacket down on the floor where one day a king sized bed would stand and pulled her down beside him. She resisted.

"It's all right, come on, baby. Let me feel you." He brought her close and Isabel melted against him. It wasn't her job to protect the newly minted relationship of Zakhi and Keren. So much was uncertain and she and Zakhi had their ways, their traditions, their favorite things. And launching one of Zakhi's newly built houses with the act of love was one of them. Their house lights ritual. After their bodies sung with bliss, they rested quietly in one another's arms. Zakhi opened an eye and looked at her.

"On this Hanukah, we not only remember the re-consecration of the Holy Temple in Holy Jerusalem, but christen the Winkler house in the once German village of Waldheim." Zakhi's mock German accent was his way of making light of her brooding which orgasm had only temporarily lifted.

"The Templars were Nazi sympathizers," Isabel mumbled. "The British surrounded the entire village with barbed wire. Students from the Technion guarded them."

"I thought you were off the Nazis."

"Old habits die hard."

"Let's take your mind off those nasty people then." Zakhi put two fingers inside of her and she arched her back. He put his mouth on hers, waited for her to moan and move to his satisfaction. Then he entered her again.

"Missionary style," he whispered, his lips hovered over hers, "in honor of the religious Templars." Air filled the small crevices between them and they stared at one another, eyes wide, pleased, joyful, mournful. She came again. Zakhi followed. They lay spent and entwined. Toes. Thighs. Arms. Hands. Cheeks. Chests. All in a job well done.

2

On the eighth day of Hanukah Isabel's true loves gave her and Emanuel a three-day holiday at a luxury hotel on the shores of the Dead Sea. The perfect gift for an exhausted writer, lover, daughter, mother facing big decisions. But before the balm and magic of the surreal Dead Sea landscape, Isabel needed to organize the house. She was hosting the Hanukah party for Uri's second grade class. The sun set early in late December and Hanukah candles were lit soon after. Festivities were scheduled for five-thirty and she had been cleaning since noon. Suri helped but she mostly kept Uri entertained and out of Isabel's way. Public spaces were orderly. Check. Disposable dishes and cutlery were set out. Check. Delicate items stowed. Check. Borrowed chairs scattered throughout. Check.

The head of the parents' committee was bringing jelly donuts. Other parents the drinks. Isabel provided the space. Check. Uri had been flying around the house for days. His teacher Idit, one of the significant female lights in his firmament, was coming to his house. Check.

Yael, on a day's leave, slept. Because of all the holidays, there was a modicum of quiet in the region and her unit enjoyed a temporary reprieve. No doubt this would be followed by fierce conflict, as if to make up for the few weeks of good will. It was dangerous to let people and troops become accustomed to calm and predictability and thoughtfulness. Aggression around these parts was turned on and off like light switches for political and military gain, but also for social management. This had become very clear to Isabel.

Home at nine a.m., Yael ate an enormous breakfast, went to the toilet, and then to bed. Eat, shit, sleep. Babies in fatigues. Isabel barely talked to her. No doubt after the party she would go out with friends. Then would come home late and wake early to be at the bus at six. She had leave from base only until eight a.m.

Suri and Isabel sat by Yael's bed and watched her sleep. The silky olive skin of her long Toledo face was flushed from body heat. Her thick black eye lashes bedded, one layer over the other. Her beautiful high cheek bones more pronounced. The child had lost weight.

"I want to keep her home," Isabel whispered to Suri.

"I miss her contagious laughter. And that Hebrew she shoots off on the phone." Suri took Isabel's hand as they stared at their beloved girl.

Quietly Isabel closed the door to Yael's room and dumped the laundry from her backpack into the washing machine. Two field uniforms caked with dirt. White tee-shirts stained with earth and sweat. Thick socks that long ago left their white behind inside black combat boots. And her dress uniform that needed to be washed and ironed for travel to and from base.

Isabel walked through the house doing the first of probably two or three additional house checks. The phone rang. Jiri on the line. Three o'clock in the Galilee. Two o'clock in Prague. Once Isabel would have said two o'clock German time. Once.

"*Dobrý den*, Isabel Toledo. I just wanted to wish you a happy holiday."

She could tell he'd been drinking. Much of Europe checked out for the second half of December. "*Děkuji*. Same to you, Jiri Stipek."

"I met some people who survived Terezin. Maybe you'll write their stories and come again to Prague?" The subtitles ran thick and fast.

She laughed. "I'm done, Jiri. No more."

"But the Europeans will never forgive the Jews for being slaughtered by them. Your books are the perfect revenge." He laughed too.

"Not my battle anymore."

"Shame, really," he slurred his words. Isabel imagined his large hands around a short glass of cognac. She leaned towards his firm soft chest. A man who understood how to create beauty out of hard surfaces. And though it was only three in the afternoon, and her final house check still needed to be done, she poured herself a glass of red wine from the open bottle on the kitchen counter. The warm liquid was rich like Jiri's voice.

"Maybe we can arrange to meet in Chelm. I read yesterday on the internet that there really was a mountain in the middle of the town. Like in the story of the wise men you told me."

"Yes, there really is."

"How did it go again, the story?"

"Jiri, I can't now . . ."

"Go on, tell me. Please."

And Isabel did despite needing to shower and dress and finish up before the guests arrived. But this was their way of holding on to one another a little longer. Who knew when they would meet or talk again. "Okay." Isabel took another gulp of wine and sat down on a kitchen bar stool. "One day the wise people of Chelm decide they need to build a new school. The men climb the mountain in the middle of town, cut trees, roll the logs down the slope, and set to work building. They saw and sand and hammer boards together."

"And when they build the walls and are ready to put on the roof, the women come around and tell the men the school needs to be in the center of town. Exactly where the mountain is," Jiri continued. "That's women for you." They laughed.

"No problem the men say," Isabel took over, "and together they heave and push, determined to move the mountain. When the women see that it's going to take time, they return home to the children. Meantime, the men get hot from all the pushing and heaving and take their jackets off. They become so absorbed with this work they don't notice a thief making off with their jackets." Isabel took a long drink of wine. The best part was coming up. "At some point one of the men notices that he can't see their jackets. Hey, he tells the other men, look how far we moved the mountain! They're all very pleased with themselves and sit down to rest."

"Yes, I want to meet you there. We'll move mountains."

"Or be robbed."

Uri and Lia came downstairs raucously. Uri smacked into walls, the excitement of the coming party setting him off like a top. And Yael woke up.

"Into the bath, boy." Isabel heard Yael yelling and laughing, running after Uri. After the bath there would be a struggle to dress him in party clothes: a relatively new pair of jeans and a New York Knicks sweatshirt laid out on his bed. Courtesy of Hal.

"I've got to go," Isabel said to Jiri. "Children's party in a couple of hours. Have a wonderful holiday. Thanks for calling."

"You too, *miláček*. See you in Chelm."

"In Chelm."

As soon as she closed the phone it rang again. Itka. Also from Prague. Thankfully it was a short conversation with promises to get together when Itka returned to Israel at the end of January. And as soon as Isabel closed the phone for the second time it rang a third. Hal in New York calling to wish everyone a happy Hanukah and successful party. By now Isabel was edgy. The house checks weren't complete. She still had to shower and dress. Emanuel was due any minute with Anna and Eva who were in from Sweden for the holidays. And the pre-party flutters began to rise up in her as well.

"Hal, wonderful you called." Isabel walked outside to the yard to make sure it was clean. "I'm putting Suri on. Happy Holiday." She handed the phone over to Suri and walked on the grass, picking up stray toys and an old chew bone of Woody's. She looked at the sky. The clouds parted. The sun came in low from the west, throwing golden light over the eastern sky and homes across the ravine. Suri closed the phone and walked onto the grass.

"Why don't you and Hal come for a few months next winter? We'd love you to be closer."

Uri and Yael sent out wild whoops from upstairs.

Suri took her hand and smiled. "That's a lovely idea. Listen to those children."

At five-thirty exactly, the doorbell rang. Twenty-seven seven-year-olds and their families streamed into the house. Within fifteen minutes the house rocked with their unbridled energy. Parents and grandparents hung back against the walls waiting for Idit to take the class in hand, to create order out of the chaos.

"I need for all the children to sit quietly, hands in their laps." Idit's voice penetrated the ruckus. The children sat themselves down on the large living room rug. Woodrow wound his way among them, found Uri and climbed into his lap. The children giggled.

Avshalom, one of the fathers known for his deep voice, his large paunch, and library of tales, came and sat before them on a low stool. He recounted King Alexander's approach to Jerusalem. 332 B.C.E.

"Alexander the Great, riding on his enormous horse, sees a purple speck on the horizon. When he gets closer he sees a man approaching on foot. When he gets even closer, Alexander sees an old man in a purple robe and a large gold plate on his chest with colorful stones and funny letters. He doesn't know that this is the name of God in Hebrew. Suddenly Alexander jumps off his horse and kneels before the old man. The old man is Shimon, the High Priest of Israel.

"What is going on?" Avshalom scanned the children's faces, "thousands of soldiers riding in Alexander's army ask themselves. Their great leader, Alexander King of Macedon, kneeling in front of an old, strangely dressed Israelite?" He paused.

The children gave all sorts of reasons. Avshalom let them express themselves and waited for a lull, which took some time in this loquacious energized bunch. But when the quiet finally came, he told them that King Alexander knelt before Shimon because he had dreamt about meeting this man in purple robes with a gold breast plate with colorful stones and funny letters. He knew he was a wise and important leader.

"For many years the Jews and the Greeks live nicely together. The Jews keep the Sabbath. The Temple in Jerusalem is active. Alexander learns Hebrew. And the Greeks who live here like it so much they start to build gymnasiums and baths, like in Greece. And the Jews like that too. Slowly over the years many begin to live more like Greeks than Jews. And slowly slowly, after Alexander is no longer alive, the Greeks become less happy with the Jewish religion. And what happens?"

The children were well versed in this part of the story. They shouted out in a discordant chorus that the Temple was desecrated with pigs and statues of pagan gods. Some children jumped right to the revolt of the Maccabees and described the battles that took place between Judah, his sons, and the heretics. They especially liked the part about the Maccabees' warrior elephants. And then they quickly got to the miracle of Hanukah. The little bit of olive oil in the clay jug.

"By lighting the Menorah," Avshalom explained, "Judah the Maccabee made the Temple pure again for Israel. The Temple filled with holy light. And not just one day, though there was only enough oil for one, but for eight days."

Isabel watched the children sit quietly, absorbed in Avshalom's every word. She wondered about building consecrations and various ways of ushering in light. Miracles were out of her league, but sanctifying space wasn't. Zakhi and their house lights ritual. Despite what he said, now there was also Keren to consider. She assumed there were always other women, but no one so important that he felt he had to tell her. Now he had. Now there was. The entire time they had been together led up to this moment when circumstances, for him, for her, changed. And Isabel knew it was time for change.

Idit took over seamlessly from Avshalom and asked Uri, since it was his house, to light the candles of the menorah. The long wooden match struck loudly against the scratch strip. The children watched Idit hand the lit match to Uri. He brought the flame to the *shamash*. It caught and Uri held the lit candle high and waited. He turned to catch Isabel's eye, then Alon's. Idit indicated that he should use the lit candle to light the other eight candles while the children called out the blessings. Uri did so carefully and solemnly.

On the eighth night of Hanukah all nine candles of the menorah lit up the room. Uri placed the *shamash* in its holder and stepped back to admire his handiwork. Then the singing began. The same Hanukah songs looped their way through Jewish Israeli lives from pre-school to homes for the aged. Lia, Asaf, Yael, Emanuel, Alon, all the children, all the parents, certainly Idit, sang these traditional songs fluently, confidently, and with great feeling. The songs always reminded Isabel that she lived on the fringe of knowing/not knowing. That she was part of this culture, but was also not. A shared experience also for Molly who stood with Isabel in the back near the kitchen.

"What's it like to share a mother tongue with a mother?" Isabel whispered.

"What?" Molly asked.

"You and Sheila, your mother, share English. Irish culture. Your common native language."

"With some Yiddish thrown in for comic relief."

"Nuances, skill, cleverness taken for granted. A natural part of your communication, right?" And when Molly nodded yes. "Something we don't entirely have with our native Hebrew speaking children, right?" Molly nodded yes again. Isabel continued. "I, on the other hand, live sandwiched between two generations who speak different native languages from me. And from each other. I don't share Suri's Yiddish nor my children's Hebrew."

"Okay."

"It's like living in the land of close to's and sort of 's."

"Mistranslations on all sides."

"Exactly," Isabel said.

"Here we'll always be immigrants, living in one culture and pasting to it points of reference from another."

"Exactly."

And because Isabel would always be American, no matter how many years she lived in Israel, when the eighth song ended and the clock ticked toward eight o'clock, in Isabel's estimation the time had come to wrap up the party. But Israeli Idit and the other parents gave no sign that events were headed in that direction. Everyone stood and joined Idit enthusiastically in singing the ninth song: *Banu choshesh legaresh./Bi yadaynu or vi'esh./Kol echad who or katan/ Vikoolanu or eytan.* We've come to chase away the darkness/Light and fire in our hands/Each one of us a little light/And together a mighty light.

When they got to the chorus everyone drove away the darkness with their feet as well as with their words and stomped hard on the ground. *Soorah choshesh hal'a shkor!/Soorah mipnei ha'or!* Out darkness, banish the night!/Out in the face of the light!

Enthusiasm and excitement peaked with the foot stomping on the word "*out.*" When the song ended it became clear to the other adults in the room that the children were spent. Idit asked that the jelly donuts be handed out. The children plowed into the dining room and crowded around the table. Alon took this opportunity to exit.

"Great job, great party," he kissed Uri who was busy licking the jelly out from the donut center. Alon made the rounds. Hugged and kissed Yael, Lia, and Suri. Shook Asaf and Emanuel's hands. Kissed Isabel as well. "Thanks for the invite," he said on his way out the door.

3

It took another half an hour before the last of the parents whisked their children out of the house. Baths and bed waiting. Lia and Asaf took Uri upstairs. Yael was on the phone with friends. Suri read in the living room. Anna and Eva watched music videos under a wool blanket in the television room. They were comfortable in Isabel's house and knew that once order returned and Uri was in bed, everyone would gather in the kitchen to make a supper of chopped cucumber and tomato salad, omelets, bread, humus, yogurts, white cheeses, olives, a pot of fresh lemon verbena tea.

"Isabel." Emanuel stopped sweeping the dining room. "Before we go to the Dead Sea, I want to know. For things to be clear between us."

Isabel kept cleaning the table and didn't respond.

"I want us to live together."

"I know." Sadness like stones in her pockets weighed her down.

"And?"

"Let's go outside."

They walked through the tidy living room through the sliding glass doors to the yard. Isabel stared up at the mass of stars in the clear black sky.

"Growing up in Manhattan I never saw stars."

"I know."

"Of course you do. I probably told you dozens of times already."

"Hundreds."

"Not nice." She punched him playfully.

He laughed and took her in his arms. They held one another in the cold December air.

"You've had weeks to think about it." Emanuel spoke into the self-conscious silence of night.

Isabel held on tight, stretching out time before the words, not sure what she was going to say. "Emanuel, I can't marry again. It's that simple. I just can't."

"I love you, Isabel. I want to be with you, take care of you."

"I know."

"You'll be as free as you are now. Things are so good. Look at us, the children. It's so great when we're all together."

"I love you. And Anna and Eva, and so much of what we have, but . . . "

She was so sorry to wound him. But claustrophobia came calling when she pictured Emanuel, or any man, sharing her bed every night, being in the kitchen every morning, in the living room every evening. Maybe she was adolescent or trapped in a midlife crisis. Maybe she was a walking and talking cliché. That's what Suri and Molly thought. And making a big mistake. But that's who she was. Now.

Emanuel began to cry softly. Isabel was overwhelmed with doubt. Why was she so sure of this no? What kind of airs was she putting on—with herself? Here was a man. A fabulous man. A loving man. What was she really resisting? Say yes, she commanded herself. Say yes and rest awhile. Say yes and create a partnership of equals never known before. With Emanuel she would be independent and domestic at the same time. And what about boredom? Suri once told her that only a boring person was bored. Deal with that.

"I really am sorry." Isabel held him close.

"Mom." Lia called from the house. "Mom?"

Her body shifted. "Just a minute."

"It's okay. Let's go in." Emanuel wiped his eyes.

"I wish I could, Emanuel, but I can't. At least not now," she said.

"Shhh," he kissed her cheek. "It'll be all right. I'll be all right. C'mon. The children are hungry."

"Can we wait to tell them?" she asked. "Not on the holiday?"

"Tell them?"

"That we're ending our relationship."

"We won't tell them anything."

"But you said we'd split if . . ."

"Maybe you'll change your mind," he stared into her eyes. "I have reservoirs of patience when it comes to you, Isabel Toledo, my weakness, my love." He kissed her hands.

"Maybe." She looked away. Upset. How could he have withdrawn his ultimatum so quickly? Molly was right; his had not been a serious threat.

"I'm sorry I made it so . . . black and white," he said.

"You should be." She turned again to face him. "That wasn't nice at all. Manipulative, even mean. I should be angry, but somehow I'm not."

"I know. Izzie, I really am sor . . ."

"Accepted." Because she felt the full weight of her no. Because she knew she had pushed Emanuel to this desperate move. Because he tried to fulfill her peculiar wanderlust, and didn't entirely succeed, but kept trying. Because she knew he loved her and she him. They held each other, her head resting on his heart. Was it time to slide back into a live-in relationship, grow from there, differently this time? Send Zakhi off on his romantic adventure with Keren or whoever he would finally settle down with? Jiri already knew she wouldn't be meeting him in Chelm or Prague or New York. And she could, she could, decide there be no others. Molly's religious friend from Dublin claimed she was married but not dead. Meaning committed to monogamy but still capable of feeling the zing of attraction when it graced one's day. She could decide to relish the zing and not act on it. The definition of maturity Molly the Greek chorus in her life chimed in. And for the first time since their relationship began, not as a default or rebound position, Isabel felt in her body the opening up of the choice to devote herself sincerely and uniquely to eminently loveable Emanuel. *Maybe, just maybe.*

"Mom," Yael's loud authoritative voice summoned them. "We're starving."

"C'mon." Emanuel took her hand.

Isabel let him lead her into the house but she stopped at the door and looked up one more time at the sky packed with stars. Emanuel observed her and waited.

"You know I'm done ghosting."

"I know."

"It's time to come clean."

Emanuel waited.

"You know I love you." Isabel brought his hand to her mouth. She kissed it feeling the burden of all the years of ghosting, of running, of seeking solace, answers, and order, tumble to the side.

"I know."

"Mom," Yael called out again.

Asaf dressed the salad with olive oil, lemon, and lots of salt. Lia's onion and tomato omelets were sliding out of the pan. Yael sat at the table, her plate already full, never seeming to get enough of home cooking. Anna and Eva were also at the table, but they waited for everyone to join. European children with proper table manners. Suri sat near them approvingly.

There was only so much a mother could do, Isabel sighed, as Yael shoveled food into her mouth, elbows on the table, reaching over others' plates for the salad and the salt shaker. Isabel tried to insist her children eat politely. Another sign of being a foreign parent in Israel. Lia complied but Yael defied her and complained relentlessly that no other parents (except for Molly) badgered their children with ridiculous nonsense such as table manners.

Uri made his way stealthily down the stairs. The excitement of the party, knowing that everyone else was sitting around the large dining table eating a late supper, knowing that tomorrow he was still on vacation from school and would spend the day with Alon and the ponies, and after that the trip into the desert, was too much for him. He couldn't sleep.

Emanuel lingered by the sink. He ran water on his hands and rinsed his face. He came into the dining room and sat near Isabel. Anna and Eva began to help themselves to food. Beautiful teenagers. One blond like her mother. The other dark haired like Emanuel. Both had blue-grey eyes and skin which blended the Scandinavian and Semitic. Isabel adored them. Should she bring together the Toledo-Segev-Jakobsson-Dor clan? Five children. Seven to twenty-three years of age. Nearly a generation's span. Yes, five children. A house full of comings and goings. Crises. Hugging. Crying. Talking. Fights. Laughter. *Maybe, just maybe.*

Uri was fast upon her.

"Oh." Isabel pretended to be surprised when he grabbed her from behind. She lifted her little boy's lithe body into the air and slid him onto her lap. He laid his head against her chest and she cocooned him in her arms.

Isabel watched her family eat and talk. Before joining them she did a quick survey of the blessedly few phone calls she would make the following morning. First to Jaim Benjamin to say she was happy the book was already in production. But no, she wouldn't go to Spain for him. Suri would bring him his key when she returned stateside. Then she would call Schine and reiterate that there would be no more books issued from her pen. Not for the former partisan in Florida. Not for Yehudit Klein in Israel. Nor for anyone else. Other writers could drive away the darkness and the silence. And when he would say, because she knew he would say, just one more, *maidele*, just one more, she would say again, and if need be one more time after that, that she preferred not to.

A wave of hunger and fatigue crashed over Isabel. As if reading her mind, Lia scooped salad onto her plate. Suri placed a slice of whole grain bread on the side and moved the humus closer. Isabel would have her rest. The Dead Sea and the minerals. The purple mountains' majesty. The winter sun. Emanuel. She looked at his handsome face in the evening light. *Maybe, just maybe.*

What could be better, Isabel Toledo, she said to herself as she leaned towards the table, Uri an indelible part of her movements. What could be better than this? On the eighth day of Hanukah, nine people and one dog sat together. A warm lit house. Night holding fast around them. A large oval table filled with winter fruits from her own and from friends' gardens. Oranges. Lemons. Pecans. Persimmons. Pomegranates. And olives. Lots of olives. Black. Green. Cracked. Spicy. And salted. The miracle of the olive. The miracle of its light.